ABOUT SHOW DOWN

A JUNIPER RIDGE ROMANTIC COMEDY

They called me America's smartest entrepreneur. So how was I dumb enough to let my dream girl get away?

Blame ego, blame my need to prove I could build a business all on my own. Hell, blame my parents—God love 'em—for thinking I'd have problems prospering with a hammer instead of a law degree.

Turns out I'm doing just fine with a chain of luxury resorts bearing my name, but it's a cold comfort when the woman I love hates my guts. Can't say she's wrong, considering how things ended.

I set out to win Lauren back, scoring a spot on her family's reality show social experiment, or whatever it's called when someone buys an old cult compound to build a tiny town. Works for me, since I'm a builder who loves a challenge.

But getting Lauren to forgive me proves way more than challenging. Between a botched baking class, sexy bumper car battles, and a bizarrely hostile fish, it's clear Lo's in no hurry to pick up where we left off.

Good thing I'm no quitter, especially when it comes to her.

A Juniper Ridge
Romantic Comedy

show
down

tawna
USA Today Bestselling Author
fenske

SHOW DOWN

TAWNA FENSKE

This is a work of fiction. Names, characters, organizations, places, events, and incidents are either products of the author's imagination or are used fictitiously.

Text copyright © 2021 Tawna Fenske

All rights reserved.

No part of this book may be reproduced, or stored in a retrieval system, or transmitted in any form or by any means, electronic, mechanical, photocopying, recording, or otherwise, without express written permission of the author.

www.tawnafenske.com

Cover design by Craig Zagurski

❦ Created with Vellum

ALSO IN THE JUNIPER RIDGE
ROMANTIC COMEDY SERIES

- Show Time (Dean & Vanessa)
- Let It Show (Mari & Griffin)
- Show Down (Lauren & Nick)
- Show of Honor (Jessie & Joe coming soon!)
- Just for Show (Cooper & Amy coming soon!)
- Show and Tell (Lana & Dal coming soon!)
- Show of Hands (Tia & Vonn coming soon!)

You might also dig my Ponderosa Resort rom-com series. That's where you'll get your first glimpse of characters from Juniper Ridge, including Val and Vanessa in *Mancandy Crush* and Dean and Gabe in *Snowbound Squeeze*. Check them out here:

- Studmuffin Santa
- Chef Sugarlips
- Sergeant Sexypants
- Hottie Lumberjack
- Stiff Suit
- Mancandy Crush (novella)

- Captain Dreamboat
- Snowbound Squeeze (novella)
- Dr. Hot Stuff

For Meah. Thanks for being my friend, pet nanny, personal assistant, tarot card wonder, cheerleader, sounding board, and an all-around awesome human. I'm damn glad to know you.

A NOTE TO MY AWESOME READERS

Hello, lovely reader!

When I first dreamed up the Juniper Ridge world, I got giddy about writing a tiny town that's a quirky little microcosm of American life. Characters bloomed in my brain in all shapes, sizes, colors, and backgrounds.

Naturally, this meant writing outside my own lived experience. While Nick Armbrust—the smart, take-charge hero of this story—is a strong and sexy Black man, I'm not. I'm also not one of the talented #ownvoices authors writing from that perspective. I'm just a white chick from Oregon who loves the idea of an inclusive, colorful, caring, and diverse world.

There are so many amazing Black and indigenous authors writing romance from an #ownvoices perspective, and I could fill 2,497 books with my recommendations. Some of my personal favorites include Farrah Rochon, Naima Simone, Beverly Jenkins, Talia Hibbert, Kennedy Ryan, LaQuette, Nana Malone, M. Malone, Nina Crespo, Robin Covington, Jamie Wesley, and Savannah J. Frierson (who also served as a sensitivity reader for this book). Go snap up their books and read along with Lauren and Alexis as they swap clandestine romance reads in *Show Down*.

Thank you so much for reading, and for joining me in our latest journey to Juniper Ridge!
Love, Tawna

PROLOGUE

TWO YEARS AGO

CONFESSIONAL 753
Judson, Lauren (Producer: Juniper Ridge)
You want me to share one of my worst memories? Nice, Gabe. How about you punch me in the tits while you're at it? Oh, stop looking like that. I'm a woman. I have tits, okay? Being your sister doesn't negate that biological fact. If you want to get technical, you've got three sisters who all happen to have—
Stalling?
I don't know what you mean.

* * *

I sip from a flute of Veuve Clicquot, careful not to smudge my lipstick. It's Friday night at Evolution, the most exclusive club in West Hollywood, and we've got a VIP suite.

"Hey, gorgeous."

My hot-as-hell boyfriend nuzzles the words against my neck. I lean into his heat a moment before drawing back to watch his fiery gold-brown eyes skim my body. They linger in the space where my pushup bra performs miracles with my pale and paltry cleavage, so I draw my shoulders back to make the most of it. I bought this strapless Oscar de la Renta in lush velvet knowing he'd love it. The heat in his gaze tells me I wasn't wrong.

I seldom am. If tonight goes how I'm thinking, Nick's about to swap the *boyfriend* title for *fiancé*.

"Hey, stranger." God, he looks good. I skim my fingertips over the warm brown line of his chiseled jaw. "Having fun?"

"Oh, yeah." He dips a palm into the curve of my waist, and I fight the urge to drag him into the nearest coat closet. "I love you in red," he murmurs.

"Is that so?" I know this, of course. I know most things about Nick, since tonight marks one year since our first date. "Glad you like it."

"Mmm." He kisses my neck again, and I let my palms take a lovely trip from his shoulders to his forearms, tracing muscles built by years of slinging tools on job sites. These days, he spends more time bossing other people with tools, but the fact remains —Nick Armbrust knows his way around a tool chest.

And *my* chest, but I'm getting distracted.

"Alexis is looking for you," he says, and it takes me a sec to go from fuck-me-against-the-wall, to let's-talk-about-your-sister.

"She caught me in the ladies' room a minute ago." I love Nick's sister, so shifting gears is easy. "She looks amazing."

Nick grins. "Mama's pestered her for years to leave her hair natural. She wasn't so sure about going full afro."

"It looks great."

"She said she had something for you?"

"Mmm-hmm." I don't tell him that *something* was a pair of Farrah Rochon paperbacks. Alexis and I agree it's best to let her brother think we've spent the past year swapping stock tips or shoes instead of romance novels. "Is she pregnant again?"

"What?" Nick squints at the corner table where Alexis is

feeding a bite of crostini to her hottie husband. "Why would you think that?"

"Watch." On cue, Abe touches his wife's belly beneath the table. His big, ebony hand lingers a moment before sliding away. The two share a private smile that makes my ovaries ache. "See?"

"Huh." Nick dots a kiss behind my ear. "We should put in our order for another niece."

"Or nephew." Delight ripples through me at his slip of the tongue. *We*. A good indication I'm right about tonight's plans.

"I love seeing our families together." His gaze moves past his sister to the tight knot of Judson offspring in the corner. Dean, Cooper, Lana—all five of my brothers and sisters are here somewhere.

A few feet away, my parents huddle in conversation with Nick's mom and dad. My soon-to-be-in-laws? I hate to be presumptuous, but all signs are there. Nick did ask me last week what I thought of public proposals. A comment on the viral TikTok video we watched together, or something more?

My money's on more.

I skim a hand down his chest. "I can't believe you managed to get everyone in one place."

Nick laughs warm and low. "There's a lot to be said for just asking for what you want."

I shiver, recognizing the quote he gave *Businessweek* last month about the success of his construction firm. Tonight, I hear it with fresh ears.

If Nick's about to ask me something, the answer is an unequivocal *yes*.

His dad says something that makes my mom laugh, and I catch myself smiling. Our parents met before we did, since Angela and Darius Armbrust are prominent entertainment lawyers, and my parents are—well, Laurence and Shirleen Judson. Enough said.

Though not enough has been said about why Nick summoned

us here this evening. I've asked him for weeks, but all he'll say is it's a surprise. Even Alexis has no clue. All Nick says is that he needed to line things up before sharing his plans.

I sip from my champagne flute and order myself to keep my voice casual. "You went all out for this soiree."

"It's a big occasion." He winks, and there go the damn butterflies in my stomach.

I know I should play it cool. That's what I'm known for, after all. *Entertainment Weekly* dubbed me the "She Shark," a reference to my cool poise on set. What the hell does that even mean? They'd never write that about a male producer.

But it's true I'm cool under pressure. Always have been, though maybe not where Nick's concerned. One look at him, and my kneecaps melt like butter.

"I heard what you did for Lana." Nick brushes my hair back from my face. "Pretty badass."

I frown. "What did you hear?"

"That you kneed that actor in the balls for grabbing her ass at a fundraiser."

Goddammit. Hollywood's getting too small.

"Repeat that to anyone, and you'll get the same." I keep enough sweetness in my voice so he knows I'm teasing, but he must see steel in my eyes because he inches back a little. "Seriously, Nick—don't repeat that."

"It's true, though."

He didn't add a question mark, so I don't bother answering. "No one fucks with my family."

Nick's chest rumbles as he chuckles. "And I dig that about you."

"Thanks." I think. Speaking of family— "I'm going to go say hi to Mari, okay?"

Nick spots her in the corner and waves. "She just getting here?"

"She came straight from taping a demo for *Shrink to the Stars*. Want to come find out how it went?"

He kisses me again before releasing my hand. "You go ahead. There's something I need to do."

The way his fingers just skimmed the breast pocket of his suit has me speculating about that *something*. Is my ring in there?

Flashing one last smile, I stride toward my middle sister, who's waylaid by our youngest. Mari looks sophisticated in off-the-shoulder Chanel, while Lana's peach complexion glows in green Dolce & Gabbana. I'm so proud of my sisters, for how they're forging their own paths, stepping out of our parents' shadows, becoming strong, confident—

"Lauren, sweetheart." Fingers clamp my arm, and Shirleen Judson—aka sex siren of seventies cinema, aka *my mother*—tugs me to stand beside her. "Lovely party."

I frown at her empty seat. "Weren't you just sitting over there?"

"I wanted to speak with you." She smiles and waves at someone en route to the bar. A director, I think? The faces blend together these days.

My mother lowers her voice. "Things seem to be going well with Nick."

"I suppose so." It's not the gushing response she's probing for, but I won't give her the satisfaction of seeming too eager. Too needy.

"Don't be coy, Lauren." She tucks a swatch of hair behind my ear, then flutters her fingers at someone strolling through the side door. "There's a reason you work behind the cameras. You're not that good an actress."

The words don't sting because I won't let them. Also, I never wanted to be an actress. I've made a name for myself behind the camera, so Shirleen Judson can suck it.

Not that I'd say that out loud. "Was there something you wanted?"

My mother sighs. "You've got an attractive man with a promising career and a good family. You're running out of time to close the deal."

This conversation again. "Marriage isn't the crowning achievement it was in your day." A low blow, but she asked for it. "I've got my own promising career. Maybe I don't care about marriage."

"Sweetheart." She rubs my shoulder, a comfort I'm annoyed to find myself craving. "Is that why you and Lana looked at wedding gowns last week?"

I blink. "How did you—"

"Or why you pulled up that photo of the pink diamond ring the morning we had mimosas?"

I clench my jaw, willing myself not to react.

She squeezes my arm with a satisfied smile. "Mothers know everything, dear." Dropping her hand, she takes a step back. "I'm proud of you, darling. Now go close the deal."

She walks away while I'm still processing her words. Is she proud of me for dating the man *Businessweek* called "Hollywood's most up-and-coming entrepreneur," or for my own career achievements?

My Oscar nod last year solidified my standing as part of Judson royalty, and God knows my mother had her own Hollywood career. It's not like she wants me barefoot and chained to a stove.

But deep down, I know I won't earn her awe until I've achieved the great trifecta. Career, beauty, and the cover of *People* magazine's wedding issue, not necessarily in that order.

Squaring my shoulders, I pivot and march toward my sisters. Mari turns and meets my eye, and I'm opening my mouth to call to her when a mic squeal slices the party chatter.

"Heeeyyy, everyone! Thanks for being here." Nick's voice is smooth as polished maple, and I turn as my heart kicks to a quick canter. He's standing on a raised platform, and when he catches my eye, he winks. "Part of why we're here tonight is to celebrate the opening of Armbrust Anaheim, so thank you all for making it happen."

I clap along with everyone, heart in a full gallop now. His modesty is one thing I admire about him, and I love that he makes it sound like the new Armbrust Resort was a joint effort.

But I know he turned down his parents' offer of seed money. He designed all those pretty little cabins himself, slinging a hammer right alongside his crew. He did it on his own, and I'm damn proud of him.

My husband.

I know I said I don't care about marriage, and I don't. But seeing him up there, dark skin like smooth mahogany under the lights, I can't stop picturing our future.

Nick clears his throat and continues. "I'd like to thank my parents, Angela and Darius Armbrust, for not disowning me when I quit law school to work construction."

A ripple of laughter moves through the room, but I keep my eyes on Nick. On the flicker of anxious pride in his eyes. I wonder if anyone else sees it.

"I'd also like to thank Lauren Judson." He turns to me and smiles. "Girl, you've been my rock through all of this."

More applause, and I demur like I learned to do before I could walk. My brain snags on the word "rock," curious if it's a clue.

"Speaking of rocks," he continues, and my breath catches in my throat. "I have an important announcement. Well, an announcement and a special request."

Oh my God.

This is happening. It's really happening.

Tears needle my eyelids, but I blink them back. With the sharp points of my manicure, I pinch the skin between my thumb and pointer finger the way I learned at sixteen.

"Do this when you think you might cry," my mother instructed on

the eve of my first major awards ceremony. *"The pain will distract you."*

But nothing distracts me from the glint in Nick's eye, the shape of him in that well-tailored suit, the fullness of lips I've kissed a thousand times as he lifts the mic again.

"Let me back up a little bit," he continues, voice cracking a little. He laughs and clears his throat, glancing at the bright light shining down on him. "Wow, this is harder than I thought. I'm not used to being in the spotlight."

Should I help? I grew up in the spotlight, so public speaking is like breathing. I edge close to the platform, breath coming quicker now.

"Let me try this again." He shifts the mic to his other hand and smiles at me before lifting his gaze to the crowd. "Ten months ago, on a trip to Colorado, I went to see one of my favorite performers."

Fondness squeezes my heart. We'd been dating two months when Nick invited me on a weekend getaway. *"We'll see Gary Clark Jr. at Red Rocks Amphitheatre and stay at this cool bed and breakfast. They've got bonfires where we can cuddle up and roast marshmallows."* He smiled almost shyly, pulling me closer. *"I know it's not the luxury digs you're used to, but—"*

"It sounds amazing," I'd interrupted, stretching up to kiss him. *"Just like you."*

And he is. This public event, the retelling of our first weekend getaway—all of this is the proposal of my dreams, if I were the kind of woman to dream of such things.

Which I'm not.

But I'm just saying—

"—the trees, the sky, the entire landscape," Nick's saying, and I realize I've missed some of what he's just said. "And I found myself thinking there's only one thing that could make this better."

He meets my eyes again and I hold my breath. This is it.

"So what I'm wondering," Nick says, tugging the collar of his shirt. "What I'm hoping, that is—"

"Yes!"

Oh, God.

That was me, wasn't it?

I glance around, and yep. Everyone's staring.

But I don't care because the man of my dreams is proposing, and the least I can do is make it easier on him. Nick cocks his head, smiling with a question in his eyes.

And I have the answer.

I take another step forward and hold out my hand. My left hand, in case he wants to slip the ring on. Nick looks at me uncertainly and pulls the mic closer. "Hold on just a second, babe." He smiles. "Almost done."

Right. Of course, he wants to get the words out. I glance at the edge of the platform and see my brother, Gabe, with his camera rolling. The upside of growing up in showbiz is that there's always someone to capture life's big moments.

Nick clears his throat again, so I put my hand down and command myself to be patient.

"Just last week, I signed the title on eight acres west of Denver." He smiles and a flush of pride moves through me. Building a rustic resort in Colorado has been on his bucket list forever, and I'm thrilled I'll be by his side as he makes that dream come true. "As part of that project, we're building a new a state-of-the-art performing arts center."

This part is news to me, but okay. It sounds amazing, and I can't wait to hear more. But come on, let's get this show started.

Nick meets my eye like he's psyching himself up for something. I offer an encouraging smile as he takes a deep breath. "Right now," he says, "I would like to formally ask Laurence Judson to m—"

"Yes, I'll marry you!"

Oh, shit.

All the blood drains from my head as I realize what he's just said.

Laurence Judson?

My humiliated heart claws for explanation. Like maybe he's seeking my father's blessing, even though it's patriarchal and outdated and—*oh, God* now my dad is striding toward the platform, grabbing the mic to thank Nick for partnering with him on a new business venture.

But everyone's staring at me.

Everyone.

Literally, *everyone.*

Shame rushes icy and bitter through my veins as I square my shoulders and refuse to fucking cry. Refuse to meet anyone's eyes as my throat squeezes tight and all those eyeballs drill into me. Disgrace tastes bitter on the back of my tongue, and it's all I can do to stay upright, to balance on these mile-high heels and hold my head up as I die inside.

How could you be so stupid?

My father's rambling on about the new Laurence Judson Performing Arts Center and his partnership with Nick. *Surprise!* They've kept it under wraps for weeks because—honestly, I stop listening because my ears are buzzing with the heat of humiliation. I fix my eyes on a potted plant in the corner, blinking back waves of embarrassment.

Do not cry. Do not cry.

My mother steps into my line of sight, her face filled with pity and concern and the tiniest hint of I-told-you-so. She'd never say it out loud.

She doesn't have to.

Nick's talking again, explaining how he plans to move to Denver for a year to oversee the project personally. *Moving*, for God's sake. The opposite of proposing.

And the fact that he never mentioned it, never said a word to me about relocating to Denver…well, I think it's safe to assume I'm not part of his plan.

I tilt up my chin and keep my eyes on my dad. Nick's wrapping up his speech, and I applaud so hard my hands sting. Now Dad's saying something and *oh my God* is this almost over?

And then, it is.

And then, my dream man is walking toward me.

I swallow hard and try to force my face into a smile. My mouth won't cooperate, so I settle for balling my hands into fists and fixing him with a shark stare. Flat-eyed, no emotion. It's what I do best.

Nick stops dead in his tracks. "Hey, Lauren." He drags a hand over his head the way he does when he's not sure what to say. "Uh—so I guess I should have warned you about that. About—well—"

"Moving a thousand miles away? Planning a project with my dad?" My voice sounds cool and calm, which surprises me. "That's your business, isn't it?"

Nick looks unsure for the first time I've known him. "There was an NDA. A non-disclosure agr—"

"I know what an NDA is, Nick." I've seen plenty in my career, and my dad's a stickler for them.

He clears his throat. "You want to go somewhere and talk?"

"About what?" I sound like an idiot, but I can't help it. Maybe we can pretend this didn't happen. Maybe we can go back to—

"I think maybe we're on different pages, Lo." He shoves his hands in his pockets, the distance between us a big, gaping hole. "Uh, marriage and all. It's not really where I'm at right now."

Like that wasn't fucking obvious. "It's fine. Everything's fine."

Everything is *not* fine, which he can clearly tell from my tone.

Nick's brow furrows. "Look, uh—I'm gonna be gone a while on this project." He pauses, choosing his words with care. "I figured since you're starting that new film, you'd be glad about getting time to yourself."

If there was any doubt Nick and I are on different pages, he just snatched the book and lit the damn thing on fire. I take a deep breath, insides quivering from the effort of keeping emotions in check. "Of course."

I need to get out of here. I need this conversation to be over so I can run to the bathroom and sob like a pathetic little girl.

But Nick's still talking, still hammering nails into my heart. "You're amazing, Lo. It's not about that. It's just—"

"Let's call it quits."

Nick blinks. "What?"

At least he's not misunderstanding. He knows I'm not talking about ditching the party and heading home to watch Netflix in our PJs with a bag of Ruffles.

Crooked House.

The code words we say when we're aching to ditch the clamor of a party crowd, the shine of a spotlight, and sneak home to snuggle.

But this is no Crooked House moment. Nick knows that.

I swallow back the sting of memories. My palms feel sticky, and I can't get enough air as my heart bangs against my ribs like it's fighting to get out.

But I slam the door on that motherfucker and look Nick square in the eye. "We need to split up."

CHAPTER 1

NOW

CONFESSIONAL 759.5
<u>Armbrust, Nick (Owner, Armbrust Resorts)</u>
Prove yourself.
You've gotta be two times better to get half of what they've got.
That phrase was hammered into me from the time I could walk.
I've done it, though. Two dozen resorts around the country.
My name on every sign shouting, 'Hey, this guy made something of himself.'
Damn right, I did. I'm at the peak of my career. Hard work has its payoff, and I've got mine. Even Mama and Pop can see it.
[scrubs hand over chin]
You think Lauren ever sees me in magazines and wonders if maybe—
Aw, hell. Never mind.

* * *

"So that's about it for the tour." Lana Judson flashes her sweet little sister smile, socking me with a fresh wave of missing my own sister. "Any questions?"

"Yeah." I tip my head toward the coffee shop beside us. "Tell me straight—are the muffins there as good as Bakelicious on Sunset Boulevard?"

She laughs and folds her fair, freckled arms over her chest. "Better, if you can believe it."

"No lie?"

"None whatsoever." She hooks a thumb toward the front counter. "Patti and Colleen run the place and do all the baking."

"I don't think I've met them yet."

"They're wildlife biologists who were here doing research when we bought the place," she says. "We basically begged them to stick around."

"I see." I'm not sure I follow, but maybe there's some link between biology and baking skills. "And you all are pretty tight?"

Lana smiles. "They're sort of the mother hens of the place. You know how it is."

Ah. Now it clicks. Shirleen Judson might be a Hollywood superstar, but her mothering left six kids fending for themselves half the time. Or for each other, in Lauren's case. As the oldest girl, she had a knack for looking out for her siblings.

Thinking of Lo has my chest pinching in on itself. "You tell your mama hi for me the next time you talk to her," I say to Lana.

She makes a face. "Will do."

"And your dad," I add, though I've kept better touch with him on account of our business relationship. "Give them both my regards."

Lana throws a mock salute, and my heart twists up tight again as I notice how she looks like Lo. Same long hair, same big smile. Lauren's less generous with hers, which I always kinda dug. Earning a smile from her was one of my favorite challenges.

Clearing my throat, I take a step toward the coffee shop. "I'm gonna head on in and check out the muffins."

"Enjoy!" Lana starts to back away, then stops. "I'm glad you took the job, Nick. It's good to see you again."

"Same." I swallow hard, annoyed by how sentimental I'm getting. "You take care."

I turn and stroll toward the coffee shop, taking my time to soak up the landscape. Ragged basalt cliffs cut the horizon like a sawblade, and a swaying sea of grass gives the whole place a farm vibe. To my left there's nearly a hundred of the prettiest little cedar cabins imaginable. It's cocky to think that, since I built them. A long time ago, back before I was in a position to be picky about taking jobs for a rumored cult.

News flash: The rumors were true. The Benevolent Order of the New Kingdom—BONK for short—turned out nuttier than squirrel shit, but they did create a nice compound.

All that's behind me now, and the place makes a fine backdrop for a reality show, social experiment, and self-contained community. That's what they're calling it now, and why I'm here.

One of the reasons I'm here.

I push through the coffee shop door, wondering when I'll get a glimpse of Lauren. She must know by now I'm contracted to build the new cabins, though she's been conspicuously absent from meetings. I've tried not to take it personally.

"Afternoon." A rosy-cheeked woman with a long gray braid looped over one shoulder steps up behind the cash register. "You look like you could use one of our new black-bottom chocolate vegan muffins."

I cock my head and take her in. "Because I'm Black?"

I expect her to blush or stammer the way white folks do. It's true Black folks are about three times more likely to be vegetarian, but I'm thinking more about the black-bottom bit.

The woman hoots with laughter. "Cooper said you don't pull any punches." She laughs some more, blue eyes holding mine in a way I find friendly instead of disarming. "He's talked for weeks about you getting here. About having a vegetarian buddy. All those meat-loving siblings give him a hard time, you know."

I do know, though I'm surprised Cooper Judson remembered my dietary habits. "I'd love one of those muffins," I tell her. "I'm Nick, by the way. Sorry if I came off like a jerk."

"Nah, you're good." She smiles as she rummages in the display case to pluck the biggest muffin from the tray. "I'm Colleen, and this is on the house. A thank you for building the cabins with all those hidden cubby holes. We've been here for years, and we're still finding new ones."

I grin as she slides the muffin on a plate. "Hidden storage is my trademark. Folks love it."

Colleen nods and pushes the plate toward me. "Especially lesbians who need all that extra space for our flannel shirts and Jeep keys."

She says it with such a straight face that it takes me a second to catch the spark in her eye. A grin tugs the edges of my jaw. "I like you." I take a bite of the muffin. "And I like this even more."

"Need anything to go with it?"

"Coffee's great." I throw her a wink. "Black, please."

"Coming right up." She sets to work pouring it as another woman steps behind her with a laptop in her hands. Colleen nods to her.

"My wife, Patti," she says by way of introduction. "Nick Armbrust."

Patti sets down the laptop and extends her hand. "I've heard a lot about you."

"Good things, I hope." I hesitate. "From Lauren?"

The two exchange a look I can't read as Colleen hands me my coffee. "Everyone's excited about the new cabins," Patti says, expertly dodging the question. "Are you building more secret cubby holes?"

"You know it." I like how they're into my trademark, even if they didn't answer my question about Lo. "I've got a couple new ideas for where to hide them."

Colleen smiles and nods at Patti. "Our son, Joe—he was here on leave and found one we'd never noticed."

"He's a Navy SEAL." Pride warms Patti's eyes. "Anyway, we're glad you're here. It'll be great to have those new cabins."

"I'll work as fast as I can." Balancing the muffin plate and a red ceramic mug, I make my way to a corner table. It's tucked behind a shelf brimming with bright mugs and bags of coffee beans, plus a few knickknacks with sayings like, "coffee is my duct tape," and "coffee 'til cocktails."

I pull out my phone and snap a picture of one that says "may your coffee be stronger than your toddler," then shoot it to my sister in a text.

Thinking of you.

Alexis has back to back trials all day, so I don't expect a response. But she fires back within thirty seconds.

Very funny. Where are you?

Biting off a hunk of muffin, I type out a reply.

First day at Juniper Ridge. Already hard at work.

I only wait ten seconds for a response.

Work. Right. You're in a coffee shop, aren't you?

Before I come up with some smart-ass retort, she's typing again.

Nice there? Good for families, I mean?

I read the words several times, trying to gauge what she's getting at. She's got a great career as a badass district attorney. Abe just made captain in the police department where he works, and their girls—my nieces, Rosa and Nala—have a full-time nanny who speaks three languages and was a finalist on *The Great British Baking Show*.

In other words, my sister and her husband are living the dream. Our mom's dream, the one she had for both of us. I lift the phone to respond when a chime dings at the front door.

I glance up to see Lauren sailing through with a dark-haired woman on her heels. "Mari's posting a digital announcement on the community bulletin board," Lauren's saying to her friend. "Everyone will see it by tomorrow morning."

"I won't." The brunette—an outdoorsy-looking lady who definitely has a little Latina lineage—hands Lauren a rolled-up banner. "It's only for people who live here, right?"

Lauren's smile shoots straight through my spleen, rippling out alternating waves of joy and yearning. "There's an easy fix for that, Tia."

The woman—Tia, I guess—rolls her eyes. "Are we having this conversation again?"

"Oh, come on." Lauren bumps her with an elbow. "You've gotta get lonely at the ranch. It's just a matter of time 'til you sign on to be our official farm babe and animal hoarder."

"Animal hoarder?" Tia snorts. "Please tell me that's not how you're promoting this adoption event."

"Cross my heart, it's not." Lauren traces an X over her perfect breasts, and it's all I can do not to remember how they felt spilling into my hands. How perfectly they filled my palms as she arched against me and—

"Lana wrote all the copy," Lauren continues like I'm not over here having lustful thoughts about her body. "I promise—it's going to be the best animal adoption event *ever*."

That's...new. Not that Lauren was anti-animal or anything, but she swore off pets when we were together. Maybe if we'd gotten a cat together, or a dog, or—

"Crap, I need a ladder." Lauren's gaze swings past, and I'm almost sure she spotted me here beside the shelves. "Back in a sec."

I try not to watch her ass in snug jeans as she hustles to a back room, pausing to make small talk with Colleen. God, she's gorgeous. More beautiful now than she was two years ago.

Oregon agrees with her. Maybe it's the fresh air, or maybe it's getting the hell away from Hollywood drama.

Or you, a voice whispers in the back of my brain. *Maybe she's better off without you.*

I tell my inner voice to zip it as Lauren marches back through the coffee shop dragging a ladder twice her size. I start to get up, then sit my ass back down. If there's one thing Lauren Judson hates, it's being treated like she needs help.

It's a trait I love about her.

Loved.

Oh, hell. Like I ever stopped loving her, even if she kicked my ass to the curb. Like it's my fault I wasn't ready for church bells and babies.

My annoying inner voice reminds me Lauren never asked for any of that. Hell, we hardly talked about the future at all. We were both so focused on our careers, I just assumed we were on the same page. Talk about misreading the room.

I order myself to stop kicking my own ass and focus on what Lauren's saying to her friend.

"…Gabe and I already scoped things out with lights and cameras," she's saying as she clambers up the ladder with the rolled-up banner in one hand. "We should get lots of good footage."

"Do you Judsons ever stop thinking of footage?" Tia's voice is teasing, but I sense it's a real question.

A question I could answer if she let me.

Yes, Lauren thinks of everyone but herself.

Yes, Lauren's got the toughest hide and the tenderest heart of the whole Judson clan.

Yes, in private, Lauren Judson is sweet and sexy and vulnerable and—

"Throw me that hammer?"

Her command jolts me back to the moment and the fact that Lauren's teetering at the top of the ladder. I get to my feet, not liking the way she has to stretch to reach the spot she's aiming for. If she loses her balance—

"Shit!"

I leap forward, not caring if I stay hidden. She's toppling sideways, a ten-foot drop to a concrete floor I personally supervised the construction of. It's hard as hell and set to make a mess of her beautiful body.

Not if I can help it.

I throw out my arms to catch her. She lands with an ungraceful "oof," her shoulder nailing me in the ribs. My breath whooshes into a grunt, but I don't let go. Not even as I stagger back, knees creaking under the soft weight of her.

Lauren looks up in astonishment, her steely eyes wide, the fierce line of her mouth rounding into a startled O. She stares me in the eye, blinking like she can't quite place me.

"Nick." She tenses in my arms, eyes locked with mine like it's the last place on earth she thought she'd find herself.

"Lo." My voice rumbles lower than I mean it to, but I don't break eye contact. I don't loosen my grip on the warm, solid, sexy woman in my arms.

She goes from tightly coiled to limp. Closing her eyes, she lets out a slow breath. "Fuck."

I fight the grin grabbing the edges of my mouth. Adjusting my hold on her, I smile down at the one face I could never forget. "Good to see you, too."

CHAPTER 2

CONFESSIONAL 768.5
JUDSON, LAUREN (PRODUCER: JUNIPER RIDGE)
HISTORY'S A WEIRD THING. LIKE, DID YOU KNOW THE WHOLE CONCEPT FOR CONFESSIONALS IN REALITY TV ORIGINATED IN DOCUMENTARY FILMMAKING? SHOWS LIKE THE PEOPLE'S COURT PICKED IT UP AND HAD LITIGANTS GIVE INTERVIEWS TO THE COURT REPORTER. IT'S BECAUSE OF THAT HISTORY THAT WE—WHAT?
OH. SURE, I GUESS WE CAN TALK PERSONAL HISTORY. [FROWNS] ACTUALLY, YOU KNOW WHAT? I JUST REMEMBERED I'M LATE FOR A PRODUCTION MEETING.

* * *

If there's one place I never thought I'd be again, it's Nick Armbrust's arms.

His big, strong, dark, sexy—

"You can put me down, please." I clear my throat. "Thank you."

"No problem." Nick takes his time lowering me to my feet, his expression perfectly bland.

But I see laughter in his eyes, feel the sharp sting of pride. The last time I saw the man, it was smack dab in the middle of the most humiliating moment of my life. This doesn't compare, but it's still the same ballpark. I hate that.

I also hate him.

I take a few deep breaths, hoping if I remind myself, my silly, thumping heart might get the message.

"Lauren." He takes his time scanning me from head to toe, and I'm annoyed by how my body tingles. "Are you okay?"

"I'm fine," I shout. "Totally great. Amazing!"

Why am I yelling?

And why am I still gripping the hammer like a serial killer? I move to stash it behind my back, but not before Nick spots it and grabs it from my hand.

"Where do you want this?"

He's talking about the sign, of course, but I decide to play dumb. "The hammer? You can put it back in my hand so I can finish—"

"The banner, Lauren." He stares at me from the foot of the ladder. "Centered above the window, or off to the side?"

I hesitate, stalling for time. Maybe for the ground to gulp me up. "Centered." There's no point in fighting Nick when he sets his mind to something. "Thank you."

"No problem." He scales the ladder like it's nothing, tacking up one edge of the banner with a few quick taps.

I'd have spent at least a minute beating on the thing, possibly smacking my thumb in the process. I should be grateful instead of annoyed. Annoyed and turned on, which is even more annoying. *God*. I can't seem to figure out what to do with my hands, so I shove them in my pockets as Tia Nelson steps closer.

"Who's *he*?" she whispers, eyes saucer-wide.

A dozen words buzz my brain, most with four letters. I pick the simplest answer.

"Nick Armbrust," I mutter. "He built the compound. The cabins, the lodge—"

"The bumper car pavilion," he calls good-naturedly as he crawls back down the ladder and moves it to the right. "That's my personal favorite."

Tia laughs as Nick scales the ladder again. "Because what cult doesn't need a set of bumper cars?"

"Amen." Nick pounds in the final nail. He takes his time coming down, and I absolutely do not admire his perfect backside while he does it.

As soon as he's standing beside me, Tia sticks her hand out. "Tia Nelson," she says. "I own Sun Daisy Organic Ranch just north of Juniper Ridge."

"She also rehabilitates sick and injured and homeless animals," I put in, grateful we're talking about Tia and not the fact that I'm blushing like a kid. "Hence, the adoption event."

Nick's gaze skims the banner, and I do my best not to notice the fiery gold flecks in his deep brown eyes or how my heart squeezes tight as a fist.

"Cool." He looks back at Tia, and I hate the bright blaze of jealousy behind my ribs. She's smart and pretty and down-to-earth, and I absolutely do not care if Nick checks her out. "Are you on the TV show?" he asks her.

Tia laughs. "Not my scene." She shoves her hands in the pockets of her jeans. "But if we can use the show to help homeless pets, I'm in."

"Fair enough."

I clear my throat. "Thank you, Nick. For hanging the banner and, uh—" Hell, he's going to make me say it. "For catching me."

"No problem." He grins and leans against the wall, chest flexing under his tight T-shirt. "Will you let me buy you a coffee?"

Times like this, I wish I'd mastered Lana's sorbet-sweet smile. I settle for my flat-eyed shark stare. "No, thank you."

There. That was easy. I start to turn away, but Nick catches my hand. "Lauren, wait." His fingers lace through mine, and I hate how my heart ticks up. "We're going to be working together. Don't you think we should clear the air?"

Tia looks from Nick to me and takes a step back. "Sounds like you have some catching up to do." She smiles and swings her gaze to mine, telegraphing the message every woman masters the moment she learns men are either sweethearts or psychos.

Are you okay? Want me to stay?

I honestly don't know what I want. Not feeling like an idiot would be a start, but we're well past that.

"We dated once," I blurt, not sure why I'm telling her. "Ancient history."

"Not that ancient," Nick adds unhelpfully.

"It went badly." I glare at him, willing him to shut the hell up.

Nick grins. "Not that badly."

My glare folds into a scowl. "Don't you have someplace to be? Cabins to build or plans to draw up or—"

"Coffee to drink?" He nods toward the table where I spotted him earlier.

Of course I saw him. I pretended I didn't, hoping he'd just go away. But I felt his eyes like a caress, dismayed to discover the magnetism still there. Nick Armbrust could be barricaded on the other side of a brick wall, and I'd still feel him.

Something softens in his eyes. He lets go of my hand, but his gaze doesn't release mine. "Please, Lauren. Just five minutes."

I can think of a million reasons to say no, but none I'm willing to say out loud. "Five minutes." I sigh and turn to Tia. "I'll let you know when the internal post goes up. We'll touch base tomorrow?"

"Sounds good." She smiles and nods at Nick. "Nice meeting you."

As she strides out of the coffee shop, I expect Nick's gaze to follow her. Not that he was ever one of those lecherous Hollywood types who see women as eye candy. That wasn't Nick's way, but Tia's gorgeous, and he's a red-blooded, heterosexual male.

Only Nick's not looking at Tia. He's watching me, his expression unreadable.

"She's single." I blurt the words without thinking. "Tia, I mean. If you're interested."

"I'm not."

"Oh." Okay, then.

I shuffle my feet, wondering if there's any way out of having coffee with him. Wondering why part of me still aches to sit down beside him and feel his heat soaking through my T-shirt.

I make a mental note to ask Patti to turn up the air conditioning. It's way too hot in here.

"Can I get you a coffee?" he asks.

"Um, sure." Why am I so out of sorts? He's just a man, a regular guy.

"You still like it black?"

Heat floods my face. "I—"

"Coffee, Lo." He grins, knowing damn well where my mind went just then. "Just the coffee."

"Yes." I clear my throat. "Actually, no. Cream and sugar, please."

"Yeah?"

"Yep."

"Anything else?"

"I'm good, thanks." I'm craving one of Patti's homemade pretzels, or maybe just something to do with my hands. But that will prolong my time with Nick, which is the last thing I need.

"Be right back." He takes his time strolling to the counter.

I glance over at the table where he was sitting when I got here. Part of me wants to choose a different one in some lame-ass attempt to assert my independence. It's petty and childish, and I can't bring myself to do it, so I amble over to his table and claim the chair he occupied minutes before. It feels like a power move, but the more I think about it, the more I wonder if he'll see it as some pathetic attempt to soak up his butt heat.

Goddammit.

See, this is why working with an ex is a bad idea.

"Problem?" Nick takes the seat across from me and pushes a steaming mug toward my left hand.

Of course he remembers I'm a southpaw. He's also got a pretzel on one plate and one of Patti's new s'mores macarons on another. He nudges the pretzel toward me and smiles.

Bastard.

Why does he have to be so damn decent?

"Lo?" He stops pushing the pretzel at me and looks deep in my eyes. "Look, I can see you're not thrilled I'm here."

"It's fine. Everything's fine."

Kill me now.

With a sigh, I pick off a hunk of pretzel and shove it in my mouth. "Thank you for this," I manage around my too-big bite. "These pretzels are amazing."

He laughs and picks up his macaron. "I'll try one next time."

We chew in awkward silence for about eight years. Or maybe I'm the only one feeling awkward, because Nick just surveys the coffee shop like he's thrilled to be here.

"This is great," he says. "Looks a lot different than when I built the place. That counter didn't used to be there, and that wall of windows really opens things up."

"Mari's idea." I can't keep the pride from my voice. "She said seeing the mountains would be more conducive to health and well-being of community members."

"How is Mari?"

"Good." I gulp some coffee. "Married."

"I saw that in one of the show trailers," he says. "Good guy?"

"The best. Griffin runs the brewery and has a daughter named—"

"Sophie, I saw." He grins. "Popular choice. That's what Alexis gave Nala as a middle name. Well, Sophia. Nala Sophia Armbrust-Davis."

"I know. We've kept in touch."

Nick cocks his head. "You suppose there's much we don't know about what the other person's been up to the past couple years?"

I shrug, not wanting to admit I've read every damn article written about him since we split. I could blame Lana, since she's the one waving them under my nose, but the truth is that I seek them out. I've got a goddamn Google alert on his name. How pathetic is that?

"We both live in the limelight," I say instead of admitting any of that stuff. "We're bound to keep tabs on each other, even if we don't want to."

"I wanted to." He looks deep into my eyes, and I hate how my stomach quivers. "I never stopped caring about you, Lo."

"Huh." I pick up my coffee and wish I could stop being a bitch. It's not Nick's fault he didn't want to marry me. That he watched me humiliate myself and then—

"Remember those s'mores at the B&B?" He picks up his macaron with a thoughtful look. "Those bonfires were the bomb. When ours went out, you relit it like some badass forest ranger."

"Wouldn't forest rangers *extinguish* fires?" It's a snarky response I regret instantly because yeah, I do remember the bonfires. I remember everything about that trip and plenty of other things Nick's surely forgotten. "Lana bought a chimenea that summer so we could figure out how to start a fire. That's how I learned."

"No kidding?" He takes a bite of the cookie, and I try not to stare at his mouth. "Or how about that time we snuck out of the awards ceremony and went to that Podunk county fair. Remember that? I wanted to win you that gigantic teddy bear—"

"Yes, I remember." I hate how my heart squeezes at the

thought of Nick gripping that giant mallet, shoulders flexing as he slammed it down to ring the bell. "Rosa loved that bear."

"She sure did." His eyes warm with thoughts of his niece, but he's watching my face with an intensity I can't read. "How about when I took you to the park? The place Lexi and I played when we were little."

My throat's closing up like a fist, and I'm fighting to keep breathing. To pretend we're just two old friends swapping sweet memories. My tongue moves before I can stop it. "The Crooked House." I swallow back a lump in my throat and sit on my hands to steady them. "That funky little play structure with the painted walls and all the weird angles."

"Man, I swear that's half the reason I wanted to be a builder." He's chuckling and shaking his head, and I swear I might kill him if he brings up our code word. The way we'd signal each other when it was time to escape some party to find quiet calm in each other's arms.

Crooked House.

We got so we didn't even say the words. One of us would hum a few bars of the old Crosby, Stills, Nash, and Young song "Our House," and we'd be out like a shot, scrambling back to his apartment where we'd tear off our clothes and dive into the safe harbor of a shared bed.

Nick's eyes hold mine, and I know he's thinking the same thing. He's going to say something. "Remember how—"

"How you asked me about hip wedding venues the week before your party?" I blurt the words before I think them through, but there's no going back. Not now. "Or when you asked me how a guy's supposed to know what kind of engagement ring a girl wants, and I said he should ask her sisters or mom or—"

"Lo." He closes his eyes, brow furrowing as he drops his head. "Shit, I'm sorry. I really was asking for a friend."

"I know that now." And I'm the fool who thought "asking for a friend" was some tongue-in-cheek code. "Did your buddy end up marrying her? The woman with the Doberman?"

"Yeah." The word comes out low and raspy, like his throat's as pinched off as mine. "He did."

"Good. Good for them." I look down at my coffee, which is cooling in its red and white mug. I take a deep breath and meet his eyes again. "If you're going to insist we play the catch-up game, can we at least focus on stuff that's not about *us*?"

His brow furrows. "How do you mean?"

"*Us*—us as a couple." I wave a hand like I'm sweeping it all under the rug. "Can we catch up on stuff that's not shared memories or whatever's been in the gossip magazines?"

He looks at me a long time then nods. "What are you putting in your grilled cheese sandwiches these days?"

The laugh bursts out so hard I choke. "That's right," I sputter, wiping up coffee with my napkin. "You kept catching me in the act."

Nick tilts his head. "I didn't know sandwiches were secret."

"They are when you've got a full-time personal trainer counting every freaking calorie you put in your body because God forbid you can't squeeze into the doll-sized gown for the Oscars." I shake my head, glad we're back on safer ground. "I mean—"

"Hey, I loved your grilled cheeses." He reaches across the table like he's going to touch my hand then stops himself. "I'll never forget that time you grilled up that gouda, veggie bacon, and apple masterpiece. Man, that thing was a work of art."

I smile in spite of myself. "A post-Golden Globes treat."

And to celebrate the first time Nick and I said "I love you" to each other. I'll never admit that out loud, and I hope he can't read it on my face.

"Bacon, spinach, and dill," I blurt. "With lots of sharp cheddar on rye bread. That's what I'm making lately. And I have them anytime I want instead of special occasions."

"Congrats." He grins. "Not just for the sandwich. For the show, the move—the fact that you look so damn happy."

"I *am* happy." It's true, so why am I feeling this big, gaping hole in my gut?

Filling it with pretzel seems smart, so I take another big bite. "How about you?" I ask when I finish chewing. "Did you learn to do all those yoyo tricks?"

Nick busts out laughing. "I forgot all about that. Man, I don't even think I still have that thing."

"Really?" My stomach wobbles as I think about what's hidden in the keepsake box in my cabin. "But you were so gung-ho to master the yoyo. Something about hand-eye coordination, wasn't it?"

"Yeah, I read some article about it." He shakes his head, dragging a hand over his face as I try not to recall the warmth of his skin under my palm. "I wonder if I still have those videos I bought."

"It's never too late to learn something new."

The instant I say it, Nick's eyes lock with mine. Crap, did that sound like a come-on?

"I mean, I've been wanting to learn how to cook." I fight the urge to wince. "Something besides grilled cheese. Lana's getting good at it, and Mari, too. I'm slower to learn."

From the look Nick just gave me, he knows I'm not talking about cooking. I clear my throat, needing to shift to safer ground. "So...violin. Did you ever end up learning like you wanted to?"

"Nope." He makes a face. "Even bought one on Amazon. Ask me how many times I took it out of the case."

"How many times?"

"Once." He laughs and picks up his coffee mug. "Guess I lost interest when I realized I wasn't an instant virtuoso."

"You mean mastering an instrument takes time and patience?" I give him my best steely stare. "Who knew?"

"Very funny, wise-ass." He regards me over the rim of his mug. "Did you learn Spanish like you wanted to?"

"Claro que sí." I clip the consonants like Tia taught me. "Porque a diferencia de ti, yo no soy una persona de mucho ruido y pocas nueces."

"Ha!" Nick claps in mock applause, and I try not to get distracted by his hands. "My college Spanish is fuzzy, but nueces—that's nuts, right?"

Oh, shit. I forgot Nick minored in Spanish. He'd planned to do immigration law and thought that might be handy. "Uh, yeah. It's an idiom, though."

"So I shouldn't take offense that I'm pretty sure you just said I have small nuts?"

Fuck.

I have only myself to blame for steering a conversation with my ex to the subject of his testicles.

"The literal translation is something like 'a lot of noise and no walnuts,'" I explain, carefully sidestepping the testicle thing. "But the phrase is more like 'all talk and no action.'"

Nick cocks his head. "You think I'm all talk and no action?"

Why the hell did I start down this path?

"It's just an expression," I say, trying not to sound flustered. "One I learned producing that film in Spain. Tia's been helping me nail pronunciation. Her great-grandma grew up in Mexico, so the accent's a little different."

"I see."

Nick holds my gaze, and I worry he *does* see. That he sees right through me and knows that beneath my cool surface, I'm a big, silly s'more-squished marshmallow. I always have been with him.

Which is why I need to get out of here.

I stand up too fast, nearly knocking over my chair. I catch it quickly, then grab my coffee mug and chug it like soda.

"This was nice," I announce as I slam down the mug a little

too hard. "Now that we've got that out of the way, I'm guessing we won't cross paths all that much."

Guessing. Hoping. Praying.

Nick eyes me, arms folded over his chest, a bemused smile on lips I wish I didn't remember kissing. I'm flooding with memories, and I have to get out of here.

He stands up and holds out his hand. I stare down at it, not sure if I'm supposed to shake it or slap palms. "Lo."

The sexy rumble sets off fireworks in my chest. "What?"

I hate the quiver in my voice. I hate even more that I can't stop picturing that hand skimming my body, caressing my—

"Ass." He shakes his head and draws his hand back. "I was such an ass back then. Flighty and cocky and untethered. But I never stopped thinking about you."

I swallow hard, my urge to flee welling up like tears. "Ancient history," I manage to croak.

"Nah, it's still fresh." He holds out his hand again. I hesitate, then slowly place my palm in his. "Truce, okay?

"No need," I say much too brightly. "We're not at war."

He makes a sound that might be stifled laughter or might be dissent. "We were always halfway between."

"Between what?" I can't believe I'm prolonging this. That I need to know the answer.

"Making war." His voice is a low rumble as he leans close so only I can hear. "Making love."

Heat floods my face as I back up to get away. My hand's still in his, and he lets go easy as I bolt. "Yes, well. Things change. People change."

He looks at me long and slow as I back toward the door. "Not everything."

"*I've* changed." I don't know why I'm so insistent. Why I can't seem to make my feet move. "I'm different now."

"That so?" His curiosity sounds real, without a trace of sarcasm.

"Yep. Yessir. Absolutely." I back into the counter and bounce off, pinging toward the exit. "Completely different person."

I spin toward the door, not waiting around to hear his response. I feel his eyes on me though, warm like a caress. As I push through the door, I suck in a breath and make my escape.

What I said is true. I am a different person. So is Nick.

But as I sprint for my cabin, I wonder if the person I am now still loves Nick Armbrust.

CHAPTER 3

CONFESSIONAL 771
<u>Armbrust, Nick (Owner, Armbrust Resorts)</u>
Yeah, I've got a history with this place. Couldn't believe it when those cult guys called me up to bid on it. Couldn't believe they gave me the job. This was back before anyone knew who I was, way before Armbrust Resorts was even a thing. Hard to believe how much has changed since then.
'Course, there's plenty of things that never change. Not one damn bit.

* * *

"Let's put the trusses over there." I wave toward the open area between the cabins I built years ago and the footings for the ones I'm building now. "Don't forget we're pouring concrete in the morning."

My construction foreman nods and tugs off his work gloves. "We still framing that cabin tomorrow?"

I can tell my crew doesn't know what to make of me doing manual labor right alongside them. It's not how most developers run things, but it's how I do it. "Yep. Let's get an early start. Six okay?"

"Yes, sir."

"Vern, come on." I've told these guys a dozen times they don't need to act like I'm some stuffy-ass CEO. "Nick. It's just Nick."

"Yes, s—Nick." He grins. "See you tomorrow."

I watch him head for his truck, grateful the Judsons found local laborers who know the value of a hard day's work. Some jobs I've done, we've struggled to find workers. That's not an issue here.

"Hey, man!"

I turn to see Cooper Judson ambling over with his movie star grin. He holds out a hand and I slap his palm before giving it a good shake. "Coop, my man! Good to see you."

"You're getting right to work, huh?"

"That's the plan." I glance at my watch, surprised it's well past six. "Probably time to knock off for the day."

"I was hoping you'd say that." He jerks a thumb toward the brewery. "Want to grab a beer?"

"Uh—"

"Root beer." Coop grins. "Promise I haven't fallen off the wagon. The brewmaster makes some kickass ginger beer, too."

"Sold." I peel off my work gloves and shove them in my back pocket. "Tell me they've got food?"

"You haven't been yet?" Coop shakes his head like I've just confessed to snorting sausage. "Their fried pickles will rock your world. And they've got this great grilled cheese—pears in it, if you can believe that."

"I'm in." And I'm thinking about Lauren. Could be the grilled cheese, but that's just an excuse. Truth is, I haven't stopped thinking about her, hoping we'll run into each other again.

She must be hoping the opposite. It's been days, and we haven't crossed paths. I don't have to be a rocket scientist to guess that's on purpose.

As Coop and I make our way along the path by the pond, he catches me up on the latest Juniper Ridge news. "Our ratings were up four percent last week, which is pretty huge."

"You've got more cast members lined up for the new cabins?"

He laughs. "Don't let Mari hear you call them cast. They're 'community members.'" He makes air quotes around the words. "And this is a 'thoughtfully planned, self-contained community,' not a reality show."

"Is there gonna be a quiz later?"

Cooper drags open the brewery door. "Your real test comes when Lauren catches you alone and starts chasing you for improvised B-roll. Best to just go with it. Easier that way."

I don't have a chance to dwell on the thought of Lauren catching me alone since the hostess hustles over and seats us in a booth. Beer taps span the length of the maple bar, while rows of whiskey, gin, and vodka line shelves behind that. I steal a careful glance at Cooper, wondering if it's tough for him to stay sober.

He catches my eye and smiles. "The veggie burger is insane. Pro-tip: Add the roasted Ortega chilis."

"Sold." I skim the list of sides. "Sweet potato fries or tater tots?"

"Yep." Cooper grins. "Trust me, you'll want both."

I browse the beverage section, spotting the ginger and root beer he mentioned, plus housemade orange and grape sodas. There's also a serious tap list boasting pilsners and porters, IPAs and sour beers. Not that I'm ordering any of that now.

Coop clears his throat. "You can order a beer, you know. It's not gonna bother me."

"I know." I lay the menu on the table . "Next time. I've got an early morning."

He stretches his arms over the back of the booth, earning an appreciative glance from a passing waitress. "This is what I dig about you, man," he says.

"What's that?"

Coop shrugs. "My siblings are great, right? But they spend half their time dancing around me like I'm about to fall off the wagon. You never do that."

"Aw, hell." Now I feel bad for even *thinking* it. "You're a big boy, Coop. You don't need me hovering like some overprotective parent."

He laughs and pours us both waters from a clear glass jug. "The sibs have that covered."

Before I can respond, a waitress appears to take our order. We both get veggie burgers with baskets of tots and sweet potato fries to share. I pick a hibiscus ginger beer, while Coop goes for grape. We've just thanked the server when a slim blonde woman walks through the door.

I watch as Coop tenses. Studying the woman, I tense, too, but for different reasons. "She's a cop?"

Cooper blinks "How'd you know?"

I shrug. "Lucky guess."

He eyes me a bit, and I wonder what's showing on my face. I've never been in trouble with the law, but I also can't forget the talk my parents gave me years before I was old enough to drive.

"Hands visible if you're pulled over," Mama urged, snatching my favorite hoodie out of the laundry. "Never wear this with the hood up."

Pop folded his arms over his chest and stared me down. "Hands out of your pockets, always."

"No sudden moves," Mama continued. "And don't ever, *ever* run if an officer stops you."

"But Mama," I argued. "If I just stay out of trouble—"

"Doesn't matter." She shook her head with a sadness I didn't understand back then. "Rules are different for us."

As I watch the cop approach, I lay my palms flat on the table.

"Hi, Cooper." She turns her smile on me and extends a hand. "I don't think we've met—I'm Amy Lovelin."

Her handshake is warm and firm, dissolving some of the tension in my shoulders. "Nick Armbrust."

"You're *Nick*." Her smile widens. "Cooper's told me so much about you. I'm the police chief. It's great to finally meet you."

She sounds genuine, and I'm not getting the vibe she's planning to pat me down.

"Got a brother-in-law who's a cop," I tell her. This detail tends to melt the ice a bit. "You've been at Juniper Ridge from the start?"

Amy nods, her smile widening. "Born and raised just a few miles from here. It's great to have you with us." She pauses, and I see her weighing something in her mind. "Look, I won't pretend there's not some really ugly history in Oregon. I just want to say I'm aware of it, and I'm committed to tackling unconscious bias and making sure all my officers are trained in diversity and inclusion."

Her candor takes me aback. I glance at Coop, who's shifting uncomfortably in his seat. "Not sure if you know it, but when Oregon was still a territory, they passed a law banning Black folks from living here," I tell him. "Someone broke the law, the penalty was thirty-nine lashes every six months until they left the state."

Coop's face darkens. "Jesus."

Amy picks up from there. "There's horrible history with police in Oregon and the KKK." She swallows, and I see it's why she brought this up. She's letting me know she's not one of *those* cops. "Everyone thinks Oregon's this inclusive, open-minded utopia," she continues, "and we *can* be. It's a beautiful, loving place filled with all kinds of people. But there's ugliness, too." She presses her lips together and looks at me. "Sorry, I didn't mean to get grim. But I didn't want to ignore the elephant in the room."

"I appreciate that." I take a sip of the soda our waitress just delivered as Coop watches Amy with an interest he's trying hard to hide.

"Did I tell you Abe made captain?" I shift a glance at Amy and fill her in. "That's my brother-in-law. He and my sister are down in LA."

The pretty police chief smiles. "I'd love to meet him sometime."

Is it my imagination, or did Coop and Amy just exchange a look? It's subtle, masked mostly by Cooper's acting chops and Amy's cop training. Still, it's something. Or maybe I'm paranoid?

I clear my throat and gesture to the spot next to Cooper. "Want to join us for dinner?"

"Thanks," she says, "but I just stopped by to brief Cooper on the application process for our new deputy police chief."

"That's right, the posting went live last week?" He's looking at her like he's interested in way more than job applications, and I wonder if she notices.

"We've already had over a hundred candidates apply." She brushes blond hair off her face and rests a hand on her belt. "Lots of interest from all over the country. There are three or four I've got my eye on."

"We should compare notes." Coop looks at me and lifts an eyebrow. "For some reason the fam has me overseeing law enforcement. Ironic, huh?"

I glance at Amy and see her expression dim. Not that Cooper Judson's legal troubles are any secret. The gossip rags had a heyday with his struggles, but still. I'm guessing Chief Lovelin's not big on guys with rap sheets. Not even reformed ones like Coop.

"Maybe I'll mention it to Abe." I'm joking, since he and Alexis have a sweet setup in LA. No way are they leaving. "If nothing else, I'll get 'em out here to visit."

Again with an odd look between Coop and Amy. And again, I think I'm imagining things. I'm about to ask what's up when the door swings open and Lauren storms through.

"Cooper! I need your thoughts on my idea for a celebrity

guest star on the season finale with the animal rescue, plus there's an issue with the bumper cars where—" The words die in her throat as she spots me. "Oh. It's you."

"Good to see you, too." I keep my grin in check, but fire flashes in her eyes.

"Likewise." Lauren looks at Amy. "Hey, Chief. Whatever you're arresting them for, they're definitely guilty."

Amy puts her hands up and backs away from the table. "No charges necessary. They're model citizens." She smiles and throws us a quick wave. "Gotta go. Cooper—we'll touch base tomorrow?"

"Count on it."

She's out the door before I have a chance to mull over how weird they were acting. I've got better things to think about anyway, with Lauren standing here looking lush and warm and a little hostile.

"Have a seat." I pat the bench beside me, not surprised when she doesn't budge. "We've got sweet potato fries on the way."

"And tater tots," Cooper throws in helpfully. "We might even share."

Lauren's stern look slips. If my girl's got a soft spot, it's salty, greasy goodness.

She's not your girl anymore.

I'd be smart to remember that.

"Join us, Lo." It's a risk using her old nickname, and I can't tell what the flash in her eyes means. "And if you tell me all about your bumper car problem, maybe I can fix it."

"Fine." She plops down next to Cooper and frowns at me. "But only because we've got an event happening out there soon, and Lana's freaking out we won't have the cars ready in time."

"What's the problem?" While I built the pavilion, I don't know much about the mechanics of the cars. But I'm willing to give it a shot.

Lauren folds her hands on the table. "Several of the bumpers are…limp."

"Limp?" Coop lifts an eyebrow. "What, like bumper car erectile dysfunction?"

She rolls her eyes at her brother. "You're such a child." Her gaze shifts to mine. "We didn't notice until Gabe and I went to scope out camera angles for the shoot. Three of the cars are just sitting there with saggy, floppy bumpers."

"Sounds like some plastic surgery's in order." I hold up my hands before she can react. "Not a childish joke, I swear. That's how the bumpers are made. These little plastic pellets get melted down and injected into a mold. Release the mold, and you've got your bumper cover."

Lauren's look turns curious. "Is it fixable?"

"Should be." I shrug and sip my soda. "Someone who works with thermoplastics would handle a job like that, but I'm happy to take a look."

"Thank you." Lauren refolds her hands. "I appreciate it."

"No problem." I'm weighing what else to say to keep the conversation flowing when the waitress returns with two heaping baskets of tots and fries. She's got a great beaded Ganesh tattoo on one burnished arm that's just like one an old foreman had.

"Cool ink," I say, hoping to ease the tension at our table. "I knew a guy with one a lot like it."

"Yeah?" She turns her arm so I can see it better, her brown skin warm beneath the bar lights. "I got it visiting my grandma in Nepal."

"Love the detail."

"Thanks. Here's an extra plate so you can share." She sets down a caddy of sauces in front of Lauren. "Ranch, truffle ketchup, and Cajun mayo. Enjoy!"

Cooper digs in as the server hustles off. "Get 'em while they're hot."

Lauren hesitates, then grabs a few of each. "This is the best thing about being here, you know."

"Fried food?" I heap a share on my own plate and reach for the Cajun sauce.

"That, sure." She swirls a fry through the truffle ketchup. "But being able to eat it. Not having to watch every little calorie because God forbid I end up on some website shoving fries in my face. Or worse, I walk the red carpet wearing anything but a sample size."

"Such bullshit." Cooper looks at me. "Ask me how many times gossip rags wrote about what I ate?"

"How many?" I'm pretty sure I know the answer.

"Zero." He holds up both hands to make a circle, then grabs more fries.

Lauren picks up a tot. "Same number as the dress size I'm never required to wear again."

"You look great to me."

She glances up like I might be pulling her leg. "Thanks."

"No problem." I grin, grabbing at a memory. "Always sucked seeing you having to sneak junk food like some kind of drug deal." I deliberately don't look at Coop, recalling what he said about his family handling him with kid gloves. "Gotta say, watching you eat chips was a thing of beauty."

Lo's eyes flicker, and I wonder if she's remembering the same thing I am. The two of us naked in bed, a bag of Ruffles between us with a tub of onion dip wedged in the pillows. She'd laugh and make a crack about TMZ having hidden cameras in the bedroom before she grabbed a fistful of chips.

Crooked House.

All it took was one of us saying those words and we knew. Our signal to shut out the world and let our guard down together.

Lauren licks her lips, holding my gaze just long enough I know she's playing the same film reel in her mind. But she jerks out of it, swiveling back to face Cooper. "So anyway, about the adoption event—if it goes well, we're thinking ahead to making it a regular part of the show."

Cooper sips his soda. "Like a public service thing?"

"Basically. We'd spotlight different people adopting animals and share stats about why it's so important to rescue instead of buying from breeders."

I grab another fry. "Won't that piss off viewers with purebreds?"

Lauren looks surprised. "Or dog breeders themselves, yes. We thought of that already."

"If anyone can spin it, Lana can." Cooper winks. "It pays to have the world's savviest PR babe in the family."

Lauren smacks him. "Your sisters aren't babes."

"They kind of are," I point out, earning a smack of my own. "Don't you remember the acronym from that documentary you did? Balanced, Authentic, Bold, Erotic—fits all three of you."

Lauren rolls her eyes, but there's color in her cheeks now that wasn't there before. "Anyway, Dean likes the idea. It's still just a fantasy at this point, but you know I like to plan ahead."

With a snort, Cooper grabs a tater tot and looks at me. "She already knows I might sneeze at noon next Tuesday and has a pack of tissues in her purse."

"Gesundheit." Lauren grabs a tot. "Anyway, we're covering the shelter idea at the next family meeting. I want your thoughts on whether we could get Cash Beckett out here for the finale."

"Cash?" Cooper's brow furrows. "Why him?"

"He did that blockbuster last year with the animal rescue," Lauren says. "Since you guys were drinking buddies, I thought—" She pauses and frowns. "Wait. Is it bad to have you talk to him?"

Cooper makes an exasperated sound. "Yeah, Lauren. The sound of his voice makes me want to snort coke off a hooker's forehead."

Lo's face goes red, and I can tell she's flustered. I'm no

stranger to butting heads with my sister, so I know I'd better change the subject.

"Where's this adoption event happening?" I probably should have looked at the banner when I was hanging it, but I was too busy reorienting to Lauren. "It's here at Juniper Ridge?"

"Not the first one, no." Lauren grabs a fry. "Most of the dogs are from Tia Nelson's ranch. She runs a rehab clinic there."

"Cats and bunnies, too," Cooper puts in. "We're having the first one in her barn."

"Right, but if it becomes a regular thing, won't you need a facility here?" I keep my tone casual, but I'm pretty sure Lo knows why I'm asking.

Sure enough, she quirks an eyebrow. "You volunteering to build us an animal shelter?"

"Possibly." Not like I don't have tons of other work on my plate, but how could I pass up a chance to get more involved with Lauren? "What sort of needs are we talking about?"

She licks her lips again, and I rethink my word choice. Or not. I'm pretty interested in Lauren's needs.

"Hard to say this early in the game," she says. "Big enough for maybe a dozen dog kennels. A separate area for cats and one for small animals like guinea pigs and rabbits."

I comb my brain for existing structures here that could work. "What's in that warehouse on the northeast edge of the property?"

Lauren frowns. "Warehouse? Oh, you mean the storage space."

"There's your answer." Cooper grabs a tot. "It's full of crap, mostly."

"Huh." I'm already thinking of ways to retrofit it as I grab a napkin and slip a carpenter's pencil from my pocket. "Something like this, maybe. It's already got concrete floors for cleanup, so with a few dozen panels of chain link fencing..." I start sketching kennels as I try to recall the dimensions of the structure. "Doggie doors leading to an outdoor area for fresh air."

Lauren stares at my hands, lingering a while before lifting her gaze to mine. "Yes, I—something like that."

"That actually wouldn't be so hard." I push the napkin toward her and fold my hands on the table. "I know someone who runs a shelter in LA. I could reach out for tips if you want."

Lauren blinks. "Already on it. Gabe's wife, Gretchen—she has a sister with tons of experience in nonprofits and animal welfare. Jessie's coming tomorrow for a consultation."

Of course Lo's on the ball. She's always ten steps ahead of the game. "I'd like to help," I tell her. "If you decide to forge ahead, count me in."

"Thank you." Her steely eyes hold mine. "I'll keep it in mind."

She licks her lips again, and for a few breathless seconds, I think she might slide across the table and kiss me. It's a crazy thought, but one I can't shake.

Lauren shakes herself instead. "So, bumper cars." The words slip out swift and rushed. "How did BONK decide a cult compound needed those, anyway?"

I laugh, mostly in surprise. Leave it to Lo to change the subject. "Oh, you'd be amazed by what didn't make the cut." I grab another fry. "They had all kinds of carnival stuff on the table."

"Like what?" Cooper asks.

"A human trebuchet. This giant medieval bucket they wanted to set up to fling people into a net. They thought it sounded fun."

Lauren's brow furrows. "Sounds like a lawsuit."

"That's what I told 'em. A park somewhere in the UK had something similar. Got into big trouble when a rider missed the net and died."

"Jeez." She frowns. "What else?"

"Something called a SpinDizzy," I say. "Also from a UK amusement park chain where they turn old construction equipment into rides."

Cooper looks delighted. "What does the SpinDizzy do?"

"It's a modified excavator with a bucket they retrofit to hold eight passengers." I flip over the napkin and sketch another picture. "The ride hoists 'em up in the air and spins around. Pretty bonkers."

Lauren grabs another tot. "Were you the one who talked them out of it?"

"Yeah," I say. "Convinced them go-karts and the water park were plenty."

Lauren rolls her eyes. "I still don't understand why a doomsday cult needed all that."

"Guess if you're preparing for the end of the world, you may as well do it with carnival rides." I glance at Cooper. "Didn't you do a film with a Ferris wheel? One of your action flicks?"

Cooper laughs and picks up his soda. "Oh, yeah. They had me climbing up the outside of it while it was spinning. That was the one where I did my own stunts. Almost shit myself when they started roping me up."

Lauren shakes her head. "I still can't believe your manager let that happen. If I hadn't been filming in Paris, I'd have shown up on set every day to roll you in bubble wrap."

"I can see that." I glance at Cooper. "You got to save the day though, right?"

"Right." Coop smiles. "The final scene had me proposing to my co-star at the top of the Ferris wheel, so it came full circle—pun intended."

I laugh because that's what the crack calls for, but Lauren stiffens across from me. Crap, it's the proposal. I try not to look at her, hoping we can pretend that didn't just happen.

When she jumps up, I'm not surprised. "Excuse me," she says. "I—uh—just remembered I need to check something for the adoption event."

"Sure, no problem." I stand because my mama raised me right, but Lauren's halfway to the door. "You still want me to come look at the bumper cars?" I call.

She spins around, hand on the door, and I swear her eyes are glittering. She blinks hard and nods. "I'd appreciate it. How about half an hour?"

"I'll be there." Part of me knows she won't. That she'll send Gabe or Lana or Cooper so she doesn't have to face me. "Good seeing you, Lo."

Her wince is so subtle that I'm guessing Coop doesn't see it. "Same."

Then she pushes through the door, hair flying behind like a superhero cape.

CHAPTER 4

CONFESSIONAL 788.5
Judson, Lauren (Producer: Juniper Ridge)
Were you there last week when Mari gave her talk on manifestations of hurt?
[eye-roll]
Of course I wasn't participating. I was filming.
Anyway, I guess some people respond to hurt with tears, while others throw themselves into work or sweep things under the rug. For some people it shows up as aggression or—
Stop interrupting. Yes, Lana. I'm aware I'm crushing the paper cup. I like it this way, okay?

* * *

If someone said two years ago I'd be standing on a bumper car platform in rural Oregon waiting for the man who broke my heart, I'd have laughed 'til I peed.

But this is my life now. And as I watch Nick striding slow and easy along the tree-lined path, I wish my heart didn't drag itself from the basement of my chest and bounce like a rabid bunny.

He's carrying a red toolbox and moving like we've got all the time in the world. *If only.*

"Lo." He touches the brim of a ballcap that says Armbrust Resorts, and I remember how his mom hated him in hats.

"Makes you look like a common laborer," she used to say. He rarely wore them, not even on the beach or lazy Sundays alone.

I shake off memories like sticky water droplets and offer my best shark smile. "Thanks for coming." I toe one of the wilted bumpers with my sneaker, reminding me even my footwear has changed. "I don't know if these things are fixable, but I can't send people out in them like this."

"Definitely not." Plunking his toolbox beside the blue and green car, Nick crouches and pokes at the flabby rubber. "I made a call to a buddy who owns a thermoplastics company in Portland. They work on these things a lot."

"You think it's fixable?"

"Not by me." He stands and dusts off his hands. "But this looks like what my buddy described. He can be out here before the end of the week to do the repairs."

"Oh, well—thank you." I bite back a flicker of irritation. Nick's habit of making assumptions, of charging confidently in one direction while I'm ambling in another wasn't great in a relationship.

But it's handy when I need help fast, so I swallow my annoyance. "Thanks," I say again. "Please have him send me the bill."

"Will do." He surveys the arena, whistling low as he does a slow pivot. "Man, this brings back memories. I always loved it here."

The word *love* rolling off his tongue makes my belly quiver. I shove back the sensation and nod. "It's pretty great. All the fresh air and outdoorsy stuff. I find myself breathing easier here."

He cocks his head, and a flash of memory hits me between the eyes. I used to say that to him, falling into his arms after I'd called a Crooked House.

"I just breathe easier with you," I'd say, snuggling against his chest.

I swallow again as Nick watches me. If he remembers, he doesn't say anything. Not about that. "Couldn't believe it when I heard your family bought this place," he says. "I've got a lot of memories here."

"Yeah, well." I clear my throat. "Knowing you built it was a big factor. We never would have invested if we weren't confident in the construction."

Nick smiles. "Thanks."

"You're welcome."

My skin starts buzzing as his eyes sweep over me. He's got his hands in his pockets, and I have the oddest feeling there's something he wants to say. After a long stretch of silence, he adjusts the ballcap. "Mama's been binge-watching the show. Pretty cool concept."

"Thanks." I shove my hands in the back pockets of my jeans, conscious of how awkward this is. Also a little romantic, though I'd never say that. Crickets chatter in the sagebrush as the sun dunks itself low over the lip of a basalt cliff. A sweet, warm breeze stirs the grassy field to the north, sending wisps of alfalfa swaying like dancers. Nick's dark skin glows in the last shreds of sunlight, and I forget for a moment what brought us here.

"Bumper cars." I clear my throat. "You think there's any chance we'll be safe to run the event in a couple weeks?"

"Depends." He steps toward the next cluster of cars, circling to inspect them. "These ones look okay. You've checked them all?"

"Pretty much." I shrug, not liking to admit when I'm in over my head. "I'm not exactly a bumper car expert, but nothing's falling off."

Nick laughs and bends to inspect the next cluster of cars. "Neither am I, but I'll give 'em a look."

He takes his time making a lap around the arena, peering

closely at each car. I stand like a lump with my hands in my pockets, hating that I'm not useful. That I don't know what I'm doing.

But Nick clearly does, even if he's no bumper car expert. He stoops and adjusts something with a screwdriver, then moves on to the next car. His attention to detail is admirable. So is the way he fills out his jeans, his backside tight and muscular and—

"Lookin' good."

I blink. "What?"

He glances up and grins like he knows damn well where I've been looking. "Your bumper cars. Can't say if they're mechanically sound, but the rest of these look solid from a cosmetic standpoint."

"Oh. Right. Thank you." I push back a hank of hair that's fallen over my face. "Does your thermoplastics guy do mechanical stuff, or just the bumper parts?"

"Just the bumpers." He tucks his screwdriver back in the toolbox and closes the lid. "But I left a message with a guy in town. Someone who helped set 'em up at the start. He can come out next week. I'm guessing you had these tuned up when you bought the place?"

"Of course." Like we wouldn't take every step to ensure safety. "I just got worried when I saw the limp bumpers. Like maybe we weren't thorough enough."

"You should be good to go." He studies me a moment, like he's deciding something. "Want to test them out to make sure?"

"What?" I bite my lip, pretty sure I know where this is going. "You're suggesting we—play?"

Is that even the right verb for bumper cars?

Nick grins and lifts his arms. "You know it, girl." He executes a dance move that definitely shouldn't be sexy. "A little bump and grind to feel things out?" He laughs and stops dancing. "Maybe more of a friendly battle."

Nick knows damn well I can't resist a challenge, but I force myself to execute a bored eye-roll. "And I called Cooper childish."

"Is that a no?" He steps closer, reminding me how tall and powerful he is. "It's all right. I get it."

"Get what?" My voice comes out oddly breathy.

"You're afraid I'll win." He's grinning as he tucks a piece of hair behind my ear, and I gulp back the urge to lean into his hand. "Hey, no worries. We wouldn't want to damage your delicate parts."

I take a sharp breath and glare. "You really think that's going to work on me?"

"Maybe?" The hopeful glint in his eyes is my undoing. "Probably not, but a guy can hope. Should I try another tack?"

I should just go home. There's no point flirting with Nick, if that's what you'd call this. But something keeps my feet rooted in place. "What else have you got?"

"Hmmm, let's see." He leans back against the wall, muscles flexing. "If I can't impress you with my dance moves or woo you with a challenge, I'll charm you some other way."

"Really." God help me, I'm falling for this. "What did you have in mind?"

He rubs his chin, pretending to think. "You still got a thing for nerdy trivia?"

"I don't."

I totally do.

"Huh." He rubs his chin some more, clearly not believing me. "Did you know the first bumper cars in the 1920s weren't actually meant to collide?"

"What?" I don't even ask how he knows this. Nick's always been a font of weird information, and I wish I didn't find that attractive. "Why are they called bumper cars then?"

"Back then, they were called dodgem. You were supposed to avoid hitting anything as you zigzagged all around the floor. The steering was built to be screwy, so it was all about dodging other cars."

"Huh." I've missed Nick's knack for weird trivia. "What happened if you hit someone?"

"You'd get penalized," he says. "Partly because they were made out of cheap tin and they'd fall apart with the slightest bump. They had to burn those first dodgem cars after one season."

I glance at the closest car, a yellow one with flames on the sides. "I trust they make them stronger now?"

"Oh, yeah." His voice is warm and fluid, and I'm not sure this is about amusement park rides. Is he spinning some sort of metaphor? "Folks started learning from those earlier mistakes. Added things like seatbelts and bumpers to soften impact. Closed off the sides to protect people's feet."

I'm fighting not to think of how this applies to us. Fighting the urge to grasp Nick's hand, to pull him close and draw his mouth down to mine as he—

"Let's go."

Nick blinks. "What?"

I swallow hard, ignoring at least half my urges. "The bumper cars." I sweep a hand to the side. "I accept your challenge."

"Yeah?" His grin spreads slow and easy. "You sure?"

"What, you're chickening out now?" I tuck my hands into my armpits and start clucking, flapping my wings for effect. "Hey, I understand. Sucks to have your ass handed to you by an ex."

That gets him. Nick's eyes blaze with mirth and something I can't read. He laughs and pushes off the wall. "Game on, girl." Grinning, he brushes my bicep in mid wing-flap. "Now who's childish?"

I don't bother answering since he's headed for a red car with flames on the side. I stop clucking and swing into the closest car, a yellow one with black stripes. It reminds me of the bumblebee Mari crocheted for me when we were kids, and I wonder what my shrink sister would think of what I'm doing.

Pushing that from my mind, I test the pedals with the toes of my sneakers. "Let's see what you've got, hot shot."

Nick hoots as he slings his big frame into the red car. "Buckle up, babe. You've got some serious ramming headed your way."

I ignore the bait, though Lauren from two years ago would have seized the shot at a flirty joke. But that's not where we are now, or ever again. We're just two work colleagues testing equipment.

Keep telling yourself that.

I switch on my car, grateful I booted up the system before he got here. I thought it might be handy for his inspection, but I didn't expect this.

He flashes a grin that sends my belly flopping like a fish. "Ready?" He grips the wheel, already buckled in. "How about I start on the other side so we face off all proper-like?"

I glance at the sky, making sure there's no clear advantage with the position of the sun. It's dragging low over the basalt ridge, casting a golden glow on the arena. I can't believe we've got the place to ourselves. A sentimental woman might see that as serendipity.

But I'm not sentimental, so I point to a spot at the edge of the arena. "Right over there." I angle my car that direction. "These babies are electric, by the way."

"I know. You've got the batteries charged?"

"Of course." Like I'd forget a detail like that. "How are we scoring this?"

Nick's already in position facing me, and I can see his brow lift from twenty feet away. "You want rules?"

I shrug. "How else are you going to know when I've won?"

"Maybe we both win." He grins and adjusts the brim of his cap. "Or we both lose."

His words feel heavy with meaning, but I'm imagining things again. I concentrate on getting myself lined up, on feathering the pedals so I know how to finesse it.

Across from me, Nick's doing the same. "The lightest touch sends you into orbit, huh?"

I ignore the innuendo since he clearly didn't mean it that way. Doesn't matter if it's true, if just the faintest, featherlight brush of his fingers used to rocket me to the moon. That's not what he's implying, and I need to stop thinking like that.

"Okay." I grip my steering wheel and ignore the thud of my heart.

It's force of habit. Just a bunch of old neurons firing because they forgot we're not in love with Nick anymore.

Maybe I'll believe it if I keep saying it in my head.

I meet Nick's eye. "Ready?"

"Always."

Deep breath. "In three, two, one…"

I stomp the gas and lurch forward, zooming at Nick. He's laughing as he careens toward me, zigzagging so I can't tell where he's going. I'm not sure if he's playing chicken or planning to hit me head-on, and the uncertainty kicks me into gear. He's getting closer, still laughing, still keeping me guessing.

Bam!

He strikes the left side of my car and I let out a yelp. He freezes instantly.

"You okay?" He eases back, concern etched on his brow.

"Please." I spit hair out of my mouth and give my best shark smile. "Barely rattled."

"Yeah?" He quirks an eyebrow. "Permission granted to go harder?"

God.

No way am I letting him see his unintentional innuendos are getting to me. They're unintentional, right? "Let's do it again."

His eyes flash, and instantly I'm back in Nick's bedroom in LA. It was the first time we had sex, and in the dizzied afterglow, I rolled over and put a hand on his chest. *"That was amazing. Let's do it again."*

He laughed then, just like he's doing now. "Always loved your spunk, Lo."

I wish he'd stop calling me that. I wish he'd *keep* calling me that so I can feel the flutter in my belly each time.

Instead, I spin around to return to the starting point.

Wham!

This jolt comes from nowhere, and I give a squeal of surprise. I whip my head around to face him. "What the hell?"

"Thought we were already underway." He backs up, grinning. "Anything goes now, right?"

"No ramming from behind." Crap, I didn't mean to say that. Nick's grinning like he caught the double meaning this time.

"Sorry," he says, not sounding very sorry. "It's rude to ram a lady who's not expecting it."

I narrow my eyes and force my voice to sound stern. "Watch it, Armbrust." I edge my car toward the starting line, keeping him in my sights. "I'm just getting warmed up."

His grin widens. "I could go all night."

I know he can, and that has nothing to do with why I just shuddered. Stomping the pedal, I careen toward him. At the last second I zip sideways, zooming around to nail his rear flank.

Wham!

"Ooof." Nick grunts with surprise, then spins around to grin at me. "Oh, girl. You're just asking me to bang you into next Tuesday."

For fuck's sake.

He's smiling his good-natured Nick smile, so I'm probably alone in hearing dirty jokes. He could recite his mother's pancake recipe and I'd probably spread my legs.

I need to focus.

I also need to get away from the wall before he pins me up against it and bangs into me over and over and—well, just…that would be bad.

"Why are you looking like that?" Nick cocks his head, watching me like my thoughts are flickering over a movie screen on my forehead.

I lift my chin and feign ignorance. "Like what?"

"Same way you used to look when we'd sneak out of a premiere to have sex in the coat closet."

The fact that I've got an identifiable look to accompany the act is a testament to how many times we did it. But I'm not letting him see he's getting to me. "I don't know what you're talking about."

"Sure, Lo." He smiles and zips back to the other side of the arena. "On three?"

I grit my teeth and clutch the wheel. "Three, two, one…"

Instead of stomping the gas, I stay still. Nick's moving fast with a gleam in his eye. I hold my breath and hold my spot, willing him to come at me. To underestimate me.

He's ten feet away, now six, and I pump the pedal a little, just enough to make the car wobble.

Four feet, three, two…

I jerk the wheel and stomp the accelerator, escaping just before impact. Nick hammers the brake, but not quick enough.

Bam!

He slams the wall behind me, jerking him back in the seat. I spin around, ready to ram him from the side like I'd planned. But the dazed look in his eye stops me. "Are you okay?"

He stares and doesn't answer. Oh, shit. He's really hurt.

I yank off the seatbelt and shove the door open, flailing as I sprint to his side. "Oh my God, did I hurt you?"

Gold-brown eyes hold mine as his slow grin spreads. "Just seeing if you still care."

I smack him hard on the shoulder. "Jerk."

"Ow." He winces and rubs his neck. "Lay off the assault, will you? I fell off a ladder last week and—"

"Shit, I'm sorry." I touch his shoulder and stoop beside his bumper car. "Should you even be doing this?"

He holds my gaze a long time, dropping his hand to the wheel. "Oh, yeah."

I search his eyes for signs of head injury or whiplash or—

"We should stop." I lick my lips and watch his eyes drop to my mouth. "Right?"

"Depends." He searches my face, trying to get a read on me. "You offering to kiss it better?"

I should slug him some more. I should get in my car and ram him again.

I should get the hell out of here before I do something dumb.

That's the last thought I have before I cup the back of his head and drag his mouth to mine.

CHAPTER 5

CONFESSIONAL 791.5
<u>Armbrust, Nick (Owner, Armbrust Resorts)</u>
My folks gave me a different view of the entertainment biz than y'all got as Judsons. That's for damn sure. Entertainment lawyers see the shadiest stuff. There's boring crap like contract negotiations, but there's lots more ugliness. My dad had a case where this hotshot director convinced some young actress she should practice kissing. Practice more than that for this scene he's shooting.
He swore they just kissed. Like that doesn't mean something. Like a kiss can't leave a big ol' dent in someone's heart.

* * *

The kiss shouldn't stun me like it does. Lo always kissed like she aimed to eat me up. Like she couldn't pick between lust and fury.

It's not 'til her tongue touches mine that my brain catches up, and I drag us both to our feet. Can't have her stooping down while I sit like a lump trying to figure out what hit me.

But I'm not sure this is better since I'm towering over her from this bumper car. Sliding my hands to her hips, I boost her up. I'm half expecting her to fight, but Lo wraps her legs around my waist and lets me lift her. The heat at her center ignites what's behind the fly of my jeans. I fight to ignore it as I kick the car door open and carry us both to the edge of the arena.

Lo gasps as I press her against the wall. Then she's rubbing against me, moving like she used to when it was the two of us minus all this clothing. The memory stirs me, and I kiss her with an intensity that makes her gasp again.

"God, Lo."

She responds by grinding her hips, leaving no doubt we're in sync. She's molten hot and hungry, and I recall why this is a bad idea. Odds are good she'll regret this later. Maybe I will. But right now, I can't ignore the feel-good friction that's got me pushing into her so she knows how much I've missed her.

"Fuck." She groans it like I've dragged the word out. Like her self-control's slipping the way mine is.

Her scent, I've never forgotten it. Spice and honey and sunshine, and something that's been iced over inside me springs up from a cold puddle.

This.

This is what I loved about Lo. This mix of hard and soft, hot and cool, prickly and liquid heat. She's every sweet sensation rolled into one tight package, and I've missed this more than I can say.

Missed *us*.

"Lo," I breathe as I kiss my way down her throat. She's a solid woman, but I've got no problem holding her like this. I could do it all night. "You taste good."

"Don't stop." She draws a quick breath as my lips graze the nerve that always set her off. The spot behind her ear that makes her squirm, makes her clutch my shoulders like I might get away.

I'm not going anywhere.

Heat seeps through her jeans at the spot where we're fixed together. My body recalls the sweet, slick junction that fit like a glove. She's burning up, moving with a mindless heat that's making me dizzy. It's like no time has passed at all. We're as hungry for this as we ever were.

She grips my shoulders as I press into her, moving with a rhythm her body picks up fast. It's familiar and fiery, and I swear I could come just like this. Lauren growls and bites my earlobe. "Damn," she breathes into my ear. "I hate how you're so good at this."

I laugh because that's all Lo. Still pinning her to the wall, I cup her ass and slide my free hand to her breast. Through the thin t-shirt, her nipple pebbles under my fingers. She squirms against me, filling my hand with her softness. "Nick—*Yes*."

I kiss along her throat, knowing there's a clock ticking. I don't see us fucking in a bumper car arena, not with families that could walk by anytime. One of us has to make a move.

I draw back to ask the question we're both thinking.

My place or yours?

Which one's closer?

But the voice that splits the silence isn't mine.

"Lauren?" A woman calls from far away. "Hey, are you here?"

I jerk as Lo stiffens in my arms. She draws a breath like a diver coming up for air. Slowly, she unwinds her legs and slides to the ground.

"Tia?" Lauren lets go and drags a hand over her mouth. Like that's gonna erase anything. I'll be feeling that kiss next Tuesday.

"I'm over here," Lauren calls, taking a step back to drag her fingers through her hair.

I've barely got the good sense to shove my hands in my pockets to hide the rod in my pants. That's when the woman from the café rounds the corner.

"You're still here." Tia rushes us, blessedly clueless about what she's interrupting.

Lauren frowns. "What's wrong?" She searches the brunette's face, scanning for injuries. "Are you okay?"

Tia's gaze flicks from Lo to me and back again, awareness dawning. "Oh. I'm sorry. I can come b—"

"No, it's fine." She smooths her hair again. "What's wrong?"

The other woman looks pained. "A few things. A burst pipe in my barn."

"Oh, no." Lauren moves, putting another chunk of distance between us. "Are the animals okay?"

"They're fine," Tia says. "I got most of them moved, but I can't find someone to fix the pipe before our event."

Lauren shifts her gaze to me. "I don't suppose plumbing's in your wheelhouse?"

"I wish it was." Especially if it'd wipe that sad look off her face. "I could make some calls—"

"Wait, what's the other bad news?" Lauren looks back at Tia.

"People keep dropping off animals," Tia says. "I guess word got out about the adoption event, and everyone just assumed I'm a dump station for unwanted pets."

"People are just *dumping* animals?" Lauren scowls. "That's horrible."

"How can we help?" I'm not sure I can solve any of this with power tools, but I'm game to try. "How bad is the plumbing leak?"

"I got it stopped, but there's standing water in the barn." Tia squeezes the sleeve of her shirt, and I realize she's soaked. "I've called every plumber around and no one can look at it until after the event."

I slide my phone out of my pocket and scroll for one of my new crew members. "I know a guy with a pump truck. Let me see if I can reach him."

I'm texting the guy as Lo talks to Tia. "Would that help?"

"I've got my own pump," Tia says, and I delete the unsent text.

"And I've got a temporary fix on the pipe. But I don't trust it to hold for the event, and if I can't get a plumber—"

"You think we should postpone?" Lo frowns, and I know it's killing her to think of screwing up that season finale. "We could maybe move it a week."

Tia's already shaking her head. "We've got over a hundred people signed up to attend. At the rate people are dumping animals, I can't afford to take in more. The ones I've already got are desperate enough for homes. We need to forge ahead, but we need a new venue."

"You're right, you're right." Lo looks at me. "Nick had an idea about turning one of our old warehouses into an animal shelter. What if we could expedite that?"

I'm not sure who she's asking, but I take a shot at answering. "I'd have to see what we're working with. The number of animals, the amount of stuff you've got stored in there now."

"We could move most of it fast." Lauren's rolling up her sleeves, drawing her phone from her pocket. "Between my brothers and sisters and their spouses, we've got enough hands to get the job done."

I like how she thinks. I like even more how close she's gotten with her family. This would never happen in Hollywood. "I could maybe spare a couple crew members tomorrow." Not ideal, since we're pouring concrete, but I want to be a team player. "We can shift gears and prioritize that project if you want."

"Let's go see what we're working with." Her gaze softens as her eyes search mine. "Did you have plans tonight?"

"Nothing I don't mind breaking." I don't add *for you*, but maybe she hears it anyway.

Her throat moves as she swallows. "Thank you."

"I appreciate it, guys," Tia says. "Sorry for the switch."

"Not your fault." Lauren pulls her in for a quick hug. "Maybe this will be better. Expedite our plans for a real animal adoption center."

I pick up my toolbox and try to wipe my brain clean from all its filthy thoughts. "Can we swing by the warehouse first to grab a few measurements?"

"Sure," Lauren says. "Then we'll run to Tia's to pick up animals that need to be relocated."

Relief shows on Tia's face. "I'd love that. I've been scrambling to move everyone, but between mopping up and dealing with people who keep dropping off pets—"

"We're on it," Lauren says, already striding toward the parking lot beside the water park. "Let's take one of the Juniper Ridge trucks so we can haul animals if we need to. Maybe I can get Lana to put out an emergency call for foster homes."

I start after Lauren, then turn back. "You need a ride, Tia?"

She jerks a thumb behind her. "I'm parked over there. Meet you at my place?"

"On our way." I grab my toolbox and catch up with Lauren in a few strides, but she's still ahead of me. "Is the warehouse unlocked?"

"I've got a key."

We're almost to the truck when she spins so fast we nearly collide. "Look," she says, cheeks flushed with color. "About what happened—"

"Lo, we don't have to do this now." The last thing I want is her putting up walls when we've already scaled a big one. "Let's talk later about the kiss."

She blinks, eyes searching mine. I hear the words she's not saying, or maybe they're just in my head.

That was a helluva lot more than just a kiss.

But now's not right for that conversation. If I push it, she'll shut me out again. "Come on." I touch her arm, nudging her toward the parking lot. "Want me to drive so you can call siblings?"

She nods with relief. "That would be great."

"Let's go."

As we hustle to the truck, I hold tight to the hope we're getting somewhere. That this could be the thing to bring us back together.

* * *

A SAD-EYED HOUND peers from an oversized crate and gives a listless "woof." No wonder Tia's eager to find homes for these guys.

"I normally have the bigger dogs in stalls." Tia hustles past the hound toward a bank of smaller kennels. "I had to move everyone fast when the pipe burst."

Lauren turns from the yowling stack of cat crates she's carting to a spot near the barn door. "We should be able to relocate most of these guys." She glances at me. "The heat works in the warehouse, right?"

"Yep. Air conditioning, too." My survey was quick, but thorough. "Did Mari say yes to finding volunteers?"

"She's on it." Lauren's glow gives away the pride she feels for her siblings. They jumped to help the instant she called, no hesitation. Dean and his wife, Vanessa, are back at the warehouse clearing space. Coop and Lana are hustling to contact foster families. "We already had community members training to be pet fosters. Hopefully, some can take an animal early."

Tia stretches to pull a leash from a hook. "I can't thank you guys enough for this."

"Glad to help." I wade through some muck from the burst pipe, grateful for waterproof work boots. When I reach a bank of smaller cages, I peer inside at a pair of rodents. Guinea pigs? "What about these guys? Warehouse or foster homes or what?"

"Ugh." Tia finishes clipping a leash to a medium-sized spaniel mix. "Those showed up this morning. Someone dumped them outside, cage and all. Like I know anything about rodents or fish or birds."

I glance at Lauren. "I don't suppose you're a secret rodent and bird expert?"

"Mari has a bird." Lauren moves closer. "Not that it makes her an expert—"

"But knowing Mari, she researched every type of domestic bird before getting one herself." It's a guess, but I see from Lo's tight smile that I'm right.

"I'll bet she'd take in a foster bird or two." She peers into a cage containing three blue and green parakeets. "These guys won't take up nearly as much space as Leonard."

That must be Mari's parrot. Crazy to think of all the Judson kids getting pets and spouses and families of their own.

"I'll be right back." Tia tows the spaniel toward the barn door. "This one missed her walk, and I can't lose ground on leash training."

"We've got it handled." I survey the barn, assessing priorities. "Seems like we could take all the small animals plus cats at the warehouse. How many dog fosters did you line up?"

"At least a dozen." Lauren scans the smaller crates. "The smaller dogs will be easier to place. Tia seemed cool with keeping some of the bigger guys and moving them to the south barn."

"Solid plan." I pull out a tape measure and do some quick calculations for how many crates we can wedge in the truck.

Lauren carries the parakeet cage to a spot far away from the cat crates, then comes back for a cage of tiny finches. "Mari will be here in a minute. She was just leaving her stepdaughter's soccer game."

I smile and jot a note on my phone. "Can't believe Mari's a stepmom. Pretty weird to see all your siblings pairing up."

"Weird." She repeats it like I haven't picked the right word, and I look up to see her frowning.

"Not weird." I try again, fumbling for a better phrase. "Just…surprising."

"Life's full of surprises." There's tension in her voice that wasn't there a minute ago, and I'm not sure how I put it there. "Gabe married a woman he got snowed in with. Dean fell in love with our CFO after they'd both sworn off relationships forever."

I'm chuckling as I shove my phone back in my pocket. "Sounds like some pretty heavy drama." I fake a dramatic shudder but knock it off quick when I see Lo's face. "What?"

She shakes her head. "You know, not everyone equates marriage with drama."

Hell. "That's not what I meant."

"What *did* you mean?"

I sigh, wishing I'd kept my mouth shut. "It's just interesting, that's all. The last time I hung with the Judson fam, marriage was the furthest thing from everyone's mind."

It's the wrong thing to say. Lauren's eyes go flat, and I want to kick my own ass. "Look—"

"You know, I wasn't the only one thinking marriage might be in the cards." She folds her arms over her chest. "You have this habit of just assuming things based only on your perspective."

Christ, what have I started? "I just meant we were all in different places back then. Take Coop, for example."

Her eyes narrow. "What about Cooper?"

"Just that he was a hardcore ladies' man back then." Maybe that's a bad example. I don't know what his dating life's like here, but I caught how he looked at the police chief. "Or Dean. Wasn't he dating that actress?"

Lauren stares at me a long time. So long, I'm not sure she's going to respond. "Dean was *engaged.*"

Crap, that's right. "I forgot about the Andrea Knight scandal." To be honest, I hardly paid attention. I was caught up in work back then.

"And Cooper was planning to propose," she continues, tilting her chin up. "Alyssa Goldman—the costume designer he was dating back then?"

I drag my brain for a face to fit with the name. "That chick with the big—"

"Catalogue of award-winning period films, yes." Her eyes dare me to correct her. "Lana and I took him ring shopping and everything."

"Jesus." I had no idea. "Can't really wrap my head around Cooper Judson getting hitched."

"And yet, the two of you were tight."

She lets the words hang there, waiting for me to get it. "I thought we were." Hell, maybe I was wrong. I was pretty wrapped up in my own life back then. Was I more clueless than I thought?

Lauren presses her lips in a flat line, pausing before she continues. "After you and I split up—" Her voice cracks, and she swallows before continuing. "When he saw how—what I was going through..." She scowls and shakes her head. "Never mind. My point is that he didn't do it. He decided not to propose."

Shit. "So I ruined Cooper's life, too?"

Rolling her eyes, she drops her hands. "You didn't ruin Cooper's life, and you sure as hell didn't ruin mine. It's a good thing he didn't marry Alyssa. She was all wrong for him and would have screwed up his sobriety."

"Still." I'm not sure what else to say. "I'm sorry."

For what, though? Being a clueless ass? Being a lousy friend, a lousier boyfriend. "I'd like to think I've learned a few things since then."

She looks at me long and hard, steely eyes glinting with emotion. "So would I."

Lo turns away, and I know better than to push it. The old me might have caught her by the arm, demanded she turn around and talk this through.

But new me sees the rigid set of her shoulders. I understand she's upset, but for the first time, I've got a fuller grasp of *why*.

"Sorry," I murmur, turning back to the cages. "I really am."

I don't expect her to respond, but she surprises me. "It's fine."

She sighs. "Look, we were both guilty of it back then. Assuming we knew what was going on in someone else's mind. Thinking our plan was the only way without actually seeing the big picture."

"You're right. I did do that."

"I'm sorry, too." Another sigh, and she goes back to moving cat crates. "Water under the bridge." Her sneakers squish as she skirts a puddle of standing water. "I didn't just reveal some big secret about Coop, by the way. It was in the tabloids. Not that you ever read gossip rags, but someone snapped a pic of us ring shopping."

"Never saw it." Probably not a point in my favor. How much did I miss having my head buried in my career? Proving myself, always *proving myself* like Mama told me to. Career connections, not human ones. That's what I've spent years chasing.

I never knew what that cost me.

I'm considering another apology when someone bangs on the barn door. I look around for Tia, but she's still off with the spaniel.

Lauren frowns. "I don't feel right answering someone else's door. I'll get Tia."

But before she can, the door shoves open, and a skinny white guy stomps through. He's talking a mile a minute, and I can't catch what he's saying. "...She was so beautiful, just one of a kind." He huffs out a breath and wrings his hands. "But now she's buried in the backyard, and I don't think I can do this anymore."

I'm not sure if it's his words or the wild look in his eye that's got me wedging my body between him and Lo. "Uh, can we help you?"

He frowns and shoves his glasses up his nose. "I called earlier."

"Oh-kay." I should go get Tia, but no way am I leaving Lauren alone with this guy. "How about we—"

"Look, I've been stripping females for years without incident."

He scowls and shakes his head. "This was just a freak thing, you know?"

"Sure, yeah." What the hell is he talking about? I glance at Lo, hoping she's got Chief Lovelin on speed dial.

Lauren frowns at the man. "Uh, we don't really work here, but if you want, we can—"

"Argh, no! It's too late." The man shakes his head. "I just need to buy a bunch of unsexed juveniles and start over."

"Right." Maybe agreeing with the guy will get him out of here. "Good plan."

But the guy's not going anywhere, and now he's pacing back and forth, yanking his stringy hair. "It's not like I'm having any luck anyway. My big male keeps flashing, so it's just a matter of time."

I don't know what he's going on about, but I need this guy to chill. "Whatever the problem is, we can figure it out."

The man snorts wildly. "Like that's an option? Please. And females are so drab and ugly anyway. They're only good for breeding, but this one's just a nasty little b—"

"Hey." Lauren's frowning, looking more mad than fearful. "We can't help you if you don't calm down."

"It's no use!" The man throws his hands in the air. "I'm just going to start selling South Americans. There's better money in them than Africans."

"Hold up." All right, I've had enough. "I think you need to leave."

"Good, right, yes." He starts backing toward the barn door. "I'll just go get her from the car."

"Get *who* from the car?" I start after him, not liking the sound of any of this. "Hang on a minute—"

But the guy's darting for the barn door, still mumbling about stripping females. What the hell?

At the last second, he turns and whips something from his

pocket. I shove my body in front of Lo, but she's reaching for what he's got.

"Here." The guy thrusts a thin rolled-up book at her. "You'll need this."

I stare as Lo unrolls it to reveal a flimsy paperback with a bright blue fish on the cover. She angles it so I can see. "'*A Definitive Guide to Cichlids*.'"

The man's already gone, and I'm hoping he won't come back. "Cichlids? That's some kind of fish?"

"Apparently." Lauren flips the pages. "Is that what he was muttering about? Stripping and flashing and—"

"Bodies buried in the backyard?" I frown at the book. "I hope so. I'm not liking the alternative."

She's still skimming, steely eyes scanning the page. "Yeah, all that lingo—he was talking about fish breeding. These bright ones —cichlids, I guess—they're mouthbreeders."

"Do I want to know what that is?"

Lo's mouth quirks like she's suppressing the same BJ thought I just had. "Look here—there's a whole diagram on it."

I peer at the page, amazed she flipped right to it. "*That's* stripping?" Looks a lot less pleasant than I pictured it.

"It says that's how you get the babies out of their mouths." She trails a finger down the page. "Fry, they're called? I guess so the mother doesn't eat them."

"Parenting at its finest." I peer closer as she flips the page to show some kind of fish maternity suite. "Times my mama threatened a lot worse if Alexis and I didn't shape up."

Lauren laughs. "Like you were some kind of delinquent? Please. Your parents raised freakin' perfect children, and they know it."

I meant it as a joke, but there's a sore spot in my chest that wasn't there before. I should drop it.

"Yeah, well." I shove my hands in my back pockets. "You weren't there the day I told her I quit law school to keep my summer construction job. You'd have thought I'd confessed to killing kittens while wearing white after Labor Day."

Lauren's mouth twitches. "But who got the last laugh there, Mr. 'America's Top Entrepreneur'?"

I shrug and skid my gaze away. "I'm still not doing what they wanted me to be doing."

Which means it's tough not to see disappointment in Mama's eyes all the time.

"My father wrecked his body working construction," she said to me not that long ago. *"I wanted an easier life for my kids. For you and Alexis. For your future kids."*

"Hey." Lauren touches my arm, resting the book on a worktable. "Your parents are proud of you. Both of them, Nick. Even if I haven't—"

"Here you go." The stranger slams back through the barn door, making Lauren jump. The guy grips an oblong aquarium with a few inches of water slopping around. As he shoves it at my chest, I wrap my arms around it by instinct. Water sloshes my face, and I look down to see a bright yellow fish bobbing around.

"Wait—"

But the man's gone again, bolting from the barn like his ass is on fire. From the gunning of an engine, I'd say he's not coming back.

Lauren steps close and peers in the tank. "I'm still replaying all the stuff he said," she murmurs. "The stripping, the flashing, the backyard burial. Is he a fish breeder or a psychopath?"

"Maybe both?" The bright yellow fish looks mad as hell wallowing in a pile of gray gravel. Not that I know what a pissed off fish looks like. As Lo pointed out, I suck at empathetic connection.

But hey, I'm willing to try. Looking at Lo, I adjust my grip on the tank. "Now what?"

We watch as the sleek gold body stops moving and stares at us with gills flaring.

"Hey, there." Lo touches a finger to the glass. "Are you okay in there?"

Gills flapping faster, the fish sucks up a huge mouthful of gravel. "That can't be good," I mutter.

Before we can do anything, the fish stares Lo right in the eye and spits out a rock. Then another, all while looking straight at Lauren.

"That's creepy as hell."

"Maybe?" Lauren cocks her head. "She just seems upset. Understandably."

I don't recall hearing this fish is female, but okay. "Does the book say what we do now?"

Lauren straightens. "You mean when a crazy person storms in shouting about burying bodies in the backyard and selling Africans, and then throws a fish at you?" She waves the book. "I didn't get to that chapter."

The tank's getting heavy, so I set it down on a battered worktable. As we watch, the fish settles into a patch of gravel and gives us the fish equivalent of a scowl.

Footsteps signal Tia's return. "Dammit!" She strides in with the spaniel. "That fish guy came? I told him not to show up."

I straighten. "A friend of yours?"

She shakes her head and unclips the spaniel's leash, ushering him into an empty horse stall. "I've never met him in my life. He called a few hours ago talking about losing his best breeding pair and how this one female cichlid won't stop killing her tankmates. I said I couldn't take her. I know zilch about tropical fish."

"And yet, here she is." I turn to see the fish making frantic circles, zipping around like her ass is on fire. "Don't they need heaters and water pumps and stuff like that?"

Lauren stoops down to watch the little aquatic demon bang its face on the glass. The fish slows its swirling, then swims to the edge and stares at Lo. Gills flapping, she spits out another rock.

"What a weird animal." I glance at Tia. "It's just the one fish?"

Tia shrugs. "I guess she murdered all the others."

"And he expects you to find a home for a serial killer cichlid?"

Lauren's ignoring us, trailing a finger over the front of the tank. "She'll freeze if we don't have an aquarium heater. Chapter two, it said they need warm water."

I'd forgotten what a speed reader Lauren is. I'm also not sure keeping the thing alive is in anyone's best interest, given what we know about this creature.

But I'm not a fish-killing asshole, so instead I ask, "What do you want to do?"

Lo looks at Tia. "I'll take her."

"Seriously?" Tia looks incredulous. "Have you had a fish tank before?"

"No, but I've got a book." She picks up the paperback. "How hard could it be?"

We all look at the fish. She spits out another rock, then hunkers down in her bed of gravel.

I make a mental note to find out if cichlids have teeth. "She seems…"

"Independent?" Lauren tilts her head. "Efficient? Tough?"

"Not the words I was looking for."

Nuts, *dangerous*, and *possibly psycho* would be more like it, but I know better than to say that out loud.

"It's why I like her." Lauren straightens with a small smile. "I'm not up for dogs or cats or bunnies, but a fish? That's my kind of animal."

I can see that. Seems wrong to say it out loud, but I get why Lo's connecting with this particular pet. "So we're taking the fish home."

"Yep." She folds her arms over her chest. "Is that a problem?"

"Not even a little." Squaring my shoulders, I pick up the tank and carry it out to the truck.

CHAPTER 6

CONFESSIONAL 799
<u>Judson, Lauren (Producer: Juniper Ridge)</u>
Remember the adjectives the tabloids used anytime they wrote about me?
Icy. Efficient. Calculating.
Like a woman turning thirty with no husband or kids becomes a freakin' Frigidaire. Like she can't have it all.
For the record, I'm very warm and fuzzy. Nurturing as hell.
Fuck those guys.

* * *

"Really, thank you again." I step back from my new aquarium and turn to face Nick. "Pretty sure your contract with Juniper Ridge didn't say anything about setting up fish tanks at midnight."

He laughs and steps close enough to peer in the tank. Close enough I feel the heat of his arms through his T-Shirt. "You got lucky finding used supplies. Not sure this girl would have made it through the night without a proper heater."

I drop a couple cichlid food pellets in the water. "It's not luck. It's the whole design of Juniper Ridge. A self-contained community where neighbors help each other out with a cup of sugar or shoveling the sidewalk when it snows."

Nick looks dubious, but I'm not sure if it's the fish or what I said. "What are the odds someone would have all this stuff just sitting around?"

We watch the fish zip back and forth like she's late for a meeting but can't recall which building it's in. There's a lot for her to pick from, between the life-sized ornamental taco, the plastic castle, and the decoration designed to look like an upturned Starbucks cup.

"The Cox family has tons of pets," I explain, dipping a hand in the water to reposition one of the plastic plants. "I'm sure their kids picked out all this stuff."

"They don't need it for their own fish?"

"They changed to saltwater tanks, so this was just sitting around." I'm keeping one eye on the fish as she inspects the taco, then bonks it with the point of her bright gold nose.

"Huh." Nick frowns as the fish finishes knocking over the taco and moves to head-butt the castle. That doesn't topple as easily, so it takes her a few tries. "Guess she's redecorating."

"Guess so." I drop another cichlid pellet in the water, which she ignores to focus on uprooting a plastic plant. "The Cox family gave Mari her parrot. They had to rehome him because he didn't get along with their other bird."

"Interesting." Nick ambles away, moving past my sofa to scan the row of family photos on my mantle. "I'm seeing a pattern here."

"In the pictures?"

"No, in Judson family pets." He picks up a photo of my whole family at Dean's wedding, then sets it down again. "You and Mari chose pets that don't play well with others."

I frown, not sure I like the implication. "Our parents raised us to be independent women."

"And I love that about you." He grins and turns away from the photos. "I love it a lot."

So why didn't you want to marry me?

The question flits unbidden in my brain, and it pisses me off. Why would I care about that now?

I settle for changing the subject. "How are *your* parents?"

"Good." There's a slight dimming in his eyes, but it's subtle. I'd never notice if I hadn't spent a zillion hours staring into those gold-brown depths. "Really well, actually."

He heads for the sofa, not waiting to be invited. Such a Nick thing to do, but I can't muster any real irritation. He spent the last few hours hauling animals and shuffling things in the warehouse, none of which he's contractually obligated to do.

As he drops onto the leather cushion, he spreads his arms over the back of the couch. Desire flutters in my belly at the sight of those muscular shoulders, the big, rounded biceps. The man takes damn good care of his body.

Stop thinking about his body.

Clearing my throat, I move away from the aquarium. "I have beer." I'm not normally the hostessy sort, so I doubt I have much else to offer. Besides, it's late. "Pretzels, too. Or wine."

"Beer and pretzels sound great." He grins. "Remember that German place with the kickass soft pretzels?"

"I'd almost forgotten."

No, I hadn't. Hofbräu's was a tiny hole-in-the-wall place we found late one night while dodging paparazzi. "They had the best Swiss cheese fondue."

Nick laughs, shooting sparks of pleasure through my chest. He's always had the best laugh. "Remember that time we went with my family?" he asks. "Thought my dad was gonna stroke out when that guy showed up with the accordion."

"Alexis loved it," I remind him as I twist the top off a glass jug

I've only recently learned is a growler. Credit my beer-brewing brother-in-law for that one. "Don't you remember? It was her birthday, so she got the serenade."

Nick's watching me from the sofa. "Can I help with anything?"

"Pouring beer in glasses isn't a two-person job, but thanks." I finish that and dump half a bag of pretzels in a bowl, then load it on a tray with the beers. "Is Alexis happy as a DA?"

Nick shrugs as I set the tray on the coffee table in front of the couch. Hesitating, I take a seat safely on the opposite end, keeping space between us so I don't accidentally straddle him or something.

"The job's pretty tough, so she's busy all the time." He scoops up some pretzels and shoves a couple in his mouth. "Our folks are crazy proud."

"Not what I asked." I pop a pretzel in my mouth and chew. "I asked if she's *happy*. The last couple times I've talked to her, she sounded...off."

"Off?"

I shrug. "Restless, maybe. And her reading tastes—they're running more toward small town romance, when she used to love all the fast-paced urban stuff."

Nick quirks an eyebrow. "You talk to my sister about romance novels?"

Crap. I forgot that's a thing we used to hide from him, neither of us wanting to seem sappy and sentimental. "My point," I say, steering the conversation back on track, "is that it's not uncommon for women to get married and have babies and want to settle someplace quieter. A simpler life than what they've got in LA."

"That so?" Nick sips his beer. "Can't say I see it. She busted ass for that job. Mama's so proud she nearly wet herself the day Lex made district attorney. No way is she throwing that away."

I hesitate, noticing it's not the first time he's brought up their parents' approval. I've always known it's a big driver for both of them but tried not to probe too hard.

"They must be really proud of you," I say carefully. "Your parents, I mean. I know they weren't thrilled you gave up law school, but they've gotta be elated about all you've accomplished." When he doesn't respond, I press it. "Dozens of resorts around the country? A multi-million-dollar construction empire? Write-ups in all the major magazines about—"

"I don't think it was her birthday." He snaps his fingers, frowning. "Nah, it was the DA thing. The day she found out she'd gotten the position."

I blink. "What?"

"That's what we were celebrating that night at the German place. Lexi's new job. Remember? The accordion guy played that song about wandering because Lex and Abe were leaving for Jamaica. One last vacation before her new job."

I shake my head, exasperated by the awkward subject change and his lousy memory. "It was her birthday," I insist. "Thirtieth, I think. Remember? She wore a bright yellow dress because she said she wanted everything to be brighter in her thirties."

Nick's frowning and shaking his head. "I don't know about my sister's clothes, but I'm positive it was the promotion. Come on—my dad ordered Dom Perignon for all the tables around us?"

If he's trying to jog my memory in his favor, he's doing the opposite. "Because his only daughter was turning thirty. Come on, Nick—there was that big Black Forest cake with cherries and fresh flowers and—"

"You know what?" Grinning, he slips his phone out of his pocket. "I know how we can settle this nice and easy."

He starts to dial, and I swipe at the phone. "You are not calling a tired mother of two after midnight on a—"

"Hey, brother." Alexis's face lights up the screen, looking delighted but exhausted. "How'd you know I'd need a break?"

"Lucky guess." He laughs and shakes his head. "Nah, I'm

kidding. Mama said you're pulling all-nighters this week getting ready for some big case."

"And you thought that was a good reason to interrupt me?" She holds up a hand before he can apologize. "Nah, it's all good. I did need a break."

"Thought so." Nick shifts close enough for his knee to bump mine. "How's that case coming along?"

"The biggest case of my career." She doesn't sound thrilled, but I wouldn't either if I'd pulled a week of all-nighters. "Something wrong, or did you just call to say hi?"

"Actually, Lauren and I want you to settle a bet."

He angles the phone so we're both in the frame, and I give a reluctant wave. "Hey, Lexi."

"Hey, girlfriend! How you doing?"

"Good." I glare at Nick. "I promise it was *not* my idea to call you at midnight to ask about accordion serenades."

"Accordion serenades?" Alexis tilts her head, her topknot of braids listing to one side. "I've heard some strange euphemisms, but that's a new one."

"Speaking of cake, it was Black Forest, right?" I scooch closer so Nick doesn't have to hold the phone out so far. "Your birthday cake. That's why we were all at Hofbräu's celebrating, right?"

"Leading the witness!" Nick shouts, fingertips grazing the ends of my hair. "C'mon, work with me, Lex. We were there celebrating your promotion. Don't you remember Mama making that big speech about working for your dreams and how proud grandpa would be?"

Alexis arches an eyebrow as she looks from Nick to me and back again. "Aren't the two of you looking cozy?"

I fight to ignore the heat rushing my face. "We were working late and—"

"Uh-huh." Alexis purses her lips. "Sounds like another euphemism to me."

Nick laughs, unfazed by the suggestion. "Aren't *you* working late right now?"

"Oooh, permission to treat as a hostile witness?" Lexi wags a finger. "Now who's dodging questions?"

Nick looks at me and frowns. "I've forgotten the question."

I'd rather move past the suggestion there's something going on between Nick and me, so I fumble around for a subject change. "Hey! I adopted a fish."

Snatching the phone from Nick's hand, I bounce off the couch and head to the aquarium. "Check it out, she's got plants and a castle and all these cute aquarium ornaments."

Alexis coos, too polite to call me on an obvious distraction tactic. "There's a cuddly pet for you."

"Do I strike you as a cuddly sort of person?" I move the phone so Lex can watch my fish auguring a tunnel beneath the taco. "She's beautiful, right?"

"You know I love yellow." Lexi's eyes follow as the fish zooms in zig-zag lines around the tank. "Does it have a name?"

"I was thinking Ann." I drop a pellet in the water and watch her circle it with deep suspicion. "As in Ann-Chovy. Either that, or Sharkira."

"*Shark*ira?" Alexis laughs, then busts into the chorus of Shakira's "Hips Don't Lie," singing a few lines as her brother bobs his head from the couch. "That gets my vote. Hey, did you read that Nina Crespo I sent? The one from her Tillbridge Stables series."

I glance at Nick, whose eyes are riveted to my ass. My fault, since Lexi's song got me dancing. "Not yet," I say. "I'm still working my way through her Breakup Bash series."

"Girl, you've gotta catch up. I got through that series in a weekend."

Nick's nursing his beer now, and I lower my voice to reply. "I'm glad you're finding reading time. I've been worried with how much you said you're working lately."

I'm glad I've got the phone angled toward me. That Nick can't see the bone-bending fatigue in her eyes. There are some things women reveal only to each other. "Well, you know how it is," she murmurs. "Always got something to prove. It's the Armbrust way."

"I hear you," I say. "If it makes you feel better, my mother asked me last week when I'm scheduling a baby. Like I might pick one up at the grocery store on my way to spin class."

Lexi laughs, but the tiredness doesn't drain from her eyes. "How is it out there?"

"At Juniper Ridge?"

"Yeah." Her eyes take on a dreamy quality. "I sure loved Oregon when I lived there."

That's right, I forgot she went to Willamette Law in Salem. "Did you make it over to this part of the state?"

"Central? Yeah, Abe and I road-tripped after I graduated. We were doing the long-distance thing back then. Did I tell you he proposed at Smith Rock State Park?"

That's barely an hour from here. "I had no idea."

"It's beautiful." She sighs, looking tired again. "I'm thinking about a change. Maybe a big one."

I bite my lip and glance at Nick. The sofa's only ten feet away, and I can't tell if he's listening. He's sipping his beer and digging through the pretzel bowl, but he could hear us if he wanted.

Conscious of Lexi's vulnerability, I keep my voice low. "Are things okay with you and Abe?"

"Oh, we're solid." She sighs. "And we'd like to stay that way, you know?"

"Yeah." I steal another look at Nick, who's setting his drink on a coaster. "I know."

He glances up, feeling my eyes on him. "You gonna bring my sister back over so we can resolve this thing?"

I'd almost forgotten the bet. Holding out the phone, I return to the couch and curl up a lot closer than before. "All right, Lexi —you're settling this."

"Hmmm...that's an awful lot of power." Her eyes bounce between us with a hint of mischief. "What are the stakes, anyway?"

"A kiss," Nick says before I can answer. "That's if I win."

I roll my eyes, trying to play it cool despite the heat rushing my face. "And I'd like my kitchen sink snaked."

Alexis smirks, but refrains from making another comment about euphemisms. "You don't have a plumber at Juniper Ridge?"

"We do, but he's focused on new construction right now. And if we pull him off that, it'll be because we need him to fix a pipe in a barn."

"Or plumb a warehouse to be a pet shelter," Nick adds, grinning.

"You two have an interesting life out there."

Lexi's words hit with an emotion I can't identify. The idea of a shared life—Nick and me—is something I spent months imagining. Years.

But this right here, the two of us in a rustic cabin in Oregon with pretzels in a bowl and coyotes yipping outside, is not what I pictured.

In some ways, it's better.

"All right, Lex—spill it," he says. "Am I right and it was your promotion?"

I shoulder my way into the frame. "Or am I right and it was your *birthday*."

"Yes," Alexis smiles.

Nick frowns. "Which?"

"Both." Lexi drags a pencil from behind her ear and jots something on a legal pad. "We planned the dinner when I got promoted. Mama's idea, but you two picked the place." She glances up, and something in her eyes makes my heart pinch. "I think everyone just forgot it was my birthday. Well, not everyone. Abe made me breakfast in bed and got me a necklace I'd been eyeing. And you, Lauren—remember what you gave me?"

I nod as my throat burns. Her own family blew off her birthday? "A gift certificate for a couple's spa date."

She smiles, and I wonder if she thought I forgot. "I know you said to take Abe, but it's been three years and I don't think I'll be dragging my badass cop husband to PureSpa. You coming back to visit sometime?"

"Maybe." I swallow past the burning in my throat. "Lana and Coop have the next tour of duty with Mom and Dad. Dean and I are on deck next month."

Lexi laughs again. "I love how you've gotta break it up by sibling pairs. Nick and I need about a dozen more brothers and sisters to deal with our parents."

"It's pretty handy." I'm just grateful we worked out a system so no Judson kid bears the brunt of our parents' care and feeding. "Anyway, I'm not sure when I'll be back down there."

"Don't wait too long," Lexi says mildly. "Who knows how long we'll be here."

Nick's brow furrows. "Lex?"

"Look, I've gotta go." She smiles brightly. "Take care of each other, all right? Second chances aren't easy to come by. Love you!"

"Love you, too," Nick says automatically before I can point out we're not back together.

And then she clicks off. I look at him and lick my lips. "I guess that settles that."

"Yeah." He looks at the phone for a long time. "That's what you're talking about, isn't it?"

"What?" He's lost me.

"Me not paying attention." He meets my eyes, looking chagrined. "With you, with Coop. Hell, my own sister."

I shrug because what else can I say? "Some people have a knack for watching other people's cues."

"And some don't look for cues at all?" He sets his beer down and runs his hands over his thighs. "I'm a self-centered asshole."

"You're driven. Focused. Independent." I don't know why I'm defending him, except the same adjectives apply to me. "Anyway, it's ancient history."

"Not really." He pauses, like he's choosing the right words. "Look, Lo. I know you don't want to talk about what happened that night. The party, the…misunderstanding. The announcement that wasn't what you thought it was."

"And yet, we're talking about it." I take a deep breath. "I'm over it, Nick. Truly."

"What if I'm not?"

My heart twitches like he poked it with a fork. "I'm sorry if I embarrassed you."

"That's not what I meant." His fingers skim the ends of my hair. "If I could go back and do it over, I would."

"No, you wouldn't."

He opens his mouth to argue, but I put up a hand. "You can't honestly tell me you'd trade all your career success to go back and get married when you didn't want to." I pause, needing him to understand this. "I wouldn't want that, either, Nick. Not for you, and definitely not for me. Everything we've done here—the whole Juniper Ridge show with my siblings. It wouldn't have happened if you and I had gotten married."

His brow furrows, and I watch him weigh my words. "You're not still mad?"

"Of course not." The second I say it, I know it's a lie. Or maybe not the full truth. "I was…hurt. Disappointed. Embarrassed."

He's studying my face, brown eyes intense. "And now?"

"And now, I'm over it." I wave my hands, pushing away another half-truth. "*Working* to be over it."

"I see," he says. "And how long did it take you to be over me?"

There's no right answer here. Not a truthful one.

I was over you that night, would be the fiercest answer. A hard shell pulled over my wounded pride.

But it's not the truth, and I'm tired of stretching it.

"I—don't know." I swallow hard. "I guess it's more gradual."

Gradual, as in still a work in progress.

Gradual, as in I may never be fully over Nick.

He nods, and I wonder if he hears my thoughts. If he has any idea how badly it crushed me to go from picturing my life with someone to planning one without him. I know I made a mistake assuming too much. But he did it, too. We're both to blame for how badly things ended.

"I'm sorry," I tell him. "I could have handled things more gracefully."

"And I'm sorry I hurt you." He rubs his thighs again, and I fight an aching urge to lie across his lap. "If it helps, I've replayed that night a million times in my mind and wished I could do it differently."

"How?" Dammit, I was ready to let the subject drop. Why am I asking questions?

But part of me really wants to know, so I ask again. "I don't mean that line you just tried to feed me about wishing you'd proposed. You don't wish that, and neither do I."

He doesn't argue. Just sits there looking thoughtful. "Well, I guess I'd have been clearer. I would have talked to you sooner about my plans." He shakes his head in dismay. "When I go back in my head and hear the things I was saying. The stuff I asked you about rings and wedding venues and public proposals…" He trails off, clearing his throat. "Well. It's easy to see how you heard what you did."

"I heard what I wanted to hear."

"We both did."

We sit there looking at each other a long time. Too long. It's late, and it's been a long day, but I don't want him to go.

Which is a good indication he needs to. I'm too fragile, too tender right now. That's a recipe for having my heart broken.

I lick my lips. "We should—"

"Kiss?" He smiles. "Or snake your sink. You pick."

I stare at him, processing his words. He's right; we both won the bet. Or lost, depending on how you look at it. Part of me wants to get up off this couch. Just point to the kitchen sink or call it a night.

But most of me—especially the parts working my mouth—are already pulling toward Nick, easing closer on the couch. He sees me coming and spears his fingers through my hair, cupping the back of my head. "Lauren."

"Wait." I lick my lips. "This isn't going anywhere, okay? We're stopping with just a kiss."

"Sure." His eyes say he's only half hearing me. "Whatever you say."

And then we're kissing. Not the first kiss today, but this one's different. Before, I felt feral and hungry. Out of control.

This kiss is slower, more cautious. Like we're afraid we might break each other. When I touch his chest, I feel coiled muscle, tense with uncertainty.

His tongue grazes mine, but he's not pushing. Not cupping my ass to pull me onto his lap. I'd go if he did, but I'm grateful he doesn't. I'm aching to throw myself at him, to be back where we left off a few hours ago. Where we left off two years ago.

But that's not what either of us needs.

"Okay," I pant as I draw back. "You should go now."

He doesn't question. Doesn't wheedle to stay and snake my drain or do any of the things my body begs him do to me. If he sees it in my eyes, he's kind enough not to act on it.

Fiery gold-brown irises search mine. "That's what you want?"

I nod, even though I'm not sure what I want. But I'm sure of one thing. "If you don't go now, we're in trouble."

Again, he doesn't wisecrack. Maybe he knows what I mean, though even I'm not sure.

"Understood." He stands and holds out a hand. "Walk me to the door?"

"Of course." I let him haul me to my feet, conscious of my legs shaking. When we get to the front of my cabin, I expect him to reach for me again. Instead, he reaches for...my bookshelf?

No, a hidden compartment beneath it. I'd never seen this one before, a twelve-inch panel he pushes back to reveal a small hidey-hole.

His fingers trace the wood grain of the panel. "I started doing more of these after you said you loved them. Putting shelves inside like you suggested." His eyes are wistful as he meets my gaze again. "In case you're wondering if I take your feedback to heart."

I blink at him, at a loss for words. But Nick just smiles, bending to brush a soft kiss on my bottom lip.

"Sweet dreams, Lo."

Then he walks out the door, exactly as I've asked him to.

* * *

"Why are all the plants floating on top?"

Four grown women cluster around my fish tank, all of us angling for a look at Sharkira. Mari's the one who's most concerned. She pokes at a plastic plant, one of three bobbing on the water's surface.

Sharkira hunkers in a corner, swishing her belly to make a trough in the gravel. She's perturbed at being ogled.

"Seriously." Mari uses her finger to steer a floating plant to the other side of the tank. "Won't they get caught in the filter or something?"

"They haven't yet." I hand a wineglass to Gabe's wife, Gretchen. She's beside Vanessa, Dean's badass bride. It's raining marriage in the Judson family.

"Thanks." Vanessa sips her wine and smiles. "Ooh, is this the pinot we had at Mari's wedding?"

Mari blushes like she does anytime we mention her recent

nuptials. "Same vineyard and varietal, but this tastes like the '17 instead of '18, right?"

"Nice palate." I sip from my own glass as the ladies reshuffle around the aquarium. "Mom and Dad would be proud."

Mari winces. "I feel bad Cooper and Lana went alone to visit. Mom gave me a guilt trip this morning."

I shrug, appreciating Mari's empathy even if I don't share it this time. "We can't all leave at once. Besides, it was their turn."

Gretchen glances up from the fish tank. "Gabe said Cooper's lining up Cash Beckett for your season finale."

"That's the hope." I quietly cross my fingers baby brother can pull this off. "It'd be a huge ratings boon if we can get him."

Vanessa's still studying the tank, holding her wineglass off to the side as her gaze sweeps the décor. "You've got a clamshell, an octopus, and something that looks like the Mystery Machine from Scooby Doo." She looks up and frowns. "Why are they all upside down?"

"It's kind of her thing." I scan the new decorations, which aren't faring much better than the first set. "I bought them at the pet store thinking she might like them more than hand-me-downs."

Gretchen tilts her head. "Not so much?"

"Not even close." Sharkira's moved beyond flipping them and is busy burying the clamshell in the corner. "I'll keep trying."

Vanessa looks concerned. "Is warring with aquarium décor normal behavior for a cichlid?"

"*Normal* is a judgment word." Mari frowns into the tank. "Maybe she likes them that way?"

"Apparently." After my hundredth time righting the blue plastic van, I decided to let her do what she wants. "Sharkira has very clear ideas how she likes things."

"Don't we all?" Mari muses.

Gretchen straightens and sets her wine on an end table.

"Thanks again for bringing my sister out. Jessie's thrilled about consulting on the animal shelter."

Mari snaps on her human resources hat. "You're sure she's comfortable being on her feet so much? It's only been a few weeks since she had the baby."

Gretchen laughs. "Jessie's not one to sit still long. Plus, I get an excuse to hold my new niece."

We've all avoided probing too much about Jessie's mystery baby. *"Sperm donor,"* Gretchen said when I asked if I'd need to secure travel arrangements for a co-parent.

I'm not sure if that's literal or a figure of speech, but it seems like a sign not to pry.

"Jessie and I checked the animals again before I came over," Gretchen's saying. "Spent a few minutes brushing and feeding everyone."

"I'm sure the parakeets love brushing." I throw her a wink so she knows I'm teasing. "Actually, didn't Mari take the parakeets?"

My middle sister nods. "Soph begged to keep them in her room," Mari adds. "We're trying it out, seeing how she does being responsible for them."

"While Lauren's responsible for the aquatic equivalent of Marie Kondo." Vanessa holds up a hand. "Wait, no—the real Marie Kondo is sweet, and Sharkira's a killer. Like what you'd get if Marie Kondo had a love child with Ted Bundy."

I pretend to be annoyed, but I actually love that they've picked up on my fish's personality. I thought I might be imagining she has one. "Is the volunteer schedule updated on the virtual bulletin board?" I ask Mari.

"It is, and people are still signing up to help with the shelter."

"I'll get some footage tomorrow." Showing community spirit and volunteerism will make great B-roll in the lead-up to the season finale. "Viewers love all the animal-themed content."

Gretchen looks perplexed, and I remember that she never even owned a TV until she met Gabe. "I still can't believe you're working this fast to get the shelter up and running," she says. "Sorry we couldn't help the other night. Gabe and I got busy and forgot we switched off our phones."

Vanessa grins and taps Gretchen's wineglass. "Is the 'getting busy' the reason you're not touching your wine?"

Gretchen flushes bright pink. "I'm not…you know."

"Knocked up," I supply, seeing no point in beating around the bush.

Mari shoots me a look. "Juniper Ridge has a strict confidentiality clause around pregnancy if anyone chooses not to disclose—"

"It's okay." Gretchen smiles and hands the wineglass back to me. "I'm just cutting out alcohol for now. With my PhD done and *Fresh Start at Juniper Ridge* up and running, Gabe and I are trying."

Trying in this context conjures up images of aggressively copulating couples wearing sweatbands. Not an image I want with my brother, plus all this baby talk makes me twitchy.

"Wouldn't we make adorable babies?"

It's an offhand comment Nick said just weeks before the proposal that never happened. My ovaries went on high alert as I wondered what it might mean. *"We would,"* I answered carefully, skimming a hand down his bare chest. *"Is that something you want?"*

"Hell, yeah." He kissed the tips of my fingers and smiled. *"I mean, eventually."*

How was I supposed to know he meant *"not anytime soon"*? Or maybe more like *"not with you, Lauren."*

I clear my throat and step back with Gretchen's wineglass. "We'll keep it on the down-low you're trying," I promise my sister-in-law. "Can I get you something else?"

"Water would be great," she says.

I start to walk the wine back to the kitchen, but Vanessa plucks the glass from my hand. "I'll take that." Grinning, she strolls to the sofa and sets the wine on the coffee table. "One of us is bound to need a refill, right?"

I shake my head and go to get Gretchen's water. "Very efficient, Miss CFO."

Vanessa grins wider. "That's *Mrs.* CFO, thank you very much."

By the time I'm back in the living room, all three ladies are grouped on my plush leather sofas. Mari's on the left side of the loveseat, while Gretchen and Vanessa sit sprawled on the larger couch. I consider the armchair, then rethink. It's only in the past year I've gotten extra close with Mari. Might as well make an effort to connect.

"Hey." I plunk down beside her, making her bounce on the cushion. "How's married life treating you?"

"Excellent." Her smile could light my living room. "Who'd have guessed it would happen for so many of us this quickly?"

Ignoring the clench in my gut, I sip my wine. "Guess you never know what twists life will throw at you."

Mari looks stricken. "Lauren, I'm so sorry. I didn't mean—"

"It's fine." I force my smile to go wider, not eager to relive my humiliation from two years ago. "Did everything go okay with the new foster families?"

She hesitates, then takes my cue and runs with it. "Ten dogs and six cats are resting comfortably in their new homes. Well, temporary homes."

"Which might not end up being temporary." Gretchen tucks a leg under her butt and sips her water.

"Why do you say that?" I glance at my bare coffee table and wish I'd grabbed snacks. Nick and I ate all the pretzels, so there's not much in my pantry unless the ladies like noshing on uncooked macaroni.

Gretchen sets her glass down. "We fostered lots of pets growing up in Alaska," she says. "There were six of us girls, plus our brother, so someone always got attached. We had a lot of foster fails."

Vanessa tilts her head. "Foster fails?"

"Pets you set out to tame and socialize before sending them to their forever home, but you end up falling in love and—" Gretchen shrugs a bit sheepishly. "It's how we ended up with at least half our animals."

I've never heard the term, but this makes sense. "Sort of why I kept Sharkira," I admit. "Something about her spoke to me." My cheeks warm when I hear how cheesy that sounds, but the ladies nod like it's normal. "Besides, it's not like anyone else would go falling in love with a surly cichlid who kills her tankmates."

Vanessa sips her wine. "It was love at first sight with Roughneck," she admits. "I saw him there in Tia's barn looking all scraggly and forlorn and all I could think was, 'that dog goes home with me.'"

"See? This is what I want to show with this adoption event." I look at Mari, certain she'll understand. "The connection people feel with the pets they end up adopting. Viewers are gonna love it."

My sister studies me with her penetrating psychologist stare, and I get the sense she's mulling something besides animals. "I love that this is your new passion project. It's…surprising."

Unease swirls in my belly, but I try not to let it show. "I just think it'd be good for ratings."

"Okay." She sips her wine with a look that says she's not buying it. "When was Cooper talking to Cash Beckett?"

"They were having lunch today." It's a struggle to keep excitement from my voice. "I know he's a douche, but the camera loves him."

"So do audiences." Vanessa's inner numbers geek springs to life. "That film where he played the animal rescue guy—*Dirty Dogs*? That grossed nearly three hundred million last year. Dean's salivating over what it might mean for sponsorships and ad revenue."

"And for pet adoption," Mari adds virtuously. She's still

studying me, making me nervous with what she might see on my face. "How's Nick?"

I swallow hard as all eyes swivel to me. "Fine, I think. I mean, he's around." Not that I watch for him everywhere I go, except I sorta do. "We're still getting used to working together."

"That's right, you used to date." Vanessa smiles. "Sorry, Dean told me. I hope that's okay?"

"Depends on what he shared." I clench my teeth, determined not to murder my brother if he spilled the big, humiliating story. "Not like it's a big secret, but—"

"He said you were a great couple," Vanessa says.

"Gabe said the same thing," Gretchen adds. "Said he always hoped you'd get back together."

"*That's* not happening." I blurt it much too loudly. "We're different people now."

Mari regards me over the rim of the glass. "We've all changed a lot these past couple years," she acknowledges. "But if the people you were a few years ago didn't work as a couple, maybe the people you are now could?"

"No." I'm shaking my head, trying to convince myself. "We broke up for a reason."

Gretchen cocks her head. "What was the reason? Sorry, I don't mean to pry. Gabe's pretty closemouthed about this stuff."

I take a deep breath, considering the most abbreviated way to tell the story. "There was a…misunderstanding." I frown at my own wineglass. "I thought he was proposing, but he was actually ditching me."

"Ouch." Gretchen frowns in sympathy. "That sounds awful."

Vanessa offers her own look of sympathy. "Something like that happened to my brother."

"You have a brother?" Gretchen frowns. "I thought it was just you and a twin sister."

"He's a lot older and lives overseas." Vanessa shrugs. "Anyway, that sucks. I'm sorry that happened to you, Lauren."

"I'm over it," I say with forced cheer. "We just weren't on the same wavelength, and that's *fine*."

Mari's wearing her concerned shrink stare. "He clearly still cared about you. It just wasn't the right time. Also, weren't you the one who broke up with him?"

"Debatable," I say, ready to move on. "So…any new community gossip I should know?"

Vanessa pounces on the subject change. "There's a new book club meeting in the café on Wednesdays," she says. "Oh! And the cooking class is already full."

"The fundraiser for the animal shelter?" I glance at Mari. "We're already selling tickets?"

"It's great, isn't it?" Mari folds her hands on her lap. "There's a lot of community enthusiasm for what you're trying to do."

I try not to let pride show on my face, even though it glows in Mari's eyes. "Anyone else going to the cooking thing?"

Vanessa flips her hair. "My cousin's leading it, so I promised I'd go."

"That's right, we're bringing Sean Bracelyn out from Ponderosa Resort." I glance at Mari. "We got all his paperwork and a background check?"

"Of course." She watches me a moment. "Are you taking the class?"

"Filming, remember? These events make great footage."

Mari holds my gaze. "You know, it's a good idea for you to enjoy some of the classes. The community enrichment activities are for family, too."

"I know, I know." I'm just more comfortable behind the camera, getting the shot like I always do. "I'll check the bulletin board for other things I can try."

As the ladies chat about yoga and the new mountain biking class, I consider what Nick and I talked about that first day. The things we always meant to try and never got around to. Maybe that's what I'm missing.

Before I realize the conversation's wrapping up, my guests are getting to their feet. "I want to see my niece before Jessie puts her to bed." Gretchen pulls on her sweater. "I got to give her a bath last night."

"I held her for ten minutes while Jessie toured the shelter." I hate admitting how right it felt cradling a fresh-baked baby. "Joy's such a sweetheart."

"Isn't she?" Gretchen grabs her purse. "Jessie left the Peace Corps to have Joy, but it feels like a fair trade."

We exchange hugs before she and Vanessa head for the door, twin magnets pulling them toward my brothers. I might hate them all if they weren't such perfect matches.

Mari and I watch from my front porch. She waits until they're out of earshot to speak again. "I didn't want to say this in front of the others, but there's an issue with applications for deputy police chief."

"Don't tell me we got resumés from a bunch of racist jerks that'll make me want to punch someone in the junk."

"No punching, please." Mari winces. "Junk or elsewhere."

"Oh, come on. It's been months since we had any good Judson scandals in the news."

Her expression looks pained, so I prompt her again. "Come on, what's the cop issue?"

"I sat down with Chief Lovelin yesterday to discuss our top candidates," she says. "One of them is...familiar."

"How familiar?" I can't tell from her expression if this is good news or bad. "Who?"

"Abe Davis," she says. "Nick's brother-in-law?"

"Alexis's husband?" A few puzzle pieces click into place. "That actually makes sense. I get the feeling they're ready to leave the city. Are you bringing him out for an interview?"

"Yes, but I wasn't sure Nick knew." Mari pauses. "He hasn't said anything?"

"No, but I could feel him out." My mind veers at the thought of feeling Nick, so I'm confused when Mari shakes her head.

"No, don't. I'm telling you because all applicants agree to have their information shared with the core operations team, which obviously, you're part of. Beyond that, it's confidential."

"Got it." I can't help wondering how Nick would take the news. "Nick's close with Alexis and Abe, so I'm sure they'll tell him soon."

"Keep it quiet for now," Mari says. "I'll try to give a heads-up before we bring him out."

"Thanks. And thank you for coming." I pull her in for a hug before she can escape. "I'm glad you came over. And I'm glad you're so happy."

"Me, too." Mari beams, though I can see she's trying to hold back. "You're happy, right?"

"Of course."

She studies my face like she doesn't quite believe me. "All right. See you at family dinner?"

"That's right, Cooper's hosting as soon as he gets back." Normally, I dread Coop's veggie-focused, bacon-less meals, but all I'm thinking now is if Nick would like it.

"Good night, Lauren." My sister gives me a squeeze and steps off my porch.

I watch her go, waving when she turns at the edge of the next bank of cabins to glance back.

Then I drop my hand and head back inside, telling myself I have everything I need. Friends, family, a kickass home. Even a pet.

"We've got it all, Sharkira." I peer at my fish, wondering if I should try different decorations. Something more serious, maybe. "We're strong, independent women who don't require constant companionship. Right, girl?"

Sharkira eyes me, then spits out a rock.

"Exactly." I wonder what Mari would say about the psychological implications of having heart-to-hearts with a cichlid. "Maybe I'm a little nostalgic about Nick being here, but there's a reason we didn't work out. A lot of reasons."

I'm glad she's not asking me to list them, since I'd be hard pressed to do that right now. Sharkira shoves her nose in the gravel and wallows around before coming up with another mouthful of rocks.

"I like my life the way it is," I continue, wondering who I'm trying to convince. "I'm happy alone. I have a *great* life."

And I'm positive there's not a Nick-shaped hole in it. I never noticed one before, so there's no reason it should be there now. "So that's that," I finish, pleased by my own pep talk. "We're just friends."

Friends who sometimes kiss. I really should stop doing that.

Sharkira watches me, mouth moving, her little side fins fluttering to keep her in place. She flaps her gills, looking like she wants to say something. It's best that she doesn't.

"Okay then. Good talk."

I swear she rolls her eyes, then turns to head-butt the octopus.

CHAPTER 7

CONFESSIONAL 801.5
<u>Armbrust, Nick (Owner, Armbrust Resorts)</u>
It's funny how you change as you get older. When I was eight, I wanted to be a superhero. My sister turned one of her dresses into a cape and pretended to be Storm. I'd chase her around shouting that I was Static Shock. I had a comic book collection this high and—well, anyway. I grew up. Maybe when Mama reminded me superhero isn't a real job. Gotta have a practical career, you know? Prove yourself and all that. I still think I'd have been a badass Static Shock.

* * *

My week becomes a blur of construction. By day, I'm supervising buildout on the new cabins. Evenings are spent transforming the warehouse, getting it ready for the adoption event. The Judsons insist on paying me overtime, and I insist right back that they donate the money to Tia's animal rescue. It's not like I'm desperate for cash, and it's a good cause.

By Friday evening, I'm ready to relax. The thought takes me back to weekends with Lo, how we always had something going on. A film premiere or work travel or some Hollywood party. Like clockwork, we'd meet each other's eyes across the room after an hour or so.

Crooked House.

One of us would mouth the words, and we'd say our goodbyes to the host, making a break for the exit. Thirty minutes later, we'd be snuggled in my bed. Sometimes we'd watch TV and eat junk food. Other times we'd end up naked, touching and tasting and—

Well. That's ancient history. I'd kill to have it again, but my odds aren't good with Lo avoiding me like she is.

"Hey, Nick." Cooper strolls into the warehouse carrying what looks like a giant box of sex toys. "Lauren asked me to pass these out."

I stare at a phallic hunk of neon green silicone and shake my head. "I'm good, man."

Coop sets the box on a low file cabinet. "There's another box with all the feathery ones."

"Feathers?" I poke something I'm pretty sure is a double-sided dong, then yank my hand back. "Please tell me these aren't used."

Cooper shrugs. "Gretchen's sister, Jessie, got them donated. I think they're new."

"If they're not, I'm gonna go bleach my hand." I frown at a black bulbous object. "That's a butt plug, right?"

"What?" Coop laughs and pulls out a knobby blue stick that has me taking a quick step back. "Dog toys, dude. You got sex on the brain or something?"

I decide not to answer that one. "I knew that."

Still cracking up, Cooper ducks outside and returns with another box. "Cat toys." He grabs a stick with feathers on the end and tickles me under the chin. "But if you want, I'll look the other way so you can take some home."

"You're a dick." I yank the thing out of his hand and toss it back in the box. "How was LA?"

"Not bad." He's still smiling, but it looks stiff now. Forced. "Kinda weird being back there, you know?"

"I hear ya. Feels like a lifetime ago we were all living there."

"It was."

"Your folks doing okay?"

"Yeah, they're great. They said to tell you hi."

"Hello." I give a mock wave, grateful I've stayed friendly with Lo's family. "Did you talk with Cash Beckett about doing the show?"

Cooper brightens. "Yeah, and get this—he was already planning a trip out here. I guess he's got friends in Oregon."

"He agreed to guest star?"

"We're hammering out contract details, but yeah." He smiles. "It's looking good."

"Congratulations, man. Lauren must be thrilled."

Coop gives me a thoughtful look, and I wonder if my face just changed. If the way I say her name gives it away that I'm nuts about her.

"You know," Coop says slowly, "you're the first person not get on my case with a million questions. About whether I—" He breaks off, shrugging. "You know."

I frown because I don't know. "What do you mean?"

He drags a hand through his hair, brow furrowing. "You're not hovering around trying to figure out if I got to LA and went on some wild drug binge. If I met up with people I used to use with and fell off the wagon." He shoves his hands in his pockets and looks me in the eye. "For the record, I stayed clean."

"I don't doubt it." It honestly never crossed my mind, which may not be a point in my favor. I recall what Lo said about my oblivion to other people's lives. "If you want to talk about it though—"

"No." Coop throws his hands up like I might hurl this box of cat toys at his head. "God, no. Can we get back to talking about sex toys or something?"

"Because that's less awkward." I unhook my toolbelt. "I'm heading over to the brewery for dinner if you want to come."

"Thanks, but I ate already." He picks up one of the boxes. "Also, I've gotta distribute butt plugs to dogs."

"Funny." I sling the toolbelt into my work tote and turn to go. I'm at the edge of the door when Coop calls out. "If you wanted to try the restaurant instead, that's where the cooking class is happening."

"Cooking class?" I fix him with a frown. "I didn't sign up for any cooking class."

"It's a fundraiser for the new animal shelter." Coop shrugs. "One of the community members organized it."

"Nice." I love how folks are rallying behind this. "Is it open to anyone?"

"Nope, it's ticketed. Sold out super-fast."

"Guess I'll skip that, then." I shift the tote in my hand.

Coop's expression turns sheepish. "There might be an extra ticket."

"Oh?" Not like I care, but—

"*My* ticket. They're cooking with wine, so I'll sit this one out."

"I get it." Not like I wanted to do a cooking class anyway. I'm looking forward to a quiet night at home with a takeout burger and a beer and—

"Lauren's there," Coop says almost nonchalantly. "In case you wanted to see her."

"Why would I want that?"

He snorts. "You're a dumbass."

The man is not wrong. "Thanks for the tip." I reach for the door. "You're a good guy, Cooper Judson."

His eyes flicker before he turns and lugs the box of toys to the kennels. "Don't tell anyone."

I step outside to find it's warmer than I expected. Fall hits hard and early here, but summer won't go down without a fight. Smells of sunbaked sage mix with spicy scents of autumn leaves and whatever's baking in the café. I've gotten to know Patti and Colleen pretty well these past few weeks, so I see why the Judsons begged them to stay. Besides being badass mama bears, they're the sweetest damn couple I've ever met. Almost like Abe and Lexi the way they look out for one another, Patti handing Colleen a spoon before she even asks for it, or Colleen catching Patti's eye across a crowded room.

It's hard not to envy that kind of closeness.

When I reach the restaurant, it's already packed. The tables are rearranged to give everyone a view of the open kitchen where a tall guy in a white chef's coat is talking and holding a huge-ass sweet potato. Intrigued, I push through the door and scan for a seat.

"Nick." Lauren's whisper-shout draws me to where she's stationed beside a camera on a tripod. I move quietly along the wall, trying not to draw attention as the chef shifts to talking about onions.

"Hey," I murmur when I'm close enough to whisper in Lo's ear. "Sorry I'm late. Didn't know this was happening."

"It just started," she says. "Have you met Sean Bracelyn?"

She gestures at the tall white guy leading class, so I assume that's him. "The chef?"

She nods. "His family owns Ponderosa Resort near Bend. That's his wife with the knives."

I glance to the guy's left where a pretty brunette wields a pair of steel blades. Her pregnant belly keeps her from getting too close to the counter. "What are we making anyway?"

"Some chicken dish with roasted root veggies, but there's a vegetarian option." Lauren points to an empty workstation near the front of the room. "I could really use someone in that spot doing veggie prep. Are you staying?"

I smile down at her, digging the sight of Lauren in work

mode. "You asking because you want me in your shot or because you want me to stay out of it?"

"In." She adjusts something on the camera. "You always look great on film."

"Aw, now you're just stroking my ego." Not that I mind. If having me in her shot will make Lauren happy, I'm game. "Tell me it's because you admire my mad cooking skills."

"You do have mad cooking skills," she agrees, tucking a shock of hair behind an ear. "Also, I want viewers to see a handsome, charismatic Black man who knows his way around a kitchen."

"Ah, the race card," I tease, not surprised she doesn't get flustered. "S'awright. I'll be your token Black guy."

She snorts and hands me an apron. "You're not a token anything except pain in my ass." She points to a sink across the room. "Hand washing station's over there. Thanks for doing this." She pauses, steely eyes sweeping mine. "I really do love how you look on camera."

"No prob." My ego digs the compliments while my heart digs the fact that Lo loves something—*anything*—about me. "Get ready to be dazzled by my culinary prowess."

I head for the handwash station, waving to Gabe as I go. He's closer to the front of the room talking with a burly Asian dude who's hovering protectively by a guy in a wheelchair. Brothers, I'm guessing. I move past and catch Lana Judson staring, blue eyes locked on the big guy. She blushes when she catches me watching.

Interesting.

Slipping past, I do my best to hear the chef's instructions, but it's hard with Lo across the room looking sexy as sin. She's dressed up tonight in tight black jeans and boots with tall heels. Her shirt is one of those wraparound things, red and silky and gaping open a bit as she bends to move a cord. She shifts left, and I catch a glimpse of the bra beneath. Black and lacy and sheer as far as I can see. I don't realize I'm staring until folks start moving around me.

"Hi, I'm Amber."

Shaking myself from a cleavage coma, I start to extend my hand to the chef's wife. "Whoops, I guess we shouldn't shake?" I gesture to the handwashing station. "Just washed up. I'm Nick, by the way."

"Good to meet you, Nick." She nudges the knife at the edge of a wood cutting board. "You may have missed Sean's talk on knife skills. I can give you a quick recap if you want?"

"Nah, I'm good." I grasp the solid black handle, whistling as I admire the steely blade. "Now *this* is a knife."

"It's German," Amber says. "Sean's a stickler for nice knives."

"I like it." I set to work chopping the sweet potato, considering how to make conversation that proves I'm interested in others. I want Lauren to see I'm capable, and besides…Amber seems like a cool woman. "Are you a chef, too?"

She barks out a laugh, dark hair falling forward. "Hardly. I run a reindeer ranch with my sister. I'm just here because my husband's worried I'm going to pop out this baby when he's not there."

"Gotta love a guy who watches out for his woman." Belatedly I realize I've made her sound like a piece of property. *Shit.* "Y'all know if you're having a boy or a girl?"

She's watching me chop the potato, brow creasing a little. "Yes, but actually—"

"Wait, let me guess." I grab a second sweet potato, taking care to keep the cubes nice and even. "My sister has two babies. Two gorgeous little girls. Everyone kept telling Lexi—that's my sister—they kept telling her how women carry girl babies up high, but Lex kept saying that's just a wives' tale. Thing is, it turned out true. I swear it's like she had a big ol' beach ball—"

"Stop." Amber bites her lip. "They're supposed to be wedges."

"Wedges?" I frown, desperate to show I'm paying attention.

"Haven't heard of that. Lots of other myths, though. People kept telling Lexi, 'Oh, if you're craving sweets, you must be having a girl.' Or something about heart rate. I can't remember exactly—"

"The potato." She touches my hand, and I bring the knife to a halt. "The recipe calls for wedges."

"Oh." Shit. Frowning at my perfect pile of orange cubes, I resist the urge to look at Lo. I'm hoping she didn't hear that. "Got another one?"

"It's okay." Amber smiles and scrapes the sweet potato chunks into a bowl. "We have plenty of these anyway. Why don't you start on the onion?"

I grab the papery orange sphere and plunk it on the cutting board. "Got it. Any special size?"

"Wedges for those, too." She winces, resting a hand on her baby bump. "Sorry, she loves kicking me in the bladder. My sister swears it's because I played soccer in college."

"Ha!" I whack the onion down the middle, severing it so the stem end's on my right and the root on my left. "A girl, huh? Got names picked out?"

Amber blinks hard, eyes filling with tears. Instantly, I know I'm an asshole. "Aw, shit—I'm so sorry. You don't have to tell me if it's personal. It's none of my business, and I know we just met, so—"

"No, stop." She grabs my wrist as a tear rolls down her face. "You want to keep the cut sides of an onion face down. It helps with the enzymes that burn people's eyes."

"What?" Aw, hell. I've screwed up again. "Guess I should have paid more attention."

"It's okay." Amber's blinking hard, swiping her eyes on a sleeve. "It's all part of learning."

Charging ahead without all the information is *not* part of learning, but that's nice of her to say. I allow myself a glance at Lo. She's watching me with a look I can't read, something between a smile and a smirk. Probably heard that whole thing.

Another instance of me barreling ahead without asking questions. I mean, I *am* asking questions. Just not the right ones.

"Hang on." Amber backs away, blinking back tears. "Let me grab you another knife. That might be a dull one. A sharp knife makes all the difference with onions. I'll be right back."

I'm such a dick. I stare down at my onion, wondering if I should go ahead. The rest of the veggie people have moved on to herbs. I watch a tattooed Black guy at the next station making smooth dicing motions, his blade working nice and precise. I could stand to hone my knife skills.

Flipping the onion over, I lop off the root end. Then the stem, trying to recall what my mama taught me about cutting onions.

"With every job you do, you've gotta give it your best," she said. *"That goes for chopping veggies or making a career. Your granddaddy didn't work himself to death so you could grow up half-assing it in the kitchen or classroom or your job—"*

"Ow." I jerk my hand back, startled to see blood welling on the tip of my thumb. Holy crap, I chopped it off.

Lauren's at my side in an instant. "Are you okay?"

Pissed at myself, I snatch a dishtowel off the counter. "It's fine. Just a little nick."

Lauren quirks an eyebrow, one corner of her mouth twitching. "Little Nick, huh?"

Her smile shoots me with a flash of memory, and I forget about my thumb. I forget everything except Lauren, on her knees in bed, fingers fisted around my cock. Was it really three years ago?

"I think it needs a name," she purred, stroking me until I felt my eyeballs roll back. *"Something...fitting."*

"Mmm." It came out like a growl as I fought to keep control. *"What, like Anaconda? Warrior King? Hammer of Thor?"*

She laughed and leaned down to lick the tip. *"How about Little Nick?"* Her tongue grazed the underside, making my breath whoosh out. *"For irony, since it's hardly little."*

A sound squeaks up my throat, jerking me back to this steamy kitchen. Lo's looking at me, her face a mix of concern and curiosity as I clutch the towel around my thumb. "You sure you're okay? You look a little...sweaty."

"It's hot in here." That's true, but it's got nothing to do with the temperature.

Her forehead crinkles. "Maybe we should have the doctor look at that. She's right over there."

Lo nods to where a full-figured Black woman commands her cutting board, chopping parsley with surgical precision. Her partner—a lanky Latino guy—stands at a safe distance, recognizing her superior skill. Smart man.

"I'm fine." I unwrap the towel, relieved to see the bleeding's slowed. "It's not that bad. Promise I don't need stitches."

"And *you're* more qualified to decide that than an MD?" Her tone suggests a test of some kind. "How about you give someone else a chance to weigh in."

I hesitate, sensing there's a right and a wrong answer here.

"All right." I adjust the towel, careful not to get close to the onion. I don't want to make a bigger mess than I already have. "If it'll make you feel better—"

"It will," she says, and grabs my arm.

My thumb's stinging, but Lo's careful not to bump it. "This way." She tugs me toward the doc, eyes flashing up at me in a way that suggests I may not have screwed up. Not this time, anyway.

Maybe there's still time to fix this. Not my thumb, but this thing between Lauren and me. What if we're not too late?

Squaring my shoulders, I march toward the doc with optimism in my step, hope in my heart, and the woman I can't get over by my side.

CHAPTER 8

CONFESSIONAL 809

JUDSON, LAUREN (PRODUCER: JUNIPER RIDGE)

Do I believe in second chances? [audible snort] Isn't there a saying about the definition of insanity being when you keep doing the same thing over and over and expecting different results? That's pretty much how I feel about—what? What do you mean it's an ableist word?
All right. Lunacy. Madness. Batshit crazy. Better?
I forget what we were talking about.

* * *

I'm scanning the shot list on my phone, struggling to stay focused. I'm here to get footage for sweeps week. The cooking segment will air a week before the episode with the pet adoption, and I need them both to shine.

But I also need to know Nick's okay. Even though Dr. Williams insisted it looks worse than it is, I'm not convinced. When I glance over, I'm not surprised to see Nick watching me right back. He gives me a hangdog grin and a thumbs-up with a flash of bandage.

Okay, he's fine. And right about not needing stitches, though I'm relieved he got a medical opinion. The old Nick could have lopped off a whole finger and still insisted he didn't need help. Maybe he *has* changed. I sure have. Old me would have leapt instantly to fears of nerve damage. I'd have pulled up contact info for a neurosurgeon before he set down the knife.

Mari's words from the other night come back to me in a rush. *"If the people you were a few years ago didn't work as a couple, maybe the people you are now could?"*

"Hey, Lauren. We still filming here?"

Gabe's voice pulls me back to the moment. I'm not here to reconnect with an old boyfriend. I'm here for footage that makes viewers binge a whole season of *Fresh Start at Juniper Ridge*.

Shoving the phone in my pocket, I ignore Gabe's knowing look. "How long do we have before Sean pulls the chicken out of the oven? I want an overhead shot."

My brother squints at the kitchen. "I think the timer says four minutes."

Crap. Not enough time to get a ladder. I glance around, looking for safe substitutes. I'm a master of improvising in a pinch.

"Could you have Carl swing that fill light over here?"

Gabe looks skeptical. "What for?"

"So we don't have shadows when we're shooting from above." I grab the handheld, already calculating the angle. "Can you get a closeup from the side? I'll come at it from above on the other side."

My brother frowns. "How the hell are you going to do that?"

"I have a plan." He'll see soon enough.

"Lauren, wait—"

But I don't have time to waste. Gabe and I work well together, so he'll get what we need. Our teamwork's solid, with Gabe grabbing the shots to make a scene flow while I snag the overhead sequence I can already picture on screen.

Spotting a step stool in the corner, I drag it to the edge of the oven. Two minutes on the timer, so I summon Chef Sean. "Could I ask you to take the chicken out slowly when the timer goes off?" I nudge the stool closer and switch on the camera. "And if you can, angle your body this way. We want to get the Ponderosa Resort logo on your chef's coat."

Sean grins and grabs an oven mitt. "My sister thanks you."

Bree Bracelyn's the marketing powerhouse behind Ponderosa Resort, so I don't doubt it. She knows how the game goes. They've booked a thirty-second commercial for this episode, so it's my unspoken duty to throw some prime product placement.

"Could you adjust your chef's hat just a little?" I take a step back and get the shot lined up. "There, that's good."

Amber steps over and scratches a smudge of smashed sweet potato off his sleeve, then plants a kiss on his jawline. "You look great."

The intimacy makes my chest ache. I deliberately don't scan the room for Nick as I take a deep breath to get centered. Putting a foot on the bottom step, I wish I'd worn better shoes. Heels aren't great for this, but I wasn't sure if I'd need to step in for a scene. Too late to change now, and kicking off my shoes in a kitchen seems unsanitary. Besides, there's a minute left on the timer.

"Okay, this is good." I take another step up and get my balance, teetering on top of the step stool. "Don't look at me. Just pretend I'm not here."

Community members cluster around, everyone eager for a glimpse of dinner. Or maybe for more screen time. They know how the game goes.

I zoom in on the oven door, stomach rumbling. I saw this dish a few weeks ago when Sean did a demo, so I know how the crisp, golden skin looks against a sea of plump veggies dotted with fresh herbs. Appealing to viewers' senses is key to keeping them watching. It's the sort of shot we'll use in teaser reels, the kind that earned me an Oscar for best cinematography.

"Careful, Lo."

Nick's voice rumbles low behind me. I don't look for him. With ten seconds on the timer, I'm focused on the shot.

3, 2, 1...

The oven dings, and I hold my breath as Sean flashes his famous smile and grabs an oven mitt. "You guys are in for a real treat." He eases open the oven door, and I zoom in, mouth watering. Man, that looks good.

The camera's rolling, so I signal the lighting guy to dial it up. "A little slower, Sean," I coax. "Perfect. Hold it right there."

I feel Nick moving behind me, though he's not saying a word. That's good, since I need to concentrate. I lean forward, loving what I see in my viewfinder. "That's it. All right, you can pull it out."

Gabe snorts because my brother is a pre-teen boy. I ignore him, intent on getting my shot. I pan over the baking sheet, following it as Sean kicks the oven door closed and shifts the pan to the counter.

"You want me to pause or anything?" he asks.

"Nope, you're doing great. Just look natural."

Not easy with a camera shoved in his face, but Sean handles it like a pro. His mom's a famous TV chef, so he knows how this works.

"Excellent." I zoom a bit tighter. "You getting this, Gabe?"

"Yep." My brother zooms in on the chicken. "Damn, that smells good."

"Right?" I lean in again, tilting my center of gravity.

That's all it takes. My heel wobbles, and I feel myself pitching forward. "Shit!"

I yelp and grip the camera as I topple. My arm flails like a pinwheel, whipping around for balance, but it's too late. I'm falling, crashing straight for the—

"Gotcha." Strong arms band my waist, pulling me back. I'd know those arms anywhere. Nick's warmth, his broad chest, his cedar smell floods my senses as he pulls me to safety.

"Nick." I blink up at him, gratitude almost drowning my own self-loathing.

Almost.

My pride's stinging too badly to let him haul me away like some misbehaving child. "Wait. I just need to get—"

"You've got it." He plants me on solid ground and doesn't let go. Eyes searching mine, he keeps his hands on my waist. "You okay?"

"Yes, but—" I spin around, desperate to save face. I hate how everyone's watching, staring with silent pity. "Let me get the shot."

I lunge forward, off-balance and unsure what I'm after. The perfect angle, a boost of confidence to cancel the embarrassment coursing through me. I struggle to right the camera as my free hand flies out to steady me on the counter.

"Shit!"

Pain sears my palm and rockets up my arm as I yank my hand off the scalding baking sheet. I'm dimly aware I've just cursed twice on camera, but it's the least of my concerns. Everyone's staring, watching me make an ass of myself. Someone giggles, and my vision clouds red.

Nick grabs me again, firmer this time. "Clear the way," he calls and hauls me to the sink. If he's expecting a fight, I don't give it to him. Just sag against his chest as he pins me at the sink and lets his lips graze my ear. "You're okay, Lo. I've got you."

I close my eyes, cheeks burning hotter than my palm as he turns on the taps and shoves my hand under cold water. The burn cools instantly but it does nothing for my stinging pride. I draw in a few breaths as Gabe orders everyone to move away, to gather in the dining room.

Blinking my eyes open, I look up at Nick. "I'm sorry."

"Nothing to be sorry for." He turns my hand over in the water. "It doesn't look so bad."

The pain in my hand is long gone, but the one in my chest isn't ebbing. "I hate this."

"I know."

I swallow, wincing as he turns my hand under the icy stream. "Thank you."

"No prob." He pries the camera from my other hand and passes it off to someone. "Lauren Judson always gets her shot."

"True." It's my mantra of sorts, but at what cost? I steal a glimpse at Nick's face, waiting for the lecture, for the teasing, for the judgment.

"That better?" He turns my hand again, frowning at the redness. "I can see if Doc Williams has some salve."

"I'm fine." I swallow again, surprised my throat works. "That's twice now."

His brow furrows. "Huh?"

"That you've had to, uh—"

"Oh, that." He grins, and tension eases from my shoulders. "You mean how you're so dazed by my manhood that you throw yourself in my arms?" Still smiling, he switches off the tap. "Girl, you know I've got your back."

I do know. It's something I've always known with Nick, even when we didn't see eye to eye. Even when we missed each other by miles in intention or understanding.

He's not a perfect man. God knows I'm miles from perfection.

But right here, right now, with his solid heat against my back, I feel safe. Protected. Understood.

"Thank you for saving me." I lick my lips and will my wounded pride to stop throbbing. "You still like soft pretzels?"

He cocks his head and wraps a clean, white towel around my hand. "The ones from the café?"

"I bought some this morning." I hold the towel in place, conscious of the burn, of the fact that I spotted those pretzels in the display case and thought of Nick. Even then, I knew where this was headed. Maybe not his cut thumb and my burned palm, but *this*. This connection I've never been able to explain but always circle back to.

Nick's watching me with curiosity in his eyes, and I realize I haven't actually invited him over. "The pretzels." I clear my throat. "Colleen makes them fresh every day. They're really good."

"That so?" He's watching me, reigning in his urge to assume. "You offering to share?"

I nod, grateful for his gentleness, his patience, for so many things about this man I used to love and might still love.

"Patti made cheese sauce to go with them." I look down and adjust the towel around my hand. "Want to come over after the shoot?"

I glance up to see his grin spreading slow and warm, like caramel on cake. His palm skims my waist, sending my heart into a sharp swoop in my chest.

"I'll be there," he says, then turns to claim his dinner.

* * *

I FIGURED Nick would walk me to my place once dinner and filming wrapped. But as I'm slowly, *slowly* learning, I shouldn't assume where Nick's concerned.

"Give me twenty minutes," he said as I packed up camera gear. "Gotta shower."

"Oh, you're not—" I stopped myself in time, changing direction. "Of course. I'll see you when you get there."

"I'll be quick." His grin left me wondering if he knows how

hard I'm trying. What a struggle it is to keep pride and assumptions from getting in our way again.

As I light a candle on my entry table, I'm grateful for the short delay. It gives me a chance to collect myself. To consider my intentions for this evening.

To stare at the candle and decide it sends the wrong message because *hello*, I'm not trying to seduce the man. We're old friends, and friends enjoy snacks together. I blow out the candle, feeling foolish as I wave the smoke away.

Then I reconsider. It's a scented candle, *apple orchard*, it says on the side of the jar. It'll make the house smell homey, and isn't that what a good hostess does?

I relight it, then quickly snuff it out. We went apple picking together, Nick and I. It was our first autumn together, heavy with promise and possibility. Would he even remember? But I can't have him reading too much into this, so really, I should skip the candle.

Or maybe I should just—

The knock makes me drop the lighter. I pick it up and twist the doorknob before I realize it seems like I'm standing at the door waiting to pounce on him.

"Hey." Nick grins when he sees me. "You burning something?"

"What? Oh—yes." I set the lighter on the entry table, then pick it up again. "Just deciding whether to light a candle."

He eyes me oddly. "You haven't had enough burning for one night?"

Crap. There's that.

Ignoring the candle, I sweep a hand toward the living room. "Have a seat. I'll grab the pretzels."

I start to turn, but Nick catches my hand. "Lo."

Looking down at our intertwined fingers, I see he's taken care to grab my uninjured hand with his uninjured one. Or is it just coincidence?

"What's up?" I ask, struggling to keep the wobble from my voice.

He rubs a thumb over my knuckles. "You seem nervous. You okay?"

"I'm fine. Totally f—" I stop, shaking my head. Enough. This is Nick. He's seen me naked. Is seeing me insecure that much worse?

I take a breath. "You know what? I *am* nervous. I don't want to give you the wrong idea, but then I'm not sure what the right idea is and—"

"Relax, Lo." Gold-brown eyes hold mine as his thumb skims my knuckles, smoothing away my anxiety. "How about we figure this out together?"

I nod, even though I'm not sure if we're talking about this evening or something else. Something bigger than soft pretzels and cheese. Taking another breath, I draw my hand back. "That sounds good."

"Excellent." His smile warms me from the inside out, and a little more tension leaves my shoulders. "How about I light the candle?"

I nod, afraid to trust my voice for fear it'll blurt out all my silly secret fears. "Would you like beer or wine or soda or—"

"Beer," he decides, flicking the lighter to bring the candle to life. He turns the jar around and reads the label with a smile. "Apple orchard, huh?"

"I'll—uh—get the beer." I hurry away so he doesn't see my face flaming. What the hell am I doing?

Gathering food gives me a chance to collect myself. I've got the pretzels in the oven set to "warm" like Patti suggested. Wrapping a dish towel around my uninjured hand, I drag the baking sheet from the oven and pile pretzels on a plate. I borrowed a little fondue pot from the restaurant to warm the cheese sauce, so I set that on a tray with the beers. Carrying it to the living room, I'm feeling slightly more composed.

Nick's not on the couch, and I see he's detoured to the fish tank. He glances up as I walk by. "Sharkira's been redecorating."

"I bought her a new castle." I set the tray down and turn to see him eyeing one corner of the tank. "She seems to want it buried."

"That's gotta hurt her face, using her nose to dig like that." Nick tilts his head. "Is that a Rubik's cube under all that gravel in the other corner?"

"Cooper brought it. It's not a real one."

"I had no idea they made this many aquarium decorations."

Wiping my hands on my jeans, I walk over to join him. "I've dug it out three times today, and she keeps throwing more gravel over it. I'm letting it be for now."

"Good plan." Turning from the tank, he saunters to the living room. As he pauses by the sofa, I wonder if he's nervous, too. His eyes meet mine, and he offers a sheepish look. "I feel like this is some kind of test."

"What do you mean?"

"If I take the chair, I'm making it clear we're not sitting next to each other. I definitely don't want that." He drags a hand over his head, gaze shifting past the leather club chair to the loveseat. "If I sit *here,* you might think I'm tricking you into cozying up close. And I know you're not a fan of tricks."

"True," I agree, biting back laughter. "And the couch?"

"The safest bet." Grinning, he moves to one end of it. "But then do I park my ass in the middle and force you to pick a side? Or do I claim one end and make it awkward for you to figure out if you should pick the other end or move more toward the middle?" He shakes his head, his expression a mix of mirth and bemusement. "So many decisions."

I'm full on smiling now, charmed by his admission. "So I'm not the only one overthinking things."

"Nope." He steps close to the sofa and pats the arm. "How about we sit down together on the count of three?"

"Deal." I move around the coffee table to stand beside him. "One," I say. "Two—"

"Wait, hold up." He grins again. "Are we sitting *on* three, or like—one, two, three, *then* sit?"

I roll my eyes. "Now you're just messing with me."

"A little bit." He touches my hand gently. It's the one with the burn on the palm, and he brings it to his lips. "Quite the pair we are, huh?"

His bandaged thumb skims the flesh between my thumb and forefinger, and I sit down because I'm dizzy. "Guess we can strike 'cooking lessons' off the list of activities we can do safely."

He laughs and eases down beside me, thigh not quite brushing mine. I capture his bandaged thumb in my palm. "I didn't see how it happened." I turn the digit over in my hand, gently touching the bandage. "I know it was a knife thing, but—"

"But you're wondering how a guy who works with power tools can fuck up so badly with a kitchen knife?" He eases back against the couch. "Same way I usually screw up. Talking instead of listening. Assuming instead of learning. But hey, I'm working on it."

I swallow hard, uncurling my fingers to show the faint red line on my palm. It doesn't hurt, at least not much, but it left a mark. "And I let my pride get the best of me," I admit. "What does that say about us?"

"A lot, actually." He stretches his arms over the back of the sofa, and I hesitate before leaning back. Not touching, not that close, but his heat seeps into my shoulders. "Lauren and Nick from two years ago would never admit all that." He toys with my hair, spreading the strands between his fingertips. "They'd have dug in their heels and found someone else to blame."

"That Lauren and Nick," I murmur. "Not the most self-aware people."

He laughs and wraps a length of hair around one long finger. "They're kind of assholes, aren't they?"

"No joke." I lean forward to pick up my beer. "They're working on it. Also, can we stop talking about ourselves in third person?"

"Nick's kinda enjoying it." He grabs the other beer glass and clinks it against mine. "To figuring out our shit."

"Cheers."

We drink and then set down our glasses to reach for the same pretzel. He laughs and lets go, grabbing the other one and dunking it into the cheese sauce. "Damn," he says as he takes his first bite. "That's tasty."

"Right?" I bite into my own pretzel, savoring the salty goodness. "The cooking class was great and all, but I could never make something this amazing."

Nick tears off a hunk of pretzel and swishes it through the cheese sauce. "Look at you all foodie with the fondue pot. Go, Lauren."

"Thanks." I sip my beer and set it on the coaster. "Maybe it's a sign I'm not totally hopeless?"

He looks up, brown eyes searching mine. "Who said you were hopeless?"

"What we were just talking about." I sweep a hand to indicate our conversation from minutes ago. "I still let my pride call the shots, and that sucks. But at least I've learned how to serve a proper snack instead of throwing down a bag of chips and calling it good."

Nick's eyes take on a warm glint. "To be fair, we usually ate them in bed. We had better things to do than search for serving bowls."

My cheeks heat up, and I take another sip of beer to hide it.

Crooked House.

Is that what we're doing here now? Hiding away together from bright lights and prying eyes? It's just the two of us, the way we used to love things back then.

"Well, anyway, it's progress," I say. "The fact that either of us can recognize when there's a better way to do something we've been screwing up."

He nods and studies my face. "Maybe there's hope for us."

For a second, I think he means *us*. As in Lauren and Nick the couple, not the two of us individually on a path of self-improvement. Or maybe it's the same thing?

Electricity crackles between us, and I wonder how it got there. Or if it ever left. Maybe it's been there all along, snapping and sizzling on slow burn while we figured out our shit eight hundred miles apart. I lick my lips and watch Nick's eyes drop to my mouth.

I swallow and decide something. "There's this thing I want to show you."

His gaze drifts to my breasts, but he catches himself and drags it back to my face. "What's that?"

I almost feel bad that what I'm offering is nothing sexual. It's more intimate, though I'm not sure he'd see it that way. Maybe this is silly.

But something stirs inside me. An urge to let him in, to let him see something I've kept private for years. It's possible he'll laugh. That he'll see me as sentimental or foolish.

I take a deep breath. That's the reason I should do it, right?

"Wait here." I get to my feet, surprised to feel butterflies kicking around in my belly. "I'll be right back."

CHAPTER 9

CONFESSIONAL 815.5
<u>Armbrust, Nick (Owner, Armbrust Resorts)</u>
Love advice? Nah, I'm no expert there. I build cabins, not relationships. [Long pause]. 'Course, I overheard my sister asking Mama the key to long marriage. Know what she said? "Girl, you've gotta play together." And at first, I'm like "aw, hell, no." No way am I picturing my parents doing the deed. But Mama keeps going, saying how she and Pop play Boggle every week. Boggle, I'm serious. Cheesy as hell, and I'm pretty sure Mama lets him win sometimes or he wouldn't keep playing. But I've remembered that for years.
Maybe she's onto something.

* * *

I don't realize I'm holding my breath until Lo walks back into the room. She's clutching a carved wooden vessel the size of a shoebox, and it takes me a sec to see it's one I built.

I need to breathe, so I order myself to do that as she comes around the sofa to sit beside me. I'm not even sad she's still dressed. Is this what she meant about growing up, growing out of bad habits?

"What do you have?" I force myself to keep it casual, to not scare her off with a barrage of questions. "I recognize that box."

There's a self-consciousness in her smile as she fiddles with the latch. "I thought you might. Do you remember what you built it for?"

Lucky me, I do. "You always had stuff like movie premiere tickets and newspaper clippings. Keepsakes you wanted to hold on to, but you never had a place to put them."

I remember choosing this hunk of purplish padauk wood, sanding the striped surface by hand. I don't do much woodworking, not that kind, anyway. But I threw everything I had into building that box.

"My treasures." She smiles and flips the clasp. "I wanted you to see what's in it."

I hold my breath again as she opens the lid. I have no idea what to expect or what my reaction should be. From the set of her shoulders, I'm guessing it's something big. Something sentimental. Something—

"A yoyo?" I blink as she pulls it out of the box. It's bright red and shiny with gold writing on it. "You got a yoyo?"

"Two of them." She extracts a second yoyo, this one yellow.

I lift the red one from her palm and peer at the words etched in gold on the plastic. "It's got my name on it."

Her cheeks pinken, but she tilts up her chin. "I ordered us each one. You were gung-ho about learning yoyo tricks, so I researched the best brand and had these custom made. They were delivered the day after you—after we—"

"I see." And I do. Not just the thoughtfulness of the gift, but the significance. All this time, she's kept these. Like she knew deep down we'd meet again. Like she held out hope we'd be here together on this couch, reconnecting our new lives.

Or maybe I'm reading too much into it. I look up and see her smile has gone bashful. "Tell me about it." I turn the toy over in my palm and watch her gaze drop to my hand. "Why you hung on to these."

"I—don't know, exactly." She shuts the box and sets it on the coffee table, then picks up the yellow yoyo. "Sometimes I forgot they were even in there. I'd go to put something away, and I'd see them and think, 'am I ready to throw those out?' And the thing is —" Her voice wobbles, and I fight the urge to help. To guess at her feelings and finish the sentence.

That's not what she needs.

"The thing is," she continues, "I never was. Ready to let go."

I recognize the gift she's giving me. Not the yoyo, but this tender truth that leaves her vulnerable and exposed. Not many people see Lauren's soft underbelly. The way she's just rolled over and shown it to me has my heart thudding in my chest.

"Thank you," I murmur.

"For what?" Her voice holds a hint of wariness.

"For showing that to me. For keeping them all this time." I don't say the rest of what I'm thinking. I can't risk scaring her away.

But still, I think it.

Thank you for not giving up on us.

I'm not sure that's what she's saying, and I'm trying not to assume. The thread connecting us is thin and fragile. I'm almost afraid to breathe wrong and break it.

Lauren stands up, palming the yellow yoyo. A flicker of challenge lights her eyes. "When's the last time you practiced?"

"It's been a while." I drag a hand over my head, trying to recall exactly why I gave up learning yoyo tricks. Too busy, I guess. "I got pretty good back in the day."

"Yeah? Maybe we're well-matched now."

"That so?" I get to my feet, rising to the challenge as I loop the yoyo string around my middle finger. "Let's see what you've got, girl."

Lo laughs and turns hers over in her palm, positioning it so the string spools over the top. She's clearly watched a tutorial or two, and I try to recall my own mess of tricks.

"Start with a basic sleeper." She curls her arm like a kid told to flex his muscles, and I pause to admire her arms. She's always had great muscle tone, maybe from lugging all that camera gear.

"And then," she continues, grinning like she knows damn well I'm checking her out, "just roll it off."

She lets the yoyo drop, sending it spinning at the bottom of the string. I follow suit, flexing at the top to watch her eyes flick to my biceps. My ego loves the way she looks at me. Like she wants to take a bite out of my arm.

I concentrate on keeping the string straight, not adding unnecessary spin. "Sleeper achieved," I say once I've got my yoyo whirling at the bottom. Flicking my wrist, I tug it back up. "All right, it's coming back to me."

Lo laughs at my accidental pun. "How about 'walking the dog'?"

"I'll give it a try." I throw a fast sleeper, getting it spinning nice and steady before easing the whirring plastic disk to the floor. It's spinning like it's supposed to with the string wrapped tight around my finger. Slowly, I let it lead me across the hardwood planks.

"Very nice." She pretends to applaud as I pass the coffee table, and I feel her attention following more than my yoyo. I turn fast and her gaze darts from my ass to my eyes.

"Excellent form," she says.

"Thank you."

Who knew yoyo tricks could be a turn-on? I'm not proud, so I'll take what I can get. "Let's see you do it."

"Piece of cake." Lauren duplicates my moves, throwing in a

little hip shimmy that shouldn't be this sexy. She's got great form, too.

"How about something more challenging?" She tugs the yoyo back into her palm, and I force myself to look at her eyes instead of her ass. "Can you do a breakaway?"

"Not sure I know that one." To be honest, I can't recall the names of most yoyo tricks. "How does it go?"

"Hold it parallel to your body like this." She demonstrates, gripping it like a doorknob, and I do the same. "Now make a sea with your hand."

"A sea?" She's already lost me. "Like—the ocean?"

"No, a *C*," she says. "The letter. Like—like—" Her cheeks flush, and I'm guessing what flashed through her mind.

"C like—*cock*?" I grin as her mouth falls open in mock indignation. "Clitoris? Come? Cunnilingus? Coochie? Chesticles? Stop me when I get it."

Lauren busts up laughing. "How do you know so many filthy words that start with C?"

"It's a gift."

"What are chesticles?" She shakes her head. "Never mind, I just got it." She reaches up and cups her breasts, and it's my turn to choke in shock.

I shake my head to get some blood back into it. "Keep doing that, and I'll forget every yoyo trick I know."

She drops her hands and grins. "All part of my evil plan." As she rewinds her yoyo string, her brow creases in thought. "Okay, so swing your arm in a C shape like this. Get it going in an arc about the level of your head."

I do my best to follow, narrowly missing clocking myself in the temple. I duck just in time, and Lauren reaches out to steady me. "You okay?"

"Oh, yeah." Even better with her hand on me. "Good thing my injuries don't impede yoyoing."

She frowns at my bandage. "Is it bothering you?"

"Nah." I turn it over, surprised there's no pain. "I could probably ditch the bandage."

"Leave it." She grins and blows hair off her forehead. "I like having you at a disadvantage."

"Girl, you're going *down*." Too late, I realize what I've said. "All right, let me try again."

This time when I do it, the yoyo arcs like it's supposed to. She nods her approval, then repeats the throw herself. "If you stick your finger out like this," she says, demonstrating, "you transition into 'Man on a Flying Trapeze.' Pretty cool, huh?"

I watch as she catches the string around one finger, sending the yoyo doubling back to land on taut twine. It looks tougher than anything I've tried before, but I'll give it a shot.

"Like this?" I stick out my finger and fling the yoyo, trying to get the arc right. Instead, I nearly nail myself in the nuts. "What am I doing wrong?"

Silence. I glance at her face and see her staring at my finger. Staring like she remembers what I can do with it. Like she's picturing all those times my fingers stroked and touched and—

"Wow." She licks her lips and drags her eyes off my hand. "God, you've got long fingers."

I laugh because it's totally unexpected. "Thought you were gonna play it off like you weren't staring."

"What's the point?" She chucks her yoyo again, bobbing it in nice, even strokes. "Are you going to pretend you aren't stealing looks down my top every chance you get?"

"No, ma'am."

"Well then." She tosses her hair. "What else have you got?"

I try to remember all those videos I watched years ago when I was learning this stuff. My memory's hazy, though that might have more to do with Lauren bending to dunk a hunk of pretzel in the cheese sauce. I catch a glimpse down the front of her shirt and feel the blood leave my brain. *Black lace*. God, what I wouldn't give to bury my face between those sweet scoops of flesh. I remember how her skin tastes, the way her breath used to hitch when I swirled my tongue around her—

"Nick. Yoo-hoo!" She snaps her fingers, yanking me back from my sex haze. "You have another trick to show me?"

Boy, do I.

But that's not what she's asking. "Uh, how about the 'Flying Saucer'?"

She sips her beer, her throat a graceful line as she swallows. "What's the 'Flying Saucer'?"

"Hang on, let me remember." Not easy with my libido pounding. I start to hook the string, but it's all tangled. "Hold up, I've got a kink."

"Do you?" She smirks and licks her lips. "Tell me all about it."

There goes the rest of the blood in my brain, rushing like gangbusters to my cock. "Jesus, woman. You trying to kill me?"

She laughs and swirls another hunk of pretzel through the cheese. "Maybe. What a way to go, right? Death by flirtation."

"You're playing with fire, girl."

That's her chance to back away. To call time-out on whatever it is we're doing. To stop it from going any further.

"'Fast Wind Up,'" she says.

I blink. "What?"

"A trick for winding the yoyo back up when it's all unwound like yours is now." She points to my yoyo dangling at the end of its string, and I deeply relate to a piece of plastic.

"All right." I take a step closer, closing some distance between us. "What do I do?"

Her eyes meet mine, smoldering and steely. "String around your middle finger like normal." She demonstrates, looping the twine around her longest digit.

"All right." I make a show of sticking out my middle finger, loving how her eyes lock on it. "Now what?"

Lo puts a palm out. "Hold your left hand up like this."

There's a faint red slash across her flesh where she touched the hot baking sheet. The urge to kiss it burns in my belly. I take another step closer and put my hand out. "Got it."

"Spread your fingers apart like a V," she says. "Ring finger on one side, middle on the other."

I do it, but all I can think about is her thighs. How they opened in an invitation I could never resist. How many times did I explore that space, tongue sweeping her sweetest folds? My mouth waters at the memory.

"Lo." My voice sounds raspy and strained and I watch her pupils dilate.

"Yes?" It's a breathy syllable pushed through parted lips.

I catch her wrist, drawing her palm to my mouth. "Does it hurt?" She shakes her head as I kiss the burn and meet her eyes. "Okay?"

Lauren nods, eyes wide as her fingers stay spread. "More," she breathes.

She's not talking about yoyo tricks. My dick throbs as I lower my mouth to her hand. I kiss the tips of her fingers, index, ring, middle. I let my tongue graze the valley between digits. Lo sucks in a breath.

"You taste good."

Her throat moves as she swallows. "Pretzel salt."

"Nah, it's you." And the taste of her skin is spurring all kinds of memories. The way it felt to lick between her thighs. Her soft moans of pleasure as I probed, swirled, tasted.

She's holding eye contact like she sees straight into my soul. I suck the tight band of skin between her fingers. My tongue skims suggestively over the tender hollow.

Closing her eyes, she gives a little moan. "Don't stop."

I let my free hand slide up to cup her hip, still sucking the space between her fingers. She groans as my tongue claims the valley between thumb and index finger.

With a soft cry, she flutters her lashes open. "Nick?"

"Yeah?"

"I want you." Her throat moves again, and I watch her weighing her words. "And if you're not on the same page, I totally understand, but I just thought—*oh*."

There's a gasp of surprise as I scoop her into my arms, then a clunk as the yoyo falls from her hand. "Bedroom?"

"End of the hall," she says, and I'm already headed there. Her weight in my arms is so hot, so right.

I reach the room and lower her to the dark purple comforter spanning a king-sized bed. She blinks up at me through a curtain of hair, her lips swollen even though we haven't kissed yet.

She clears her throat. "I just want to be clear," she says. "I can't do a relationship now, and I'm not ready for l—" Her lips clamp together, holding back the one word that could change this.

I ignore the pang in my chest as Lo continues. "This is just sex."

I nod, grateful for the clarity. The lack of it derailed us before, so it's good going into this with our eyes open. My dick swells with need, even as my heart tells me to slow the hell down.

"I can do that." I sink onto the bed between her thighs.

Her arms bracket my back, fingertips tracing my spine. I move in the cradle of her thighs like I was made to fit there. Like we've never spent a day apart. I tilt my hips to press into her heat. We're both fully clothed, but I swear I could come like this.

"God, Nick." She breathes into the crook of my neck. "You smell like—"

Sawdust? Sweat? Pretzels?

"—like *you*," she finishes, and it somehow makes sense.

I laugh and nuzzle her hair. "You smell like *you*, too." And she does, like spice and honey and sunshine and a million things missing from my life these last couple years. How did I think I could live without her?

Dragging my nose from her hair, I remind myself of her words.

Just sex.

Just sex.
Just sex.

I've done it before. Never with Lo, but I'm sure I could do it again.

But as I sink into the heat between her thighs, skating a path of kisses over her collarbones, I'm not sure it'll be enough.

CHAPTER 10

CONFESSIONAL 821
<u>JUDSON, LAUREN (PRODUCER: JUNIPER RIDGE)</u>
YOU WANT ME TO SET AN INTENTION? MARI, COME ON WITH THE —FINE.
I FULLY INTEND TO HAVE GRILLED CHEESE FOR DINNER. YOU SAID IT'S ABOUT FINDING MY BLISS, RIGHT?
I GUESS IF I'M REALLY GETTING BLISSFUL, I WANT A GLASS OF WINE. A BUTTERY CHARDONNAY, OR MAYBE ONE OF THOSE CRISP PINOT GRIGIOS FROM OUR LAST TRIP TO THE WILLAMETTE VALLEY. AND WE ALL KNOW WINE'S BETTER WHEN IT'S SHARED, SO I SUPPOSE IT JUST MAKES SENSE TO HAVE NICK COME OVER AND—WHAT?
WHY ARE YOU SMILING LIKE THAT?

* * *

Just sex.

Like that could ever be enough with Nick.

But it has to be because God knows I can't handle heartache like before. We're two people who know each other's bodies, good together in bed. That's all this can be.

I drag my nails down his back, memorizing miles of muscle through his T-shirt. "You feel fucking amazing."

He laughs and draws back to look in my eyes. "How about we get some of these clothes off?"

Circling my palms on his shoulders, I look at him from under my lashes. "You first."

"A'ight."

He sits up, and my body howls in protest. I'm expecting him to tug his shirt off, treating me to the slow striptease I crave. But Nick's never one to do the obvious.

"Arms up." He doesn't wait for me to obey. Just grabs my shirt and tugs it up, stripping it over my head.

I laugh and sit up, grateful I wore my nicest bra. From the way his gaze sweeps my breasts, he's appreciating it, too. "Not what I meant, Armbrust." It's my turn to grab his shirt, and he's more cooperative than I was. Lifting his arms, he lets me strip off the blue cotton and toss it aside.

My eyes feast on the smooth span of his chest, the dark flow of abs rippling to the waist of his jeans. I draw a hand up, the pale of my palm a contrast to his burnished flesh. He's hot and hard and fucking magnificent, and tonight, he's mine.

I take my time tracing muscles, drawing my fingers over rounded pecs and biceps made for holding a woman in his arms. Not just any woman, *me*, at least for now.

"You having fun there?" His voice is tinged with humor and a hint of strain.

I take my time touching the valley between his pecs, moving down, memorizing each mound of abdominal muscle marching toward the waistband of his jeans. "Becoming reacquainted with your flesh," I say mildly, squeaking as he grabs my hand. "Hey—"

"My turn." He rolls me onto my back and catches the front clasp on my bra. "Very pretty. Let's lose it."

He flicks it open with one hand, mouth descending on my breasts as dizziness drowns me. I try to fight it, to say I wasn't done touching him. But his mouth on my nipple stops the words in my throat, and I give up fighting. His tongue swirls and tastes, laving one nipple and then the other as I lie back and clutch his head.

I somehow snake a hand between us, reacquainting myself with the fine row of abdominal muscles. Gripping the thick length of him behind rough denim, I stroke him until he groans.

"Baby," he breathes. "I want to be inside you."

It's too soon; we're supposed to savor this, aren't we? But I feel myself nodding, panting with a hungry need to feel him sliding inside me. It's been ages, so don't we owe ourselves this first frantic taste?

"Off," I grunt, fumbling to shuck his jeans. "Need these gone."

His chest rumbles with a chuckle as he helps me peel off the jeans and boxers. My bra is long gone, and Nick's making quick work of my pants. I suck in my stomach, wondering if he'll notice the extra roundness in my belly. If he'll judge my choice to trade twice-daily workouts for pretzels and bacon and—

"God, you feel good." He pushes me back, but stays seated to gaze down on me. "You're so fucking beautiful, Lo. More than I remember."

I lick my lips and try to pull him down onto me. "You look good, too."

"Wait." He catches my wrists with one hand, pinning them over my head. "Let me look at you."

Self-consciousness sweeps through me, but I tip my chin up. "Like you haven't seen it before."

"Not like this." There's a reverence in his voice that steals my breath away. So does the palm he's trailing up my belly, between my breasts, over the left one until I gasp. "I want to memorize you."

It would sound cheesy coming from any other man, but his words have tears prickling my eyes. I blink them back, needing to keep emotion out of this. "If you're not inside me by the count of ten—"

He laughs and grabs the waistband of my jeans. "Or you'll what? Take care of yourself? Not a chance."

Stripping my panties off, he drags them down my thighs and shoulders his way between them. He licks his lips and heat coils in my belly. "I'll take all the time I need." He lowers his face between my thighs, tracing a long, slick line between my folds to reach my clit. "And you'll like it."

I want to argue. To tell him he's not in charge. But another swirl of his tongue has me clutching his head and begging him to keep going. "Nick." I blink back stars behind my eyelids. "Fuck, you're good at that."

He always was, and the vibration of laughter just adds to it. Tongue swirling, Nick licks me like he's spent two years starving. Like I'm the only thing that could fill him.

As my fingers clutch bunched shoulder muscles, I know he's the only one I want filling me. All of him, not just the thick, hot shaft I feel brushing my leg. His tongue swirls my clit and I gasp. "I'm close."

"I know."

Of course he does. He knows the precise moment to slide two fingers inside, curling to hit my g-spot as I shriek. He's possessing me, claiming me, and I fight that thought even as my body clenches to claim him, to draw him deeper.

"Oh, God!" The scream rips my throat, and I close my eyes, hips bucking as his fingers, his tongue, tilt me over the edge. Shockwaves rock me to the edge, a thousand peaks of pleasure carrying me up and over.

When I come down, he's kissing my thigh. I clutch his head, blinking as I struggle to get a grip. To pretend he didn't just rock my world.

But he looks up and meets my eyes, and he knows. That goddamn smug smile—

"Hey." His grin widens.

I blow hair off my face and try to look nonchalant. "Hey yourself."

"What's up?" He keeps grinning, knowing damn well I'm too pleasure-soaked to offer some clever retort.

I try for blunt instead. "You planning to fuck me or just stare?"

He turns his head to kiss my thigh. "Staring's nice." Another kiss, this one on the other thigh. "Tasting. Touching. Teas—"

"Nick, seriously." I sound borderline frantic, which is not the cool vibe I want. I paw at his shoulders, eager to draw him up my body and inside me.

But the jerk is in no hurry. "You need to be somewhere, Lo?"

I grit my teeth against a flutter of pleasure as his lips brush my clit again. I could come again like this. I want to, I do, but there's something I want more.

"Please." I hate how eager I sound, but if that's what it takes—"Nick, please." I lick my lips, fighting to keep myself from sounding desperate. "I need you inside me."

"Ahh." He slides up my body, and I'm not sure what I said to change his mind. "Now we're getting somewhere."

"What?" I blink, then moan as fingers replace his mouth on my most sensitive flesh. "What do you mean?"

"We've escalated from *want* to *need*." He smiles, fingers working my clit like he alone holds the key to my pleasure. "Feels like progress."

My breath's coming faster, which makes it tough for me to argue. The less I say, the better. He's right, I've rounded the bases from want to need, but I know what comes next, and it scares the hell out of me.

Love.

No. I'm not doing that again. Stifling a groan, I slap at the nightstand. I hope I've got condoms in there, though God knows if they're expired.

"On it." Nick grabs his discarded pants. "There's one in my—"

"Got it!" I yank a condom from his wallet like a magician pulling a rabbit from a hat. I'm caressing him with one hand, squeezing his thick length as I wonder how fast I can get him inside me. "My turn to play."

"Oh, yeah?" His gaze is watchful, heated. He's fighting to play it cool, but his eyes flicker each time I stroke from root to crown. I'd forgotten how big he is, how fully he fills my palm.

Or other parts of me. Enough waiting.

I roll him onto his back, an impossibility if he weren't willing. But he moves easily, dragging in a breath as I roll the condom on. "God, Lo."

I spread my legs on either side of his hips, left hand gripping his shaft. I hover there but don't sink down. Not yet. I want to savor the heat in his eyes, the look that says he's on the brink of breaking in two.

"Oh, that's nice." I rock my hips, dragging the tip of him through the slickness between my legs. I can see his control slipping. "How about just the tip?"

"How about you bring those sweet tits down here?" Catching my shoulder blades, he drags me down to feast on my nipples.

My breath hitches as I go back to teasing. His head is so thick, so hot and rounded, that I feel stretched to fullness just from this. I sink down harder, earning a groan from him.

"Fuck," he breathes against my breasts. "So good."

I don't know if he means my breasts or what's between us. This crackle of electricity, this invisible, taut wire connecting us. Our attraction's been a low buzz since he got to Juniper Ridge, but it's now an electric scream.

"Lo," he groans as I sink down harder. "Baby, what you do to me."

"I know." I'm losing it, too, and it's not my magical snatch doing it. It's something that's always been there between us. I take him all the way to the root, crying out as I clutch his shoulders.

Nick's eyes search mine. As I start to move, he slips a hand between us. His uninjured one, his thumb finding my clit like a magnet. "That's it. Take what you need."

What I need is more. More than sex, more than friendship, more than a casual thing. I'm a fool to think I could ever be casual with Nick. What's blazing between us, it's nothing I can control.

As orgasm closes in, I cry out and throw my head back. "*More!*"

It's an awful word to shout at a man buried balls deep, but he understands. There's not a thing lacking with his cock, his hands, his body beneath me.

If anything, he's too much.

The orgasm slams into me like a freight train as a realization hits from the other side.

I love him.

I scream. From pleasure and shock and the spellbinding wonder that I've fallen back in love with this man I vowed to hate.

As he groans and thrusts up into me, I fear I'm not alone.

And I know we're in for a world of hurt.

* * *

I DON'T LET Nick spend the night.

Maybe I should, but I've got a built-in excuse. "I'm meeting my sisters for breakfast," I told him, snuggled in the crook of his arm. "Six thirty. Really early."

"Got it." He sat up, brown eyes lit by a knowing smile. "No sleepover then."

"It's not that I don't want—"

"Nah, I've gotta get up early, too." He had his pants on in seconds, pausing to bend and kiss me. "This was great."

"It was, wasn't it?"

I clutched the comforter in one hand, hoping he hadn't learned to read minds in our years apart.

Because the truth—the one I admit only to myself as I'm shuffling across campus with the sun barely peeking over the horizon—is that last night was way more than that. *Great* is for Wagyu steak and vintage Chanel.

What happened between Nick and me was beyond great. Outstanding. Otherworldly. Over-the-top, breathtakingly, stunningly—

"Hey, Lauren."

Mari's voice spins me around, and I wait for her to catch up. "Morning, Mar."

She cocks her head, studying my face. "You're looking very—"

"Tired?" I supply before she can guess something else.

My sister frowns. "No, that's not it. The opposite, actually. *Tranquil*. Did you get a massage or something?"

I shake my head, though it might be easier to lie. "I'm trying this new face cream." We've reached Lana's place, which is where we're meeting. "Very refreshing."

"Face cream." She gives me her shrink side-eye but doesn't call me out. "You'll have to give me the name of it."

"Right. Okay." I raise my hand to knock, but Lana yanks the door open. She peers at me with bright blue eyes, honey blonde hair pulled in a high ponytail. "Oh my God. You had sex?"

I sigh and push past into the cozy little cabin. "Tell me you have bacon."

Lana laughs and trails me like a cheerful puppy. "Bacon is only for sisters who share."

Mari snickers and follows, polishing her glasses on her shirt. "*I'll* share for bacon, but I think the middle sister's story about learning to make chili is less exciting than the older sister's story of making—"

"The beast with two backs?" I supply so she can't call it what it actually was.

Making love.

I push that from my head as Mari studies me with her curious shrink stare. "Congratulations," she offers.

There's no point denying it. Not with these two bloodhounds on the trail. "Thank you," I say and stride past them to the sofa. "We have a couple minutes before we need to call Mom." I drop onto Lana's couch and pull out my phone. "Want to go over my show notes for—"

"No way." Lana stops at the edge of her kitchen, hands on her hips. "I'm dishing up quiche. *With* bacon," she adds for my benefit. "Which gives you approximately five minutes to decide how much you're sharing about whatever's got you smiling like you spent the morning rolling in sunbeams and chocolate sauce."

"Beautifully put." Mari takes a seat beside me and sips from the mug of tea she brought with her. "You don't have to tell us anything you don't want to."

Such a shrink suggestion, but I know better. "*You know who* will just keep hounding me." I glare daggers at Lana, who's in the kitchen pretending to ignore us. "It's fine," I tell Mari. "There's not much to tell."

"The hell there's not." Lana comes out balancing three slices of quiche on small plates. She hands one to each of us before dropping beside me on the couch. "You hooked up with Nick after years of spitting every time someone said his name. That's *huge*."

I fork quiche into my mouth and do my best to keep a bland expression. "I slept with an ex. Big deal. We've all done it, right?"

Lana crosses her legs primly. "I'm the pure and wholesome baby sister, so of course not." She lifts her coffee mug, which is printed with a dozen pink stick figures fornicating. "Back to you. Was it good?"

Mari sits up straighter. "That's a personal question she's not required to answer." She glances at me and grins. "Unless you want to."

I sigh. "It's just sex, okay?"

The hell it is. Even my sisters look dubious, and I'm sure not buying it.

Lana gives up first, sighing as she taps her iPad on the coffee table. "You're not getting out of this. But I'm giving you a break because Mom's expecting us."

Only the great Shirleen Judson could orchestrate a long-distance birthday breakfast with her daughters before the sun's fully up. I inspect both my sisters, looking for things she might nitpick. "Lana, here." I hand her a tinted lip balm from my pocket before turning to Mari. "Turn your wedding ring around so the stone's visible."

Mari gives an exasperated sigh. "Don't you think we're old enough not to care what she thinks?"

"Of course."

But they do care. We all do, which is why we're jumping through her birthday breakfast hoops from a thousand miles away.

Lana finishes with the lip balm and hands it back, while Mari sets aside her quiche plate and adjusts her ring. She shoves her hands between her knees, but not before I notice they're trembling.

For all my sisters' professional accomplishments, for all their confidence and bravado, they're still Shirleen Judson's daughters.

And I'm the oldest, so it's on me to make sure this goes off with minimal bloodshed. Straightening the Gucci top I haven't worn in a year, I tap Lana's iPad to start the call.

It rings twice before our mother's face fills the screen. "Hello, lovelies." She scans us like we're soldiers lined up for inspection, then rewards us with her movie star smile. "Wonderful to see you up and around so early."

I can't tell if it's a jab about our sleep habits or a reminder she's calling the shots. Either way, I'm not biting.

"Hi, Mom," I say. "Happy birthday."

Lana scoots closer on the sofa. "Happy birthday," she sings.

Mari parrots the greeting as our mother sips from a bottle of expensive mineral water. "Thank you, girls."

I feel Mari stiffen, probably biting back a retort that three accomplished, professional women are not "girls."

I jump before Mari can paint that target on her back. "Kind of a big deal to get all four Judson women together at once," I say, putting extra emphasis on *women*. "You're looking good, Mom."

Technically, she's looking like she hit the Botox too hard, but Lana leaps to agree. "Not a day over twenty-five."

Our mother eyes us with suspicion but no furrow in her brow. Credit the concrete in her forehead. "Thank you." She sets down her mineral water and frowns. "Is that quiche?"

"Lana made it." I fork up a bite with a huge hunk of broccoli and wave it in front of the screen. "Lots of wholesome veggies."

Lana smiles and gamely doesn't mention the bacon. "Are we interrupting Pilates?"

"Sergio's just leaving." Our mother waves at the handsome trainer packing his gear beside the turquoise-tiled pool. "I asked Elaine to serve breakfast in the west courtyard this morning. Egg white omelet and fresh blueberries. Mari, dear—you're wearing glasses and not contacts?"

Mari shoves the glasses up her nose, vibrating with a retort about feminine beauty ideals. I put a hand on her knee, and she stills.

"They test well with audiences," I interrupt, squeezing Mari's knee. This is the language our mother understands. "Seventy-one percent of viewers prefer Mari with glasses."

Lana nods and edges closer in the frame. "Plus, she looks freakin' gorgeous."

Our mother, on the other hand, looks dubious. I cut her off before she can say something snarky. "Any plans this afternoon, Mom?"

She switches the phone to her other hand and pushes through a door, striding down a hall that leads to our parents' expansive patio. "Your father has a business meeting until one. We're taking the helicopter to dinner."

"Sounds nice," I say, even though it doesn't. It sounds like my old life, which I don't miss that much. I sip the coffee Lana set in front of me, appreciating that it's laced liberally with cream and sugar. The real stuff, not low-cal substitutes we pretended to like in our past lives.

Mari leans in, her curls brushing my arm. "Did you catch the last episode of 'Fresh Start at Juniper Ridge?' The one where—"

"Marilynn Jean Judson." Our mother sighs. "What on earth are you wearing?"

Frowning, Mari looks down at her outfit. "Uh, designer leisurewear?"

"We're filming a segment on casual Fridays," I interrupt before our mom can launch her lecture on dressing for success. "Did you read Mari's article in *The Journal of Positive Psychology*? A more relaxed dress code boosts productivity by more than seventeen percent."

"Is that so?" The great Shirleen Judson pushes through her French doors like she's entering an awards ceremony. "Well, I'm glad to see at least one of you still dressing appropriately. Lana, darling—are you planning to see Cash Beckett when he arrives?"

I hear my sister's teeth grinding behind her cheerful smile. "I'm giving him a tour at ten this Tuesday," she says. "Standard protocol for anyone joining the community for more than a day."

Our mother makes a clucking sound as she settles at a patio table beneath a big umbrella. The Pacific glitters like emeralds behind her, but the view doesn't compare to our mother's unbending beauty. "You know he's always had a thing for you." She accepts a cup of coffee from a well-dressed server, no doubt minus any cream or sugar. "Cash is an attractive man with a bright future and—"

"And Lana's doing just fine on her own." I catch my baby

sister's eye to make sure she's okay with this. A quick dip of her head tells me she'd rather not engage.

There are a zillion reasons I'd never want Lana dating Cash Beckett, but that's beside the point. "So dinner tonight, huh?" I steer the conversation back on track. "Is it just you and Dad, or are you meeting other couples?"

Our mom fixes me with a look, and I fix her right back. I don't care if she zeroes in on me as long as she leaves my sisters alone. "We ran into Angela and Darius Armbrust last week and invited them." She narrows her eyes and studies me. "Are you getting on well with Nick?"

I press my foot into Lana's, signaling her to keep her mouth shut. Her PR instincts are strong enough to hold a flat expression, but her twitching toes tell me she's loving this. "He's doing excellent work," I say. "The new animal shelter is coming along nicely."

"That should play well for ratings." Our mother clears her throat. "Speaking of ratings, it looks like you lost ground last week. Do you think you need to change your public relations strategy?"

For God's sake.

Lana's straightening to argue, but I can do this with a lot less angst. "I've been using that moisturizer you sent." I lean forward, forcing my face into the foreground so she forgets to torment my sisters. "Good stuff. Smells nice."

Lana shoots me a grateful look as our mother's eyes narrow. *Bring it on*, I think, lifting my chin.

"It's lovely, isn't it?" Our mother smiles and sips her coffee. "A woman needs all the help she can get once she's past a certain age."

The blow doesn't land hard because I don't let it. "So you've said." I give her my best shark smile. "We're lucky to have a role model who's so great at hiding her age."

She stares at me like she's not sure if that's a compliment or insult. "Angela is concerned Nick will get too comfortable out there," she says. "She's hoping it won't get in the way of his plans to build another resort on the east coast."

"You can reassure Angela no one's making Nick too comfortable." What I want to say is that it's none of Angela's business what her son does with his career, but that will just prolong this. "What's Dad giving you for your birthday?"

She smiles and thanks the server setting a pure-white omelet in front of her while Lana scoots her own quiche plate out of the frame. "A pair of diamond earrings from Brandille's new collection." Our mother peels back the top of the omelet and makes an exasperated sound. "I told them no cheese. Honestly—"

"Brandille makes lovely earrings," Lana says cheerfully. "I handled her launch campaign a few years ago. You're lucky to get a pair."

"Oh, I know." Ignoring her omelet, she starts in on the blueberries. "It was lovely to have you and Cooper visit, darling."

She lets the words hang, a silent chastisement for those of us who stayed behind. Mari can't resist biting on that one.

"It's a challenge getting away from the set," she says. "All six of us are very involved in filming. Maybe you could come here sometime."

"Perhaps," she says as Lana and I shoot her an incredulous look. "I trust there are accommodations?"

"We keep several empty cabins for guests." Lana squeezes my knee outside the video frame. "And you know they're nice, since Nick built them."

Hearing his name has me focusing every ounce of energy on keeping a bland expression. I do not need my mother sniffing around my love life. Lucky for me, she's more focused on her disappointing breakfast.

"We'll consider a visit sometime in the future." She drags her fork through a pile of fresh herbs, gauging the caloric content. "Thank you for the flowers, by the way. They're lovely."

"You're welcome." Lana folds her hands primly. "We know how much you love lilies."

"There's something else arriving today," Mari says. "I'm sure Elaine can sign for it if you've left by then."

"Wonderful." With an exasperated noise, our mother sets her fork down. "Thank you for the call, girls. I need to hop off and deal with this omelet fiasco."

The fiasco looks just fine to me, but there's no need to drag this out. "Happy birthday, Mom. We love you."

My sisters chorus their own I love yous before Mari reaches out to disconnect the call.

"Thanks for getting the flowers," I say to Lana. "What's the other package?"

"A bracelet from Bulgari's new collection," Mari says. "Don't worry, I signed all our names."

"I did the same with the bottle of wine I sent last week." Handling our mother is a full-contact sport, and I'm glad we're on the same team. "Think Gabe or Dean or Coop sent something?"

Mari shrugs. "I reminded them last week. If they did, they know the rule."

"Right." Everyone signs the other five sibs' names for any gift given to Mom. "Thanks for not pressing the Nick issue."

Lana picks up her quiche plate and leans back with a sly little smile. "Which means you owe us some details. Come on, we'll keep quiet."

I sigh and grab my own plate. "I told you, it's no big deal. Just sex."

"Mm-hmm." Mari's giving me her shrink stare as she sips her tea. "Some people do have the ability to separate sex from emotional attachment."

I fix her with a look. "And you're suggesting I'm not one of those people?"

She shrugs and sets down her mug. "You said it. Not me."

"I think it's great." Lana reaches for the coffee carafe and refills my mug. "You're kidding yourself about the emotional attachment, but it's nice you're giving him a chance."

"A chance to get into my pants," I correct, as annoyed by my accidental rhyme as I am by their implication. "We have good chemistry. That's all it is."

"Whatever you say." Lana rolls her eyes at Mari. "You're not buying this, are you?"

Our sister adjusts her glasses. "I think it's up to Lauren to set the parameters of her relationship in a way that makes her comfortable." Her amber eyes flicker. "But in my professional opinion, you're screwed."

I sigh and poke at my quiche. "Screwing is the whole point."

Mari watches me for an uncomfortably long time. "You want my clinical advice or my sisterly advice?"

"No." I pick up my mug, hoping she knows me well enough to realize I want both.

She does. "You do an excellent job protecting your family," she says slowly. "And an even better job protecting your own heart."

"Whoa, that's deep." Lana grins and sips her coffee. "Also, true."

Mari ignores us and continues. "While walls offer protection from things that might do you harm, they can also prevent the good stuff from getting in."

I clutch my mug tighter so she doesn't see my hands shake. "Speaking of good stuff getting in—"

"Come on, Lauren." Lana swats me, sloshing coffee onto the knee of my skinny jeans. "Mari's right. You and Nick were always great together. A team, you know?"

I do know, and it kills me. Say what you will about Shirleen and Laurence Judson, but they've always been a team. Not the loving, playful kind of team I envied with Nick's parents, or with Alexis and Abe. But there's no question my parents had each other's backs. It's what I always wished for with Nick, even beyond the idea of matrimony. What I thought we had, what we were building back then—

"Things are different now." It's such a lame point to make that I'm not even sure what I mean.

Mari nods slowly. "But the love is still there."

I shrug, even though it wasn't a question. "Maybe."

It's the closest I've come to admitting I might still be in love with Nick. That I never stopped loving him.

Both sisters' eyes fill with kindness. Lana touches my arm. "What if you told him?"

"Ha!" I slosh coffee from my mug, feeling awkward and embarrassed. "Because jumping the gun has gone so well for me in the past?"

The look they exchange blooms with sympathy. "Saying you love someone is never a mistake," Lana murmurs, her natural perkiness shifting to something more subdued. "Whether you say it out loud, or just to yourself, it's a big deal to admit it."

Before I can make a crack about where she got her psych degree, the actual shrink chimes in. "It's one of the bravest things you can do," Mari adds. "And you're one of the bravest people I know."

I swallow hard, as moved by the flattery as I am by what I've shared. Am I really admitting I'm in love with Nick? The idea makes me edgy and exposed, and I'm ready to change the subject. "Look, can we talk about something else?"

Mari gives me a long look, then nods. "Such as?"

My brain fumbles for something simple. Something unconnected to emotions or relationships or heartache or—

"The filming schedule." I clear my throat. "Are we pretty confident Cash Beckett will guest star?"

Mari shrugs. "He seems into it. I ordered a full background check just in case."

"Good." Having a star of his caliber could be key to turning our ratings around for sweeps week. "Let's be sure to keep him happy."

Lana rolls her eyes and forks up a bite of quiche. "Don't say that around Mom. She'll have all kinds of ideas for how I can do that."

"God, no." Cash might have star power, but I don't want the man anywhere near my baby sister. Or anyone's baby sister. "You think Coop can handle it okay having him here?"

No one answers right away.

"He's doing well," Mari finally says. "But we should watch carefully. He seems solid, but relapse can happen to anyone."

Lana picks up her coffee mug, thumb skimming two stick figures executing a perfect reverse cowgirl. "It's easy to fall back into old habits." Her blue gaze locks with mine, and she gives a small smile. "So I've heard."

"I don't find that's the case at all." I stab a hunk of quiche, making sure to spear a big bite of bacon. "I've got everything under control."

Swallowing the lump in my throat—along with the quiche—I pray that's the truth.

CHAPTER 11

CONFESSIONAL 825.5
ARMBRUST, NICK (OWNER, ARMBRUST RESORTS)
*You want me to talk about breaking old habits? Huh.
All right, I loved my pacifier as a kid. No, I mean really loved it. Like Mama worried I'd head off to grade school still sucking it. Yeah, I know...go ahead and call it some kind of oral fixation, but it wasn't like that. There was just something comforting about it, you know?
'Course, Mama knew I'd get ribbed something awful if I showed up at school with it, so she made me a trade. My pacifier for a new Playstation. Even then, it was a tough call.
I still think of it as my first business deal.*

* * *

For a week after my night with Lauren, I can't stop thinking about her. If I'm honest, that's been the case since I got here, but it's tougher since we broke the touch barrier. My senses all refilled with reminders of what it's like to be with her. The smooth silk of her skin, the honey smell of her hair, the soft burst of breath just before she comes.

But I push all that out of my head and text her something cool and casual.

I'D LOVE *to see you again.*

SHE USUALLY TAKES a day or two to respond, but her reply comes quickly.

I'M AT THE WAREHOUSE. *Wow! It looks amazing. Nice work.*

I SMILE AND SWITCH DIRECTIONS, texting as I walk.

HEADING OVER. *I'll give you a tour.*

I REALIZE that wasn't an invitation, but I'm too old to play games. Besides, I'm dying to see her. And with a legit work reason to do it, why not? I shove a breath mint in my mouth, annoyed with myself for caring. We went years without kissing, without touching or talking or having any contact at all. Now I can't last a few days without it?

Pushing through the warehouse door, I stop short at the sight of Cash Freakin' Beckett. He's leaning close to Lauren, touching her elbow as she talks. Her expression's mild, but I watch as she sidesteps his hand to put distance between them.

My blood's boiling as I stride toward them. "Afternoon."

"Nick." Lo's smile holds a hint of relief. "Have you met Cash?"

"Haven't had the pleasure." I shake the guy's hand, reminding myself not to crush his fingers. Being a jealous asshole isn't a great look for me. "Nick Armbrust."

"Good to meet you, man." Cash shakes with an easy grip, then shoves both hands in his pockets, looking movie star cool. "You're the guy who designed this place, right?"

"I had a lot of help."

"Cool, cool." He glances back at Lauren. "What time do you want me on set tomorrow?"

"We start filming at eight." She looks at me. "You don't need to change up the construction schedule. I'd like to get some B-roll while it's going on. The buildup to the adoption event and all."

I don't love the thought of cameras trailing me around, especially if Cash is here. "Are you the one filming?" I ask Lauren.

"Of course. Well, Gabe and me." She rocks back on her heels and smiles. "Actually, I'd love to get a few minutes with you—"

"Yes," I blurt before realizing she wasn't finished. "I mean, yeah. Sure."

She smiles like she knows exactly what I'm thinking. "I'd like to walk through with you and get a sense of what might make good shots. Places you'll be working tomorrow, where you don't want us setting up. That sort of thing."

"Sure, yeah." I drag a hand over my head, wishing for an easy way to get rid of Cash. "Now's good if it works for you."

Thank God almighty, Cash steps back. "I'm meeting Coop for beers, so I'd better go."

Lauren narrows her eyes. "Cash—"

"Relax, okay?" He puts up his hands. "I won't let him drink."

My hackles rise again. "He's a grown-ass man," I point out. "No one *lets* him do anything, but he needs our support."

"Okay, *okay*." Cash backs toward the door, hands still up. "I'll have a Coke, all right?"

Lauren's frown eases a bit, but she still doesn't look happy. "No scandals, Cash. Seriously—we're not that kind of show."

"Got it." He throws her a mock salute, then turns and strides out the door.

When he's gone, I look at Lauren. It's on the tip of my tongue to call him an asshole, but I hold it back. Hollywood's full of assholes, and I tolerated plenty growing up there. But I won't pretend I don't hold extra distaste for one with a strong creep-factor toward my girl.

"He can be sort of a dick," she says, reading my mind. "But he's a manageable dick, and good for ratings. I can handle him."

My brain short-circuits at the thought of Lauren handling dick, and I have to force myself to focus. "How long is he here?"

"A week or two. He's got some business to deal with while he's here."

"Business? In rural Oregon?"

She shrugs "Not my business." She sweeps a hand toward the big bank of kennels behind us. "Got time for that tour you promised?"

"Sure thing." I take a deep breath to get re-centered.

"I still can't believe you got so much accomplished in such a short time."

"I'm motivated," I say, throwing her a wink as we move past the pack of barking dogs in kennels on the end.

She stops and bends down to pet one shaggy brown and white beast. "Tell me more about how you designed these enclosures."

That I can do. "We built each kennel with access to an outdoor play area for fresh air." I reach through the gate and scratch a lazy-eyed hound in the next dog run. "Specialty orthopedic beds that are comfortable for older dogs. Jessie sourced them at a great deal."

"I'm so glad we brought her out here." She pauses to pet a pile of puppies in a central holding pen. "And I love how you say '*we* built' when I know for a fact you're the only one slinging a hammer here."

I shrug and keep moving. "It's a team effort."

It's true, but it's also true I've worked myself to the bone for this project. My ego's glad she noticed. "Let's see the cat room."

I lead her down a narrow hallway, its walls lined with posters about spaying and neutering. There's one for the upcoming adoption event, and I cross my fingers we'll have the space ready in time.

At a pale-yellow door, Lauren pauses. "What's in here?"

"Storage." I open the door and show her inside. "Packed with donated pet food. Lana's PR campaign has it flowing in faster than we can store it."

Lauren beams. "She's so good at that."

I love how proud she is of her sisters. "Coop's been working around the clock, too," I add. "You've seen the TV ads he's starring in?"

She laughs and starts walking again. "I *produced* the TV ads," she says. "But you're right. It's been a great team effort."

We keep walking, passing banks of cages filled with hamsters and rabbits. The door to the cat room opens, and Jessie Laslo slips through with an infant strapped to her chest in a colorful sling. Gretchen's sister is working overtime tapping contacts in the nonprofit world to bring this project together. She's a cool lady, and I can't believe she's busting ass so soon after having a baby. I guess Alexis did the same, which goes to show how many badass women I know.

Lauren's face lights up as Jessie approaches with one hand on the bundle snuggled against her chest. "There's that little sweetie." Lo gives me a bashful grin. "I got to hold baby Joy all morning."

"She's so tiny." I study the infant, marveling at how much she sleeps. "My nieces pitched fits anytime my sister put them in one of those things."

Jessie smiles and turns to give Lauren a better view of the baby in the sling. "She took to the wrap right away. I'm hustling back to Gretchen and Gabe's in a sec to feed her before my luck runs out and she starts screaming."

"Look at these cheeks." Lauren makes kissy noises, quiet so she doesn't wake the baby. "How do you not just gobble her up?"

Jessie laughs and bounces baby Joy in her sling. "Sometimes I sit by her crib for hours just watching her sleep. Is that creepy?"

"I'd do the same thing," Lo says.

The thought of Lauren as a mother twists my insides in a million tiny knots. She meets my eyes like she's just read my mind, and something warm spreads through my belly.

"Gotta go." Jessie steps around us, supporting the baby from beneath. "You'll lock up?"

Lauren nods and catches the door to the cat room. "Have a great night."

We watch Jessie leave, looking through the window as she makes her way down the path to Gretchen and Gabe's.

"It's been great having her here," I say as we resume our tour. "She's a sharp cookie with tons more nonprofit knowledge than I've got."

"And Joy's just delicious." Lauren looks thoughtful. "Have you noticed her eyes?"

"Jessie's?"

"No, the baby. They're almost exactly like Patti's." She pauses to scratch a surly Persian through the bars. "Dark around the outside, sort of amber in the middle with rings of green around the iris. I've never seen anyone else with eyes like that."

"Huh." I'm realizing how much Lo notices. About people around her, their uniqueness, their needs. "You want kids, Lo?"

The question startles her. "Um—yes." She gives a stiff laugh. "I suppose eventually."

"Good." I put a hand in the small of her back and guide her down the next hallway. "You'll be a great mom, you know?"

She looks at me like I've done a somersault down the hall. "Thank you. That means a lot, coming from—well, your mom's great. And Alexis—" she breaks off, shaking her head. "Between your family and Patti and Colleen, I've seen plenty of good mothering up close."

"Mama's pretty great."

It's true, but I can't help hearing her voice in my head. The echo that pushes me always.

"Prove yourself, son. Your granddaddy didn't work twelve-hour days in the hot sun sending his kids to college just to have his grandson turn around and throw it in the trash."

Grandpa worked construction, slinging a hammer long after his body should've given out. He always wanted his own company. A crew of his own, maybe a contractor's license stenciled on the side of a big, shiny truck.

He never quite got it. Worked his way up to foreman, but always for someone else. He spent years wrecking his knees and shoulders to put Mama and Uncle Gary through college. Gramps was proud to do it, but it took a toll. Mama's been clear from the get-go she wanted more for me. More career strategy, more time behind a desk to save my body.

Prove yourself.

Prove you can do more, be *more.*

It's a lot of pressure, but no worse than what Lo got from Shirleen Judson. Better, probably.

I clear my throat, eager to move on. "Still gotta fix the ventilation system," I explain as I lead her around a corner and back into the hall. "There's some painting left in here. But I'm motivated to get it done."

"Nick, this is amazing." She pivots to look at me with admiration that makes my chest pinch. "Motivated, huh?" She leans back against the wall, arms folded like she does on movie sets to let the actors know who's in charge. "Tell me about this motivation."

Her flirtation is a switch from the cold shoulder I've gotten all week. "Um, well—"

"Is it your intense love of animals?" She's teasing, flirting, dropping all kinds of cues I can't quite read. "That's your motivation?"

"Sure, that's part of it." I shove my hands in my pockets, determined not to reach for her. Not to scare her away.

"Hmm." She steps closer, pretending to think. "Or were you motivated by promotional potential for your brand?"

She knows that's not it, but I'll play along. "The prime-time ad is a bonus." I match her sexy tone, but something's building inside me. A pressure in my chest I can't explain.

"Oh?" She leans closer, hair tickling my arm. "What else motivates you?"

"Lo." I'm at my breaking point, but I force myself to push gently. "What are we doing here?"

Her gaze flickers, and she starts to step back. "I want—I mean, I thought you wanted—"

"Nah, don't do that." I reach out to catch her around the waist, pulling her close. Screw pride. I'm not letting that drive a wedge between us this time. "You've been dodging me all week, and now you're interested?"

I watch her throat move, watch her eyes flash with uncertainty. This moment here, it's where the Lauren I know tapdances around the truth. Where she plays it cool, telling me she's been swamped with work, she's been focused on family, she's been—

"Scared." She licks her lips and gives a sheepish look. "I've been a big, fat chicken."

Warmth pools inside me. Slowly, I reach out and cup her face. "Of me?"

"Of feelings." She flings a hand like she's swatting a fly, flustered and impatient. "Of making an ass of myself again. Of feeling the way I felt…*before*."

I nod because I get it, though I'm not sure she means that night of the party or the weeks that followed. Long nights of hurt and anger and wondering if we'd find our way back to each other.

I recognize what a brave thing she's just admitted. "I feel ya there," I say carefully. "I'd like to avoid a replay if we can."

"So why are you being so...so...*cool?*" She's blinking hard, and if I didn't know better, I might think she's close to crying. "Why aren't you freaking out the way I am?"

It's the most exposed I've seen her in a long time, and I take my time answering. "Know what was missing before? Between you and me, I mean."

She shakes her head and looks down at the floor. "If you say 'anal,' I'm out of here."

I laugh because that's classic Lauren, making jokes when she's feeling vulnerable. "Communication," I say softly, and her chin tips up again. "And honesty."

These are scary words. Big words. I won't blame her if she runs. She's looking at me like I have the answers, so I take a breath and try again. "What if we added those ingredients?" I ask gently. "If we give this another shot?"

She doesn't move. I'm not sure she's breathing. "You want to give it another shot," she says slowly. "Us, you mean?"

"Yeah." And since I'm the one tossing out words like *communication* and *honesty*, I keep going. "A relationship. Whatever that looks like, I mean. Not just sex."

"Not just sex." She rolls each word on her tongue, deciding how they taste. Then she nods. "Okay."

Did she just agree?

I clear my throat. "Okay?"

"Okay." She says it with a lot more certainty this time, and a laugh surges up my throat.

"No joke?" My hand's still cupping her waist, and I stroke it like I'm soothing one of the animals watching this whole thing from nearby kennels. "Gotta admit, I thought you'd make me work harder that time."

She drops her hand and grabs for my dick. No, not my dick. My hand, lacing our fingers together as she looks earnestly in my eyes. "No more games." Her throat moves, and I see how hard this is for her. "I want you. And I want to see if we can make this work. Also, I want you."

I lift my hand to tuck a strand of fallen hair behind her ear. "What was that last part again?"

"I want you," she repeats, putting her free hand on my chest. "So much."

"Damn." I start the kiss slow and tender, barely holding back. I want her, too, but I want her to be sure.

She kisses back with more certainty, a message unspoken. It's not long before I'm pressing her back against the wall, her body arching into mine like she wants to feel every inch. By the time she draws back, her breath's coming in short little bursts.

Steely eyes search mine as she licks her lips. "Closet."

"What?"

"That storage closet you showed me." Her flirty smile is back. "There's a cabinet in there that looks about the right height."

Cupping her ass, I draw her tight against me. "Leave it to you to scope out the sex potential of a storage closet."

"Producers know how to scout a scene." With fake haughtiness, she tugs my hand and starts down the hall. "It's the upside of dating one."

"Yes, ma'am." As she pulls me down the hall, I'm checking out her ass, eager to have my hands on it again. I almost miss it when she whirls back around.

"Wait." She bites her lip. "Is it okay to say we're dating?"

"Of course." We're at the edge of the closet now, so I nudge her back against the wall and kiss her again. When we come up for air, I look deep in her eyes. "Is it okay to call you my girlfriend?"

Her eyes flash as she nods. "Yeah. Yes, I think I like that."

"Me, too." I take a deep breath against the words swelling in my chest, fighting their way up my throat.

I start to push them back before remembering.

Honesty.

Communication.

I need to go all in.

With a deep breath, I look her in the eye. "Is it okay," I begin, brushing a kiss behind her ear, "to tell you I love you?"

She stiffens, and I get ready to backpedal.

"Wow," she breathes.

Wow?

Not the reaction I wanted, but better than running away screaming. Still, I need damage control. "Lo—"

"I mean, *wow*." Her smile spreads as she lifts her hand and shoves me in the chest. "Jerk."

I frown. "What?"

She grins wider as her other hand comes up to clutch my ass. "You beat me to it. I wanted to say it first."

"You—really?"

She nods, squeezing my left cheek to pull me tight against the heat between her thighs. "I wanted to be brave and put myself out there this time."

Heart swelling as much as other parts, I lift her hair off her neck to dot a kiss behind her ear. "You being competitive or romantic?"

She laughs and presses a palm to my chest. "According to my sisters, neither one. Brave is what they called it."

"Your sisters?" I draw back, pretty sure I've heard wrong. "Say what?"

She nods and drags her hand between my pecs. "We talked about letting down walls. About how I've fallen in love with you again and—"

"Wait, whoa, hold up." It's my turn to grab her ass, mostly to keep her with me. "You told Lana and Mari you *love* me?"

There's the tiniest flicker of uncertainty in her eyes. "You're mad I told them before you?"

"Hell, naw." I pull her closer, craving her more than ever. "Mad? Are you kidding me? I'm fucking *ecstatic*."

I kiss her hard this time, not caring that we still haven't made it to privacy. We've got a dozen dogs watching, and any member of my crew could come barging in, but I don't care one bit.

When we break apart, we're both breathing hard. Lo's looking at me curiously. "I mean, technically, they asked if I still love you, and I said 'maybe,' but that's close, and I just thought—" She trails off, frowning. "Why does it matter that I told my sisters?"

"Because it's a risk." I fumble for words, not sure what I'm trying to say. "If you just say it to me, it's secret. I could say 'I'm just not feelin' it', and you could walk away with your head up, no one knowing but us. But you brought in witnesses, Lo. That's huge."

Her hand slides from my ass to the front, gripping my dick for real this time. I'm expecting a *huge* crack, but she grins instead. "You're saying I won?"

I can't tell if she's teasing, but I'll indulge her. "I wouldn't go that far—"

"No, I think it's clear." She rubs me through rough denim, bringing my cock to attention. "I'm the champion."

"Ha!" I kiss her throat, loving the heat of her body. "I don't think so."

She gasps in fake fury. "What do you mean?"

I touch her cheek again, unable to get enough of her skin. "You've gotta say it, Lo."

"Ah." Her response morphs to a moan as I kiss her throat again. She digs her nails into my scalp, pressing her sweet pussy against me through dueling layers of denim. "Hey, Nick?" she breathes.

"A little busy here," I mumble from the depths of her cleavage.

"*Nick*," she says more urgently.

"Yeah?" I dot more kisses over the tops of her breasts, losing my train of thought.

She pushes back, breasts heaving as her eyes lock with mine. They're wild and hungry and filled with so much love that I don't need to hear the words out loud.

"I love you." She slams a palm against the door. "I love you so fucking much it's insane."

"That'll do it." God, I want her.

She licks her lips, reading my mind. "I really fucking love you." She shoves the door harder, struggling to push it open. "Now fuck me, please."

"That's a lot of fucks." Grinning, I reach behind me and twist the door handle. "Also, that might've gone better if the door opened in instead of out."

She laughs and yanks it open. "Shut up and make me come."

"That I can do." Pushing the door shut, I turn and boost her up on the cabinet. I don't bother with lights. I know this place inside and out.

I know Lo the same way, so why does she feel new? The sweetness of her skin, the fullness of her breasts, the softness in her belly that I love so much more than the washboard abs she used to have.

I'd never say that out loud. Even I know the limits of honesty, but I feel it in my core as I strip her naked and drop to my knees. Her legs part as I cup her bare ass and pull her to my mouth. Her thighs cushion my cheeks as I lick into her, earning a loud groan.

"Oh, God. *Nick*."

I laugh as dogs start howling on the other side of the door. "Shhh," I whisper, licking her again. "The animals will give us away."

"Right." She gasps again, nails digging into my shoulders. "God, what you do to me."

I do it again, not because it thrills her but because I'm so goddamn happy to have her again. To be here with her, even if it's with a million pounds of dog food around us.

"Don't stop," she breathes as my fingers slide inside. I've done this enough to know I can make her come in two minutes, but I'm taking my time. I'm savoring the taste of her, the slick softness of her folds. I want to catalogue every inch of her, to make her scream my name. To hell with the canine symphony outside.

Her thighs grip my head. "Wait, no—"

"You okay?" I sit back and peer at her in the dark, letting my eyes adjust. "We can stop if you—"

"No, that's not it." A stream of light beneath the door illuminates her mouth as she bites her lip. "I um…I'm still on the pill. And clean according to my last appointment."

Is she saying what I think she is? "You know I'm a hard-ass with condoms." I was when we dated, at least until we'd both had checkups and some long conversations. "Got a clean bill of health at my last checkup."

"Okay." She breathes the word on a sigh as she draws me to my feet. "I trust you."

I'm smart enough to know she's not just talking about STDs. I remember the first time we ditched the condom, the level of trust involved. Are we there again? I know I am, but I didn't know she was.

I lick my lips, tasting her sweetness as I ache to be inside her with nothing between us. "You sure?"

She nods and pulls me close, clutching my shirt like she thinks I'll get away. "Positive."

Certainty swirls in my head as the rest of me spins with other sensations. Lauren's hand on my fly, her clever fingers freeing me from my boxer briefs. Her thighs parting again, hands on my ass as she draws me into her heat. I tense, wanting to slow down. Wishing I could save this memory forever. I can't stop myself from sinking deeper into all that slick, glorious snugness. I draw a ragged breath and pray for the endurance to make this last.

"*Oh.*" She breathes it like a prayer, equal parts reverence and amazement. "Oh, Nick."

I'll never get tired of how she says my name. I start to move, burying myself inch by inch. Giving her a chance to adjust. To get used to me again, to *us*, to this new version of what we are together. Every twitch of muscle, every fizz of nerves feels new, but like we've done this a thousand times. Like we'll do it a million more before we draw our last breaths.

"Lauren." I drive into her as my restraint snaps its chain. "God, baby—you feel so good."

"I love you." She chokes out the words like she can't stop them. Like they're as sure as the orgasm I'm holding back. "Nick—I love you so much."

I dip my mouth to her ear and growl a reply. "I never stopped loving you."

She melts into me, heels spurring my ass cheeks as I thrust harder. I'll never last like this. It's too good, too sweet, too perfect.

Her walls squeeze tight around me. "Nick," she pants. "Nick, I'm cl—"

My kiss smothers her words. I know she's at the edge, and I'm there with her. We tumble over together, bodies colliding, breath blending as her cry shatters the silence.

"Oh, God!" She claws at my shoulders, making me glad I didn't get my shirt off.

"Lo." I chase after her, pleasure punching me in the gut as I pump into her.

I love you I love you I love you.

I breathe the words to the drumbeat of my heart as she clenches around me. It's loud and chaotic, and my elbow knocks a bowl of pet treats off a shelf, but I don't stop. Not with dogs howling and Lauren crying out and a hundred bits of kibble bouncing around my feet.

Her contractions ebb as mine do the same. My breath's

slowing down as I stroke her hair, trying to get my bearings. To reorient myself to this new version of pleasure.

"Damn," I breathe into her hair. "That was—that was—"

"Amazing?" Her smile sounds in her voice. "Incredible? Stupendous?"

"Fucking phenomenal."

She laughs, and I start to draw back. We've got a mess to deal with, but I can't stop smiling. As I start to pull out, I hear the front door open.

"Hello?"

Lana's voice echoes in the warehouse, and Lo draws a finger to my lips. "Shh." She giggles and unwraps her thighs from my hips. "Quiet."

With the canine chorus getting louder, Lana wouldn't hear us if I drove a backhoe through the closet door. I nod anyway. "She have any reason to come in here?"

Lauren shakes her head in a sliver of light, looking disheveled and so fucking gorgeous I want her all over again.

"Why would my sister—"

That's all she gets out before the door flies open. *Starts* to fly open. Reflex sends my hand flying to the knob, and I yank it closed quick. "Need something, Lana?"

Lauren covers her mouth and giggles.

"Oh." Outside, I hear Lana backing away. "Um, nope! I'm good. I'll come back later. If you see Lauren, tell her I borrowed her floral Gucci sneakers."

I look at Lauren in the half light, still struggling to hold back laughter. "Hey, Lo."

She lowers her hand, struggling to keep a straight face. "Yes?"

"Your sister borrowed your floral Gucci sneakers."

She erupts into laughter, not hiding a thing as the warehouse door shuts in the distance. I let go of the doorknob as she slides off the counter and takes the hankie I'm handing her.

"It's clean," I promise as I turn so she can tend the mess we just made. Once upon a time, this part felt awkward and silly. This time, it's one more stage of intimacy. "Need help?"

"You're offering to assist with mop-up?" She smiles and moves around me to pluck her clothes off the floor. "This must be next-level romance."

I grunt and straighten my shirt. "Smart-ass. You're the one who wanted it in the closet."

"Hey, I wasn't kidding." She's still smiling as she pulls on her clothes. "Clean hankies, holding the door, getting nailed in a closet full of Purina? It's the stuff every woman dreams of."

Her tone is teasing, but something in her eyes says she's serious. That we've reached next-level closeness. Sounds weird, but I feel it, too. Pulling her against me, I don't care that I look ridiculous in a shirt and no pants. "I love you, Lo."

"I love you, too." She nuzzles my neck and squeezes my ass. "And I'm really not kidding. This was incredible."

"Yeah. It was." For the first time in my life, I see a future that includes this. No, not just this. I see family and forever. Love and laughter.

And I see it with Lo.

Stooping down, I plant a kiss behind her ear. "Thanks for giving us a chance."

"Thank you for not giving up on me." She draws back, grinning as she looks me in the eye. "I love you."

"I love you, too."

Maybe this time, that'll be enough.

* * *

THE WHOLE NEXT week becomes a blur of construction on the new cabins, building out the animal shelter, being trailed by cameras, and of course, sex with Lauren.

A lot of sex with Lauren.

If you'd asked me years ago if it was possible to top the red-hot connection we had back then, I'd have laughed my ass off.

I'd also have been game to try.

But this, what's between us now? It's like a whole different level, and I could die a happy man.

I'm thinking about more, though. The quarter mile it takes me to walk from the jobsite to her place, it's all I think about. In the past week, I've stayed only one night in the cabin they gave me when I got here. Lo's place is bigger, and besides, she's got Sharkira. It's funny how fast we've fallen into cohabitation, my toothbrush next to hers in the bathroom, my boxers in a top drawer of her bureau. It's something I resisted last time, but I can't stop smiling about it now.

What if I stayed when the job's complete? Maybe moving in together here at Juniper Ridge. My work takes me all over the country, but home base can be anywhere. Maybe with Lauren.

I'm almost to her place, thinking about a shower and the dinner I plan to make. My famous goat cheese polenta with ratatouille. I made it a lot the last time we were together, and I'm hoping there's an encore of how we ate it in bed together, legs touching beneath the sheets.

As her cabin comes into view, I jerk to a stop. There's Lauren, which gets my heart galloping good, but she's not alone. She's on her porch swing sitting beside a tall, slender woman.

My sister.

I blink to clear my vision. "Lexi?"

My sister looks up, hand on a pile of paperbacks between them. Alexis smiles and lifts a hand to wave. "Look who decided to roll in." She looks at her watch, gold bracelets jingling as Lauren gets to her feet.

"You're here." Lo looks from Lexi to me. "I just found out this morning. She wanted to surprise you."

"I'm surprised." Stunned, actually. "Aren't you in the middle of a big case?"

"Mistrial." Alexis touches her hair, fluffed curls held back by a pink and orange headband. "You're looking good."

"So are you." My heart restarts, and so do my feet. I stride toward her, still not sure what's going on.

"Good to see you, brother." Lexi stands slowly, taking her time like it hasn't been months since we've hugged. "Get over here and greet me proper."

I take the steps two at a time. "Is Mama okay?"

Panic grips me by the balls as I search Lexi's eyes for answers. I just talked to Mama last night, but if something happened—

"Mama's good." Her smile seems warm, but there's exhaustion in her eyes. "Daddy's fine, too. And Abe, before you ask. The girls are great, and—"

"Lex, give me a hug." I drag her into my arms and squeeze hard, breathing in her familiar scent. "It's good to see you."

"Same, brother. Same." Her arms feel wiry and strong as childhood memories rush back. Riding bikes in Crooked House Park. Dominoes on the back deck with Mama fixing veggie tagine in the kitchen. That time we turned our treehouse into an office to play lawyer after Pop gave us his old briefcase.

I squeeze my sister harder as Lo smiles at us over Lexi's shoulder. Lauren's humming something, and it takes me a sec to catch it. Some seventies R&B hit by Peaches and Herb—"Reunited," that's it.

I draw back to look at Lexi. "You're a sight for sore eyes."

"Yeah?" Her golden gaze sweeps my face as her expression turns serious. "Think you could get used to seeing me here?"

I cock my head. "Come again?"

Alexis takes a deep breath, fingers tightening on my shoulders. "I'm moving here, Nick."

CHAPTER 12

CONFESSIONAL 831
<u>JUDSON, LAUREN (PRODUCER: JUNIPER RIDGE)</u>
I DO THINK FAMILY HISTORY PLAYS A ROLE IN HOW WE ALL END UP WITH CERTAIN HANG-UPS. IF YOUR FATHER'S AFRAID OF FLYING OR YOUR MOTHER THINKS MEN ARE SHIT, YOU'LL GROW UP WITH THOSE THOUGHTS PLANTED IN YOUR HEAD LIKE FACT. IT'S COMMON SENSE, RIGHT?
[GLARES]
I DON'T KNOW HOW PEOPLE SHED THOSE HANG-UPS, GABE. WHY DON'T YOU TELL ME?

* * *

I watch Nick's face as his sister drops her bombshell.
I'm moving here, Nick.
I'm expecting surprise. Expecting joy. Expecting—
"What the hell?"
Not that.
Nick's brow furrows as he looks from Lexi to me and back again. "You're the district attorney for one of the biggest counties

in the state of California. How are you planning to do that from here?"

Alexis straightens, going from baby sister to badass lawyer in two seconds flat. "People change jobs all the time, Nick. You have a problem with that?"

The question—posed in Lexi's brusque lawyer voice—would spur lesser men to back down. Nick just stares.

"Does Mama know about this?"

Alexis throws her hands up in exasperation. "How about, 'I'm happy for you, Lexi.' Or maybe 'Congrats, Alexis—you must be excited.'" She stacks her hands on her hips. "Listen to you."

Still frowning, Nick looks at me. "You knew about this?"

There goes my shot at giving them privacy for this. I shift to stand shoulder to shoulder with my friend, keeping my face calm as I look at Nick. "I knew it was a possibility. It wasn't my story to tell."

"What the—" He stares at Lexi, opening his mouth to say something else. Whatever it is, I doubt it's what Lexi needs.

"Nick." I touch his arm, noting the tension of coiled muscle. "Your sister's had the travel day from hell."

It's not the only reason he needs to cut her some slack, but we'll start there.

The rigid set of his jaw eases just a little. "Yeah?"

She nods, and there's a glint of tears in Lexi's golden eyes. She's one of the strongest women I know, and seeing her at a breaking point splits my heart in two.

Shaking her head, she stares at her brother. "I am so. Damn. Tired."

"Tired?" His brow furrows as he studies her face. "You been taking those vitamins Pop told us about? That iron supplement really helped me with—"

"Nick!" She claps her hands, making us both jump. "I need peace. Tranquility. Calm."

His eyes flicker with understanding. "Hell, why didn't you say so? You know I'll hook you up with a sweet cabin at any of my resorts. Just say the word and—"

"Honey." I grip his arm tighter because his sister's close to decking him. His intentions are good, but he's missing this by a mile. "You know how we've talked about life changes? How you and I aren't the same people we were two years ago?"

He nods, still frowning. "What's that got to do with this?"

"Think about who you are now, who *I* am now, and how we're better versions of ourselves." I glance at Lexi, hopeful I'm not overstepping. The gratitude in her eyes nudges me forward. "Now think about what it took for us to get here. Then hear your sister out, okay?"

Lexi folds her arms and stares at him like he spilled ketchup on her prized Fendi handbag. "You're a lucky man, Nick. If your girlfriend hadn't saved you, that pretty jaw of yours would have the imprint of my rings right now."

I glance at Lexi's hand, the sparkler on her ring finger looking awfully lethal. I reach for her hand and give a reassuring squeeze. "Thank you for sparing him. That's the new anniversary ring?"

Her face brightens as she holds up her hand. "Seven years. Can you believe it?"

"It's gorgeous." Flashier than I like these days, but stunning against Lexi's dark skin. I glance at Nick and see the tension's easing in his jaw. He still looks baffled but less apt to shove his foot in his mouth. "I know this is a surprise," I say to him. "And believe me, I know surprises can be…disorienting."

His eyes warm as he watches Lexi. "I really am glad to see you."

She sighs and gestures to the porch swing. "Come on. We need to talk."

"Yeah, we do." He glances at me, expression shifting to sheepish. "Thanks, Lo."

"No problem." I back toward the house, wanting to give them privacy. His eyes hold mine, and I will him to be gentle with his sister. To respect her choices, even if they're not ones he'd make.

He nods like I've spoken and looks back at Alexis. "Sorry," he says. "It's just—a shock." Dragging a hand over his head, he gestures to the swing. "Come on. You want to tell me about it?"

Alexis makes a sound like "hrmph" but marches toward the swing and pats the seat beside her. I swoop in and clear away a big stack of paperbacks. Nick's eyes drop to the covers, a Kennedy Ryan release with the new Robin Covington peeking out beneath that. He lifts a brow but doesn't comment.

Wise man.

"I've been unhappy for a long time," Alexis says as she settles on the swing and waits for Nick to join her. "It's a good week when I work fewer than eighty hours. Do you know the last time I put my girls to bed?"

I know the answer already—two months—so I turn and duck through the door. "I'll be back with wine," I call over my shoulder.

I already know she loves red, and Nick—well, I doubt he'll care at this point. I stack three glasses and a bottle of pinot on a tray, dumping a bag of salt and vinegar chips in a bowl as an afterthought. I'm getting the hang of this hostess thing.

On my way past Sharkira's tank, I spot her shoveling gravel over her newest decoration. "Come on." I touch the glass, but she ignores me. "I thought for sure you'd love the dragon."

I ordered it online, certain my fierce fish would sense a kindred spirit. The only thing she's sensing is a strong urge to bury the damn thing. As I watch, she heaves another forehead full of gravel, making the dragon tail vanish. Sighing, I shift my grip on the tray and keep walking.

Back on the porch, I hand out the glasses and try to get a read on the tension.

"Because it's a good opportunity for Abe, that's why." Alexis huffs and lifts her wineglass to her lips. "The girls need their mama home more. They need family meals and bike rides to the park with their parents. I don't expect you to get it, seeing how you don't have kids, but—"

"No, I get it." Nick's gaze shifts to me. As his gold-brown eyes search mine, he takes a breath. "Crooked house," he murmurs.

Lexi cocks her head. "Say what?" She looks from Nick to me and back again. "Are you talking about that old raggedy park?"

Nick's throat moves as he swallows. "Something like that." He puts a hand over his sister's, squeezing softly. "And I really do get it. Sorry I'm being an ass. I just want—"

"You want me to be a bigshot lawyer." Lexi shakes her head. "Like Mama and Daddy. But I've done that. It's not what makes me happy."

"And you think this place'll make you happy?"

"I think I fell in love with Oregon a long time ago," she says carefully. "Small towns especially. Even ones where there aren't many folks who look like you and me." She flicks a glance at me and shrugs. "They've done a good job making sure there's a nice mix of people here. Good people. A community where my girls can grow up strong and proud and safe."

He's still frowning, trying to wrap his head around this. "So you're gonna what—give it all up and bake cookies? Become president of the PTA?"

I watch her hackles rise, glad she loves pinot too much to dump it on his head. "You've got a problem with women making their own choices?" She shakes her head, muttering under her breath. "For your information, there's a law office in town. All female attorneys who understand flexible schedules. It's run by a friend from Willamette Law."

I clear my throat, needing to put in my two cents. "We have opportunities at Juniper Ridge, too," I add. "A good lawyer won't go hungry for work around here."

Alexis takes a sip of wine. "Plus, Abe's new job pays well. And with housing included—"

"Okay, you're right." Nick throws his hands up, recognizing he's outgunned. "I'm sorry I'm getting all up in your business. I'm just surprised, that's all."

"Well, get with the program." Alexis throws me a wink, and I suppress a smile.

"Come here." He sets his wine on the porch rail and stands so he can drag her to her feet. Lexi squeaks and holds her wine out to the side. "You know I love you," he says. "This place is great, Lex. You're right about the diversity thing. They've done a good job with that here. You and the girls and Abe are gonna love it."

Warmth floods the space around my heart. Maybe it's the sweet sibling moment. Maybe it's that I had a hand in building this place.

Most likely it's seeing the man I love let go of family baggage. That we're both learning to do that.

Stop getting ahead of yourself. You've jumped the gun before and look where it got you.

But I'm here now and grateful to be part of this.

Clearing my throat, I lean on the porch rail with my own glass of wine. "There's a water park," I put in. "I'm sure Lana showed you."

Alexis laughs and reaches for the chips. "Lord, I haven't heard the end of that all day. Rosie hasn't stopped talking about it since we showed her the pictures. Then she saw it in person, and you'd have thought we chartered a private jet to fly in Santa Claus, the Easter Bunny, and Peppa Pig for her birthday."

Nick looks around. "Where are they now? Abe and the girls?"

Alexis grabs her glass again. "Abe took them to the café. We promised cupcakes if they behaved for the tour."

Little girl laughter rings in the distance, and we watch the path as Abe and the girls approach. Rosa skips beside him, while Abe carries Nala on his shoulders. The second Rosa sees Nick, her face lights up.

"Uncle Nick!" She squeals and rushes him, bounding up the steps with braids flying.

He's dropping to his knees and swooping her up in his arms. "Rosie girl, you're getting so big!"

"I'm this many!" She holds up her small starfish hand displaying five sticky fingers. "Mama says I can have pink water wings when we go to the slides."

"If they have them." Alexis looks at me. "We saw yellow and blue in the gift shop, but I'm not sure they had pink."

Abe releases me from a bearhug and hands over Nala. "I'm almost positive we have pink," I assure them as I cuddle the little girl against me. Lana handles ordering, and no way would she let the pink ones run out. "I'll check for you, okay?"

Alexis shoots her husband one of those married people looks. "Sounds like someone's offering to take the kids to the water park to give Mom and Dad some alone time."

"Yes," I say for both of us, bouncing Nala so she squeals. "We'd love to."

Nick claps Abe on the shoulder as the two wrap up the longest bro hug I've ever seen. "I think we can handle that."

We. I love that we're speaking as a team, making decisions as a unit. Is this what it could be like?

As my gaze skips to Lexi, I watch her wrap both arms around her husband, snuggling into his chest like he's her safe harbor. The intimacy makes my own chest squeeze tight, and I look up to see Nick watching me. He nods like he's thinking the same thing I am.

Like for the first time, we might be on the same page.

* * *

"Could I get that screw right there?"

I grab the sharp steel spiral and hand it over because I'm a mature adult who doesn't turn everything into a sex joke. Also because it's ten p.m. two days before the adoption event, and Nick and I are working late evenings to get things ready.

"Thanks." He curls his fingers around mine, pulling me close as he sets down his cordless drill. "Don't think I'm not hearing the dirty thoughts running through your head right now."

I tilt my head to kiss him. "Guilty as charged."

"And I love that about you."

Love.

It's amazing how casually we're throwing that around. No, not casually. That implies we're not sincere, and if anything, I mean it more now than I did two years ago.

Breaking the kiss, I dust my hands on my jeans and look around. "We're close, yeah?"

"Yeah." He finishes screwing the shelving into the wall and steps back to admire his work. "Jessie's bringing some big cat tree by in the morning. That'll have the playroom complete."

"I can't believe we've pulled this off."

He grins and tucks the drill back in its case. "We make a good team, Lo."

"Is this where we do one of those teammate high-fives and pat each other's butts in tight pants?"

"Nah, it's where I tear off that tight little tank top with my teeth and fuck you against the wall." He winces and shakes his head. "Actually, raincheck. I've got knots in my back from setting all those fence posts outside. How about a bed?"

I'm liking the thought of Nick taking my clothes off with his teeth, so location's not important. "Deal. And since I'm the world's best girlfriend, I'll work out those knots with my new massager."

"Have I mentioned I love you?" He slings an arm around me and walks us both to the door, pausing to lock up. "Lexi met with that lawyer group this morning."

"She called me on her way back to the airport." I fish for my phone to use as a flashlight, but Nick's already pulling a headlamp from his pocket.

"The job sounds like a good fit, huh?"

"Mari's helping to get the paperwork in order," I say. "It helps that Lexi's already licensed to practice in Oregon."

"And her new office would let her work part time." He shakes his head, making the beam sweep out over the lake. "Leave it to Lex to work things out just right."

I glance over, surprised at the ease in his voice. "So you're good with it? Alexis and Abe moving here, I mean?"

"Yeah, I'm good." He clears his throat, looking thoughtful. "Not my place to judge, is it?"

"No, but she cares what you think. That she has your support."

"She's got it." He's quiet a long time, mulling something bigger than his sister's move. "I appreciate what you said. About people needing to experience new things and go their own way to become the best version of themselves."

I'm not sure I used those exact words, but his phrasing's better. "I happen to love the guy you've become."

"Yeah?" He squeezes my hand. "I've been thinking about my parents. About how hard they've pushed us to prove ourselves."

"They've always wanted what's best for you."

"I know. Thing is, I got to thinking they knew better than me. That I could never make them happy with the path I picked."

I don't know if that's true, but it's not my place to say. "Do we ever stop trying to earn our parents' approval?"

"You tell me."

We're at the front porch of my cabin now, and I pull out the key. Old habit, since there's not much crime at Juniper Ridge, but Chief Lovelin likes reminding us not to let our guard down. "Want to shower before bed?"

"With you? Yes." He ducks through the door and ambles toward Sharkira's tank. "But I have something for you first."

"Are you talking to me or the fish?"

"Yep." He grins and reaches into the tote that holds his drill. "I was going to save this and give it to you on adoption day, but I'm guessing we'll both be too busy to—"

"Oh my God!" I gasp when I see what's in his hands. "Is that a replica of the Crooked House?"

"Sure is." He hands it over, smiling as he watches my face. "Jessie helped me research the right kind of inert plastic to use. Aquarium-safe adhesives and all that. And my buddy who works with plastics—the guy who fixed your bumper cars? He helped, too."

I cradle the house in my hands, blinking back tears. It looks just like the one from Nick's childhood playground, right down to the quirky roof with alternating slopes and sides painted in primary colors. "I love it," I say, blinking as I meet his eyes. "It's absolutely perfect."

"Should we let Sharkira be the judge?"

I hustle to the kitchen sink to give it a quick rinse. "Would you mind grabbing those other decorations out of there? The unicorn in back and the shark with the pizza in its mouth?"

"Not a fan of the animal theme, huh?"

I return to the living room holding my new house. "She knocked the shark over first thing. Probably saw it as competition or something."

Nick's frowning as he pulls the unicorn from the tank. "I thought you said this was a unicorn."

"It was. She somehow got the horn off. Don't ask."

He sets the rejected toys aside, laying them on the dish towel I hand him. Carefully, he positions the house in the back corner. Sharkira swims over, gills flaring. She stares at the intruding arm, then the house as Nick pulls his hand from the tank.

"That's a good sign, right?" He stoops to peer through the glass. "Doesn't she usually head-butt things within the first five seconds?"

"Or bury them in gravel." I don't have the heart to say there's almost no chance this decoration will fare differently from the others. It's the thought that counts, and Nick's put a lot into this. "Nick."

He straightens and looks at me, dark eyes searching mine as one corner of his mouth quirks up. "The fish house makes you want to tear off my clothes with your teeth?"

I laugh because it's true, but not the whole truth. "Even if she doesn't love it, that's seriously the best gift I've ever gotten."

He cocks his head and studies me. "Didn't one of the gossip rags write about how every Judson kid got a brand-new Porsche at sixteen?"

"Mine was a Ferrari, but that's beside the point." I wrap my arms around his waist and press my body to his. My nerves kick into gear, thrumming with the need to have him again, but I need to say this first. "It's a sign that you see me. That you're paying attention to what matters, what I care about, what I need. And you'll go out of your way to meet those needs."

He smiles and brushes the hair back from my face, big hand lingering on my cheek. "Always," he murmurs. "I've always got your back."

As I stretch up on tiptoe to kiss him, I'm certain that's all I could ever want.

CHAPTER 13

CONFESSIONAL 833.5

Armbrust, Nick (Owner, Armbrust Resorts)

I do think some people are born entrepreneurs. Doesn't matter if you're toting a hammer or a briefcase. There's this mindset for men and women wired to take risks and take charge.

I was ten when my granddaddy taught me to use power tools. Built this big doghouse by myself, and we didn't even have a dog. That thing was dope. Skylights in the roof and its own front porch. Sold it to the neighbor for two hundred bucks and bought more lumber to do it again.

Mama was so proud. "Way to take initiative, son. Ambition. Action. Autonomy—that's what it's all about."

Had to look up that last one in the dictionary. I vowed from there on out to be autonomous. To make Mama and Pop proud all the time.

* * *

"That's a wrap." Lauren strides to where Cash Beckett cradles a puppy against his chest. His red Balenciaga T-shirt is tight enough I'm not sure it isn't glued to his chest. I overheard someone in costuming say it cost more than a grand, which is nuts. A thousand bucks for a T-shirt?

I'm reminding myself not to be a judgmental prick as he steps close to Lauren to hand off the puppy. His hand grazes her breast, and as she jerks back, my blood goes cold.

No way was that an accident.

Seeing red, I start toward them with a hand on my toolbelt. I've gone two steps when Cooper steps between Lo and Cash. Scowling, Coop shoves the guy. "Get out of here." Cooper turns to Lauren. "You good?"

She folds her arms and presses her lips together as Cash skulks off toward the door. Lo says something I can't hear, and Cooper takes out his phone. I'd kill to know what they're saying, but a soft female voice distracts me.

"Entitled prick." Chief Lovelin's growl is so quiet that I'm sure I wasn't meant to hear.

I'm not even sure I heard right. "What's that?"

Amy looks startled. "Sorry." She clears her throat and pushes her blonde ponytail off one shoulder. "Your brother-in-law's great, by the way. I'm counting down the days to his start date."

"Abe's a good guy." I'm still trying to figure out if her insult was meant for Cooper or Cash.

Coop's striding over, so I give up guessing and hold up a hand for him to slap. "Hey, Nick," he says. "We're heading over to grab some tots if you want to join us."

"We?" I'm hoping Lo's included in the group, but Cooper shakes his head.

"Cash." He makes a face. "I know you're not a fan."

"I'll sit this one out." I'd rather nail my nuts to the wall than grab a beer with Cash Beckett. "Gotta run into town for some supplies."

"Sounds good." He glances to where Cash is striding out the door, stopping to leer at a female sound tech who can't be over twenty.

Cooper sighs. "Get your hand off the hammer, Armbrust."

He's not even looking at me, so I don't know how he guessed. Hell, I didn't realize my hand crept to my toolbelt again, but there it is, grazing the claw hammer.

Entitled prick is right, I think as Cash gives up on the sound tech and ambles out the door. Coop looks back at me.

"Seriously, it's handled."

"What's handled?"

"Cash." He says it with such a grim expression that it's hard to believe they're friends.

"Handled," I repeat. "You're gonna play nice with a guy who groped your sister?"

"My sister can handle herself." Coop's voice surprises me with its fierceness. "She can do more damage with her tongue than you can with that hammer."

He has a point. "I wasn't really going to hit him."

Maybe scare him a little, sure…

"Amy's a good cop." His expression goes dark, like he can't believe he's saying this. "Not that I'm normally on that side of the law. I'm just saying, she'll nail your ass to the wall if you beat the shit out of Cash in front of her."

My gaze flicks to where Amy was just standing, but she's vanished. Cooper stares at the space like he's willing her to reappear.

I clear my throat. "So you're just gonna let him get away with being a prick?"

Cooper shrugs, but there's an edge to his expression. "We need his face un-punched for the shoot. Besides, I texted Mari."

"What's Mari got to do with this?" I glance back at Lo, who's busy bossing the sound guy like nothing even happened. Like she's sexually harassed on a daily basis.

Fucking show biz.

"Mari's meeting us at the brewery," Coop says, which doesn't answer my question.

I look back at him, curiosity piqued. "She's gonna bust out the company's sexual harassment policy and beat him with a copy?"

"Maybe a little more than that." Cooper shoves his hands in his pockets. "She's talking to your sister right now. Composing a legal threat that'll put the fear of God into him."

I like the sound of that. "All right."

"Lauren's idea," he says. "Trust me, Judsons know how to hit people where it hurts."

I glance over at Lauren, remembering the time she kneed someone in the balls for hitting on Lana. "I've heard."

Feeling my eyes on her, my girl looks over and smiles. Moments later, she's standing by my side. "Gentlemen." She slides an arm around my waist and angles up to kiss my jaw. "Did you hear *Entertainment Zone* is sending a film crew? Our plan to have Cash Beckett on the season finale shot the ratings through the roof."

I shove back my ego's unease and force a smile. "I'm proud of you, babe."

"Thanks." She looks at Cooper. "Shouldn't you be keeping Cash out of trouble?"

He backs away from us with a smirk. "We're seriously fucked if I'm someone's babysitter."

Coop's out the door before Lauren can reply. Just as well, since it gives us our first moment alone together all day. She scans the room, taking a deep breath as she surveys all we've accomplished these past few weeks. "Tomorrow's the big day."

"It's going to be great." I reach up and tuck some hair behind her ear. "You sure you don't want to come to town with me? Grab dinner, get your mind off things for an hour or two?"

She shakes her head, hair tickling the back of my hand. "I know it looks like we're ready, but there's still a lot to do on the production side." She bites her lip. "How nicely would I have to ask if I wanted a double order of chips and salsa from Pepe's on Third Street?"

"Chips and salsa?"

"It's one thing I can't get here on the compound."

"Oh, you'd have to ask real nicely." I lower my head so my mouth's close to her ear. "Or maybe not nice. I'm thinking *bad*. Really, really bad and dirty and—"

"Perv." She laughs and swats my ass. "You've got a deal."

"Let's shake on it." I catch her hand in mine, bringing her fingers to my lips. "You know I'm kidding. I'll get you all the chips and salsa you want."

Lo grins and squeezes my ass. "And I'll give you all the bad, dirty things you want."

I step back, needing to cool off before I pull her into the storage closet again. Now's not the time. "Better go. Hardware store closes at five."

"You've got an early day tomorrow?"

"Lumber's showing up at six. I'm guessing it's a late night for you?"

She sighs and blows hair off her forehead. "Probably an all-nighter. Sorry."

"Nah, it's good." I stroke the soft skin on her forearm, desperate to keep touching her. "I should probably sleep at my place tonight."

"Probably so." She sighs again, surveying set construction. Lighting equipment lies jumbled everywhere, with camera and audio gear covering every surface. "I'll miss you."

"Same. Want me to bring your salsa here or drop it somewhere?"

"I'll love you forever if you bring it here." She smiles, and I wonder if she means it. Not that our future's tied to tortilla chips, but is she really thinking forever? I sure as hell am.

"I'll swing by as soon as I get back."

She makes a face. "Sorry in advance I can't eat with you. It's gonna be *go-go-go* all evening. We've got a two-hour production meeting starting at six. All Judsons on deck." She gives a wry look, fatigue flickering in her eyes. "Season finales are a big enough deal without tying them to a community-wide pet adoption event."

"I understand." I bend to kiss her one last time. "Love you, Lo."

"I love you, too." The kiss lasts a lot longer than I mean it to, and my head's humming by the time I step out into the late-afternoon sunlight.

The drive to town takes twenty minutes, and I skip the air conditioning in the truck. Driving with the windows down feels freeing, with wisps of piney breeze whipping through as Gary Clark Jr. nails the guitar riff on "This Land." He played it that summer Lo and I saw him at Red Rocks, and I can picture her in my mind, dancing barefoot with her hair in the breeze. Even then, I knew she was something special. We'd dated less than two months, but my heart was already a goner.

So what if it took my brain a little longer to catch up? We're here now, finding our way back to each other. We're even talking about a future. Not marriage—not yet—but I'm sure it's headed there. If you'd told me two years ago I'd be thinking like this, I'd have laughed in your face.

Shaking off the sappy thoughts, I focus on my job. The trip through the hardware store takes longer than I expect, and it's after five when I'm finished. I hop back in the truck, getting five blocks before realizing I have no idea where Lo's restaurant is.

I pull off to the side, angling up against the curb before I slip out my phone. I'm scrolling to Yelp when something catches my eye. Glancing up, I'm jarred to see I'm parked beside a school. A shiver rips up my arms. As safe as I've felt at Juniper Ridge, it's different in small-town USA when you're the only brother for miles. A strange Black man lurking outside a school is gonna get looked at. Dropping my phone on the passenger seat, I twist the key in the ignition.

That's when I see him.

Cash Beckett, I'm positive. He's got dark glasses and a ballcap, but I'm sure it's him. Same pasted-on red shirt, same stupid-ass ripped jeans. Same swagger, like he owns the world.

Like he owns the teenage girl beside him.

I stare as he slings an arm around her. She's in a black and green cheerleader outfit, bookbag hooked over one shoulder. As I stare, Cash leads the girl to a black Mercedes. It's got tinted windows and leather seats that gleam in the sunlight as he opens the door.

I hold my breath, watching as he hands the girl into the car. Christ, she can't be more than fifteen. I grip the wheel tighter as Cash touches the small of her back. It's a familiar touch. A touch that makes her look up and smile.

And then the door closes. I let out a breath, watching as Cash swaggers to the driver's side and gets in. Through the tinted windows, I can just make out the shape of him leaning toward her.

I've got a bad feeling about this.

Snatching my phone off the seat, I snap two quick photos. I can't make out much behind the tinted windshield, but I get the license plate. The shape of two people looking awfully cozy in the front seat.

My heart hammers as Cash starts the car and peels out, moving quicker than I'm ready for. I crank the wheel, hustling to follow, but I'm facing the wrong way.

The Mercedes whips past, followed by a school bus that takes its sweet-ass time getting out of my way. By the time I'm headed the right direction, I've lost sight of them. *Dammit.* Which way?

I pause at a stop sign, glancing left to right. Maybe they went straight? My head's pounding and I fight to think of where Cash Fucking Beckett would take an underaged girl. I've gotta help her.

And I have to do this for Lo. If the asshole gets busted for statutory rape, the Judsons can't be tied to that. There's still time to nail him before they tape a whole finale with his stupid face filling the screen. I can fix this for them, for Lo. For the girl who won't have someone like my parents looking out for her.

I gun the engine, deciding to go straight. My brain buzzes with headlines I've seen over the years. Shit about Cash, what a womanizer he is. Not just women, either. My dad represented a young actress years ago, a girl barely old enough to vote.

"Let's just say Cash Beckett likes them young," Pop muttered over dinner as Mama shot him a look. "What? I'm not saying anything you can't see in the tabloids."

"Makes me sick," Mama muttered, shaking her head. "A man should have some decency."

I'm determined to be the decent man. To find fucking Cash Beckett if it kills me.

I cruise down Main Street, scanning for the black Mercedes. For anyplace that might be a magnet for an aging movie star. He wouldn't take her back to Juniper Ridge, would he? Or maybe her house. Should I call the school? No, there's no one there at this hour, and besides—some petty little part of me wants to nail the son of a bitch myself.

There!

There's a black Mercedes up ahead, parked at an angle outside an upscale chain hotel. I squint at the car, but there's no sign of them. It's parked by a dumpster, and I grab a spot a hundred yards away. As I peer through the windows, my heart sinks to see it's empty. I grab my phone and scan the photos I took minutes ago. Definitely the same car.

Now what?

I consider calling Lo.

But by now she's in her production meeting, which is not the time to drop a bomb on her. Cooper or Mari? Nah, they're meeting, too. Even if they answer, what can they do from the compound?

I drag a hand over my head, ordering myself to think. No way am I calling 911. I don't know much about the cops around here, but that doesn't feel like the right move. I won't be the guy who phones police because someone looks suspicious.

But shit, I can't sit here doing nothing.

Amy Lovelin?

Better. At least it's not a random call to some small-town police department. We're friendly and I trust her judgment. Hesitating, I lift the phone and hit speed dial for the Juniper Ridge switchboard.

"Chief Lovelin, please," I say when someone answers. My heart's jumping out of my chest, so I force myself to take a few deep breaths. I wish Abe was here. He'd understand what a tough spot I'm in.

But I'm pretty sure Amy's no fan of Cash Beckett, so she'll believe me. Better yet, she'll know what to do.

She answers on the second ring. "Chief Lovelin speaking."

"Amy, hi." I clear my throat. "It's Nick. Nick Armbrust."

"Hey, Nick." Her voice sounds steady, but there's a hint of concern. "Everything okay?"

I take a deep breath, not sure how to say this. Every second I waste is one more where that bastard's alone with an underage girl. A chance for him to take advantage, to hurt her, hurt Lo's reputation—

"Cash Beckett," I say. "Um—"

"If this is about what I said earlier, I apologize." Amy releases a ragged breath. "That was unprofessional to let my personal feelings cloud my perception of a situation."

"Amy, stop. It's not that." I clear my throat. "Actually, it *is* that. You're right about him being an entitled prick, but there's more."

"What do you mean?"

I close my eyes and pinch the bridge of my nose. "I just watched Cash pick up a young girl in front of a high school." I fight to keep my voice even, to report only the facts. "He had his arm around her. Hugging her, getting all up in her personal space. She got in his car and then…" I swallow hard, fighting to separate facts from my worst-case scenario fears. I can't be the jackass who sends the cops swarming for no good reason.

But I know what I saw. And I know what kind of guy Cash Beckett is.

"I took pictures of the car," I continue, "but you can't see much. I tried to follow and then lost them, but his car's outside a hotel now."

Amy's silent a long time. So long, I think the call's dropped. "Amy?"

"You're sure about all those details?"

I replay my words, making sure I haven't embellished. It's no secret I can't stand Cash, but I don't need to exaggerate. I saw what I saw.

There's not a single damn reason a superstar actor should be lurking around a high school in bumfuck Oregon.

"Yeah," I say into the phone. "I'm sure about what I saw."

"Okay." Amy goes quiet as I glance back at the hotel.

My feet twitch with the urge to get out. To go door to door until I find her. Probably another thing that wouldn't go great in small-town USA, a big Black dude beating on hotel doors.

Amy's voice breaks the silence. "You've still got eyes on the car?"

"Yeah. Sitting right outside the hotel."

"Okay," she says. "Where you're at now, that's outside my jurisdiction. But I know a lot of cops there, and I'm going to call this in. Nick?"

"Yeah?"

"You did the right thing. It's better to be safe than sorry with stuff like this."

"Sure, okay." I stare at the hotel, hating the sick feeling in my gut. "Could you tell them to hurry?"

"I'm hanging up now."

I scan the hotel windows, wondering which room they're in. "Should I stay here in case someone needs to question me?"

"No. I have your number. You said you've got photos?"

"Yes."

"Could you forward them to me?" She rattles off her direct line and I jot it on the back of a receipt. "You can head home, but please keep your phone on in case they have questions."

"All right. Got it." I fire off the images, then put the phone to my ear. "Thanks for dealing with this."

"Thank you for calling it in. They'll handle it as discreetly as possible, and it'll all be okay."

"I hope so." For the girl's sake. For Lauren's sake. For the sake of the Judson reputation. "Keep me posted if you hear anything."

"Will do."

We hang up, but I don't pull away. I sit staring at the hotel until the cop cars roll up. Two of them, no sirens, but the officers are in uniform.

I feel itchy and suspicious sitting here watching, but I can't look away. Can't stop wishing I could watch Cash Beckett get marched outside in handcuffs.

Glancing at my phone, I pull up Lauren's name in my contacts. I hesitate. Does she need to know about this now? She said she's got a long night. Knowing her guest star might end up in jail won't help things. Not tonight, anyway.

I recall how often my dad bailed out guys like Cash Beckett. Creeps who think they're above the law, directors who want scandal brushed under the rug so they can keep filming. The Judsons have a lot hinging on this finale. How far would they go to save it?

I remind myself that's not what it's about. I called police because I suspected crime. *Period.* I'm choosing not to tell Lauren because I don't want to stress her out. *Period.*

So why is my gut twisting like a wrung-out washrag?

Fingers hovering over my phone's keypad, I fire off a message to Lauren.

On my way to Pepe's. Need anything besides chips and salsa?

I expect she's too busy to answer, so I'm surprised when she responds right away.

Could you make it a triple order + cheese enchiladas? Sharing with Lana.

My jaw clenches. I pause again, wrestling with my conscience. Should I say something?

No. I can't. The last thing she needs right now is more stress. Something else to worry about, to pile on her already overloaded plate. If Cash gets busted, she's better off without him. My girl is resilient. She can handle it if it happens, and if it doesn't…well, no sense freaking her out tonight.

Thumbs paused on the phone screen, I text a response.

No problem. Love you!

I set the phone down, dragging in a breath as I glance at the hotel. Still no sign of Cash. Just his sleek, fancy sportscar at the edge of the lot, black paint gleaming under a sun sinking lower in the sky.

You did the right thing.

It'll all be okay.

As Chief Lovelin's words play in my brain, I pray to God she's right.

CHAPTER 14

CONFESSIONAL 840.5
Judson, Lauren (Producer: Juniper Ridge)
You learn fast in showbiz not to make the same mistakes twice. Don't skip panties no matter how much you want to wear that high-cut gown. Don't work with the director known for grabby hands. Those lessons I didn't learn the hard way because my mother fed them to me with my Gerber.

It's a figure of speech, Lana. It was the nanny, okay? Can I finish my story?

Some people repeat mistakes again and again, and I feel sorry for them, but that's not me. I'd rather skip the kickass Atelier Versace gown with the cutouts if it means I won't end up flashing my meat curtains to five million YouTube viewers.

* * *

"Could you put down the breakfast sandwich and get that mic moved over there?" I direct a sound tech to the corner near a pen filled with wriggling puppies, then pivot to the next task. "Gabe, you've got the—"

"On it." My brother glides past with a boom mic as gratitude grabs me by the heart. We're lucky we work well together. It's ten minutes to show time, and I'm only mildly freaked about the gazillion pet adopters lined up outside.

"Here are the forms." Jessie sets a stack of adoption contracts on the table, one hand bracing the sleeping infant bundled on her chest. "Dog contracts are here, and these are for cats. I need to feed Joy, but—"

"Got it." I check the lighting equipment before swiveling back to Jessie. "Thank you for everything. Really. We couldn't have done this without you."

"No problem." She smiles, still cupping the baby's small body. "I'm going to go put her down at Gretchen's, but I'll be right back."

"Perfect." I'm already turning, scanning the room for our star. It's hardly the first time Cash Beckett's been late to set, but I swear I said the call time is firm.

"Lauren." Nick's low rumble spins me around as my heart kicks up. "How's it going?"

"Not great." I keep scanning, wondering if Cash got tied up at his *Entertainment Zone* interview. "I've got eight-zillion things happening at once and a buttload of people at the door." Remembering not to be a work-driven bitch, I soften my voice. "Thanks again for the food delivery. Sorry I couldn't chat last night."

"It's cool." Nick's steady presence soothes me more than his words. "Can I help with anything?"

I huff out a breath. "You can help me find Cash Beckett. He was supposed to be here an hour ago."

Nick's eyes dim. "Right. Um, look, I—" He clears his throat. "Haven't seen him today."

"No one has." I scan the room, watching Cooper string leashes outside each kennel. Any Judson who's not manning a camera has been put to work preparing for the rush of pet adopters. "Tia stayed up all night bathing a zillion dogs so they're ready for show time."

"That's great." He clears his throat again. "So, hey, I was wondering—"

"Sorry, hon." I touch his arm, stealing a glance at my watch. I've got five minutes to find our guest star. "Can we catch up later?"

"Sure." His brow furrows as he takes a step back. "Do your thing. I'm here if you need me."

"Thanks, Nick." I stretch up to kiss him, then duck back before it turns into more. I need to focus. It's almost ten a.m. and nearly eighty degrees outside. We need to get that crowd inside. The longer guests stand in the sun, the crankier they'll get. Not the vibe I want for our feel-good finale.

"Has anyone seen Sadie from craft services?" I shout.

Lana swoops in, blond ponytail swinging. "Already on it," she shouts as she jogs past. "Cold drinks for the folks in line. I'll grab a Gatorade for you."

God, I love my family. "You're an angel."

I spot Cooper in the corner talking to Nick. My boyfriend looks casual and sexy in a pale blue T-shirt, and I fight back a rush of distracting thoughts as I approach. "Coop, have you seen Cash?"

He frowns. "Shouldn't he be here by now?"

"That's the problem. He's not."

My brother slips his phone out of his pocket. "No missed calls. You've tried texting?"

"Only about a thousand times." God, of all the mornings for a prima donna movie star to flake out on me—

"Look, guys." Nick drags a hand over his head and looks uneasy. "Hypothetically speaking, what if Cash can't make it? Coop, you're a big star—couldn't you step in?"

Coop laughs and shakes his head. "Not me. Cash has the clout on pet adoption. He did that blockbuster last year about the animal rescue, plus all those Humane Society ads. How about I run to his cabin and check—"

"Lauren. Problem." Lana's voice spins me around, and I catch the red Gatorade she's handing me. "We've got the crew from *Entertainment Zone* outside."

"Already?" We knew they'd be on set, but I wasn't expecting them right at the start. "Did Cash not make his pre-show interview?"

"That's one problem." Lana frowns. "We've got a PR disaster on our hands."

Before I can ask, the doors crash open, and a camera crew rolls in. Not a Judson in the bunch, and I'm instantly on alert. Anchorman Richard LaGrande—a slick-but-fading star my family dubbed Big Dick after his exposé on Coop going to rehab—spots us across the room. He charges at us, camera tech jogging behind.

"Lauren Judson." Dick beelines it past a cluster of kennels. "Is it true Cash Beckett got arrested last night for sex with a minor?"

Oh, Jesus.

Lana shoves in front of me, eyes blazing as she swings into PR mode. "We aren't at liberty to comment on anything besides our need to get these pets into safe and loving homes. If you'd like, we can—"

"Come on, give us the scoop." Dick flashes a made-for-TV grin that makes me want to deck him. "Throw us a bone for coming all the way out here."

The camerawoman zooms in on me, and the lights feel way too hot. I clench my hands and try to back away. "Why don't you wait outside," I suggest. "Get B-roll of the pet adopters or something."

"But Cash Beckett." Dick's frowning as he holds out a mic. "We heard it on the police scanner."

The camerawoman scans the room like she thinks Cash could be hiding in a kennel. "We drove to the hotel last night, but we were too late to get anything. Just a bunch of cop cars in the parking lot. If you could give us a quote—"

"No comment." I back away with blood pounding in my head. What the hell is happening?

Cooper shifts closer to Lana, dragging a hand through his hair. "Hey, so that interview you wanted. About my sobriety anniversary? I could reconsider. What do you say we go someplace and talk?"

Dick's eyes narrow. He's wanted this interview for ages, and I can't believe Cooper would throw himself on the fire. Actually, I can. That's exactly like my little brother, but I can't let him do that.

Besides, if what they're saying about Cash is true—

"Give us a chance to find out what's going on." I hate sounding clueless, but we have to know what we're dealing with. "Lana?"

She shrugs, clearly as clueless as I am. "Maybe Dean knows something?"

Big brother CEO is back in his office handling last-second details. If this thing blows up, he'll have a mess to deal with from investors. Advertisers will jump ship the second there's a hint of scandal.

Especially the sort they're talking about here. Did we miss something in our background checks? If I did something to put a teen girl in trouble, I'll never forgive myself.

I fix Dick with a stare. "What exactly did you hear?"

Lana frowns, and I'm sure that's not how the PR handbook says to handle this. But my heart's racing a million miles an hour, and everyone's staring. Lighting crew, sound techs, even my siblings. They're watching our big-bang finale crumble around us, and I need to fix it fast.

"Well." Dick grins, a squirrel with a big nut. "Apparently, he got caught in a hotel with a fourteen-year-old local high school girl. By tonight it'll be on all the major stations, so if you give us the scoop, we'll help you—"

"—control the message." Lana rolls her eyes. "Good one. Back off so we can figure out what's going on."

A realization dawns, dripping relief into my veins. I might know what's happening, and it's not what they think. I scan for Mari, wondering how to get out ahead of this. How much the law lets us say. "Be right back."

I step aside, letting Lana handle Dick and his crew. This is her specialty, and I've got mine. I'm still hunting for Mari when Nick steps in front of me. He's frowning, but there's a slight glint in his eye.

"Don't." I tip my mouth to his ear so I can whisper. "Do not be smug about this. I know you can't stand Cash, but—"

"Hey, Lo—that's not what it's about."

I frown and draw back. "What *what's* about?"

He drags a hand over his head. "You were busy last night. I took care of a problem."

I order myself to breathe. Not to freak the hell out. "What. Did. You. Do?"

Before he can answer, the doors open again. Tia's at the front of a shouting crowd looking bewildered. The mob moves fast, circling the dog kennels, calling out to each other.

Tia catches my eye and gulps. "I've never seen so many people this fired up about pet adoption."

"It's the cameras." Or the fact that we hyped the hell out of this. Everyone's eager to find a furry friend, to adopt a pet in need. Beyond the warm fuzzies, it's a star moment for community members.

Several of them glance over, sensing something's off. Lana's waving her arms at Dick, but a few folks zero in on me. A chiropractor named Carrie pokes a horticulturalist named Shelly and whispers in her ear. Curiosity flares like wildfire, shifting two dozen sets of eyes to us.

I've gotta do damage control.

Squeezing my eyes closed, I breathe through the chaos of barking dogs and squealing kids and hushed conversation. When I open my eyes, Nick's watching me.

"We need to talk."

"You *think?*" I'm fighting not to sound snippy, but being caught off-guard does not bring out my best self. "Closet."

I grab his arm before he can respond, towing him toward the storage room we christened. It feels like a lifetime ago, like something far removed from the chaos around us. Dick's thrusting his mic at random strangers, doing his best to get a quote from a personal trainer named Cal.

I spot Gabe across the room, and thank God he had the foresight to get our cameras rolling. Dick's camerawoman spots me moving toward the closet with Nick and tries to follow. "Lauren," she shouts. "What does it mean for *Fresh Start at Juniper Ridg*e that your guest star has a problematic reputation for—"

"No comment," I shout, and drag Nick into the closet.

He hits the light and stands blinking before me. The self-assured glint lingers in his eyes, and I fight my irritation. I need information, not surging anger.

"Spill," I demand. "What do you know?"

He touches my arm. "I wanted to take care of things, okay? I knew you were busy, so I—"

"Nick." I grit my teeth, biting back swells of stress and shame as someone outside the door shouts my name. "I need you to tell me what happened."

He sighs as some of the cocky glint leaves his eyes. "I saw him with a teenage girl, okay? I had to call it in. I had no choice, and I knew you could roll with whatever happened so—"

"You had no choice." My head's pounding as Gabe's voice echoes on the other side of the door.

Where's Lauren?

Why isn't she handling this—

"So, you saw him with a young girl, and you assumed the worst." I take a calming breath. "Child sex trafficking or statutory rape?"

"Pretty much." Nick's jaw clenches. "I didn't want him to get away with it."

"Very admirable of you." I don't bother keeping the snark from my voice. "And you thought if you told me, I'd let him get away with something?"

He frowns. "You had your hands full."

I throw up my hands, which he's lucky are empty at the moment. "Pretty sure I could take a break to deal with the arrest of our goddamn guest star."

His eyes darken as he glances away. "I've seen too much stuff like this get swept under the rug. I thought—"

"You thought you knew better than me how to handle this?"

"Babe." Nick's hand is still on my arm, and it's all I can do not to yank it back. "Cash Beckett is a jerk, okay? A loser and a creep and a—"

"Father." I cross my arms and stare at him. "Cash Beckett is a father."

He stares at me. "Say what now?"

I take a deep breath, trying not to shout. "It came out in the background checks." Because *of course* Judsons do our due diligence, which Nick fucking knows. "He's only known for a few months. It's not public knowledge."

His perplexed look shifts to downright confusion. "The girl," he says. "She's—his daughter?"

I nod because it's safer than slugging him. "He knocked up a waitress way before he got famous. The kid did some DNA test at school and it went into a database, so Cash tracked them here to Oregon and—you know what? This is none of your business." I take a deep breath and try not to lose it. "His publicist worked to keep things quiet so Cash could get to know his kid in private."

But now that's blown to hell.

Nick's staring at me like I ran over his foot with a bumper car. "Hell, Lo. I didn't know."

"That's right, you didn't." I ball my hands into fists, needing to get back out and do damage control. "But you could have asked me. You could have called or texted or—"

"You were busy," he interrupts. "I didn't want to throw you off your game."

"By telling me something vital to the filming of our final episode?" God, he knew how important this was. "Why didn't you tell me last night? Or hell, tell Cooper or Mari or—"

"You were all swamped." He shakes his head as a mulish expression sets in. "Even Coop blew me off when I tried pulling him aside. You barely had time to inhale dinner last night. You didn't need one more thing on your plate."

I clench my teeth so hard they squeak. "I'd have *made* time for something this big."

"Come on, Lo." He tries a smile, but it doesn't quite work. "You're the master of rolling with change, and I knew if it came to that—"

"That wasn't your call to make." Wait. Realization rushes through me. "You're the one who called him in."

He doesn't deny it. "I had to," he says. "The guy's a prick, Lauren. It seemed reasonable he'd be sniffing around underage girls."

I close my eyes, tamping back my frustration. I fight to put myself in Nick's shoes, to think of what I might have done if I'd seen an older man with a young girl. I'd have called the cops, too.

When I open my eyes, Nick's watching me.

"You still could have texted me," I say. "Even if you had to get police involved, we needed to prepare for this. Instead, you let me be blindsided."

He takes my hand, lacing his big fingers through mine. "I didn't want you to worry."

"Jesus Christ." I yank my hand back, making him frown. "Can you not see how this is so much worse?"

His brow furrows, jaw clenching like it does when he's getting defensive. "Do you really want a guy like Cash wrapped up in your show? I thought you were aiming for a family-friendly—"

"For fuck's sake!" I'm so angry I can't see straight. "None of this was your call to make. Do you realize what you've done? To our show, to a man's career, to a young girl's *life*? This wasn't about her at all."

It's his turn to look pissed. He's got one arm braced on the wall as he glares at me. "I handled a situation to the best of my ability with the information I had."

"Rather than—oh, I don't know—gathering the *right* information?" I shake my head, needing to deal with the crisis outside. "Never mind. I need to work."

"Lauren, wait."

I ignore him and yank the door open. I step through it to see the *Entertainment Zone* camera zooming in on me as Lana struggles to herd them the other direction. "Out," she's saying. "You're done here for now."

Big Dick feigns confusion. "But you invited us here. You said—"

His words fade as the front door bangs open, and Cash Beckett strides in. He's disheveled and scowling with Amy Lovelin right behind him. "Fucking small-town cops," he's muttering.

Amy heroically does not deck him. "Here you go," she says, propelling him toward the camera Gabe's manning. "You're welcome for the ride."

I don't want to know why she had to give him a ride or what he's been through in the past twelve hours. He looks unshowered and pissed off and gunning for a fight.

Lana's jaw clenches as she throws her shoulders back and marches over. When this is done, I'm buying her that pony she wanted as a kid. Maybe six of them if she can fix this with her PR magic.

But we're nowhere near fixing it yet. Community members swarm, dog adoption taking a back burner to the drama unfolding around us.

"Lauren, is it true?" Jaya Cox approaches with her daughters. The girls wear traditional Indian dresses from their dance recital this morning, a program Jaya organized herself. "Is there really a child predator in our—oh, God—he's here."

Spotting Cash, she pulls the girls behind her and hurries from the building, both daughters shouting about a cat they want to adopt.

Great.

Over by the door, I spot Griffin Walsh. Mari's husband stands with arms folded, shielding his pre-teen daughter as he watches Cash warily. God, this can't get much worse.

I cup my hands around my mouth. "Everything's okay." I wish I had a megaphone. That I believed the words I'm saying. "This was all a big misunderstanding."

Cash snarls from the other side of the room. "Some fucking misunderstanding."

A young mother behind him gasps and covers her daughter's ears. "Watch your language," she snaps. "There are children."

I stare at Cash and try to stay calm. "We're dealing with it, okay?"

He chokes out a furious little laugh. "I should sue. I've already called my lawyer. And my agent says—"

"Cash, I'm gonna need you to take it down a notch." Or get the hell out of here. I need him to stop making a scene. I need everyone to stop staring at me like I'm responsible for this.

I am, though. This is all on me.

Amy Lovelin approaches, eyes filled with concern. "Lauren, I'm so sorry."

"It's not your fault." I deliberately don't look at who's standing behind her near the door. The man who pledged to trust me, to let me handle things myself. To never throw me under the bus again.

I didn't want you to worry.

I was looking out for you.

I am so goddamn tired of men doing that. Of the man I love leaving me to flap in the breeze while people stare and whisper and point.

I take a deep breath, willing myself not to panic. To breathe through the barking dogs, the crying kids, the concerned looks from community members. Tia hustles by with both hands filled with leashes, a sea of tail-tucked dogs skulking at her ankles. "I'm taking them outside," she says. "All this tension isn't good for them."

"I understand." I also know I'm missing out on the footage I need. "Are the cats okay, or should we move them?"

Before she can answer, someone starts yelling. "Don't take the cats! My daughter has her heart set on that orange tabby. Just because some pervert wants to…"

I stop listening. I close my eyes, cheeks stinging with shame and humiliation and the sick sense of everything going off the rails. This can't be happening again.

It is, though. And there's one common factor.

I scan the room for Nick, not sure if there's anything he could say to make this better. An apology, a hug, an attempt to calm the chaos.

That's when I catch sight of his back, his dark head above a swirling sea of bodies. He doesn't feel my eyes on him. Doesn't look back as he pushes through the door and leaves me alone to face the mess.

"I'm heading back to the ranch." Tia pauses beside me, dark braid frizzed and unraveling. "You sure there's nothing else I can do?"

"Are you kidding?" I dust my hands on my jeans and gesture to the empty kennels. "You killed it today. I can't believe we found homes for everyone."

Her smile is weary but bright. "I wasn't sure we'd find placements for a few of them."

Jessie looks up from photocopying adoption paperwork. "Even the lab mix with stinky ears and bad gas." She smiles and adjusts the baby slung across her chest. "I was worried about fame-seekers adopting for the wrong reasons, but all the pets found amazing homes."

Pride blooms in my chest, but its petals are wilty. My body sags with fatigue, and my limbs feel heavy. None of this has anything to do with the event, so I force myself to share their smiles. "Thank you. Both of you."

"Thanks for letting me be part of it." Jessie drops her chin to kiss the baby's soft head, and something squeezes inside me. How silly I was to think I'm anywhere close to that kind of happiness. "I'm heading out," she says. "Great work, Lauren."

"Thanks again." I glance at my watch and see it's after eight. Our event ended hours ago, but there's still so much to do. Between snuffing out PR fires and coddling Cash Beckett, it's been a long day.

"Go home, Lauren." Lana puts a hand on my shoulder. "You've been working like a dog all day."

I nod at the empty kennels. "None of them left to compare work ethic."

"And you did it," she says. "*We* did it."

"You handled way more than your share." I stifle a snort recalling my kid sister getting in Cash's face, insisting he apologize to Chief Lovelin before Lana would help with his personal damage control. "I still can't believe how you handled him."

She shrugs and tucks her hair behind one ear. "Once he knew we couldn't keep his kid out of the media, he saw the upside."

"Exploiting his secret daughter to repair his image?" I stifle a groan. "I thought we left Hollywood to get away from shit like this."

Lana's back straightens even as her eyes go soft. "His publicist is a good guy. He'll be careful, even if Cash isn't." Lana bites her lip. "Speaking of good guys—"

"If you're going to talk to me about Nick, don't."

Stacking both hands on her hips, she stares at me like I've spit on the floor. "Fine. I'm here if you need to talk."

"I know." That's one thing I always know. My family has my back no matter what.

I turn back to the next pile of projects, then stop. "Wait. Why did Cash have the girl at a hotel?"

"Her mother hates his guts." Lana shrugs like that's no surprise. "I guess it's where they've met privately the last couple months, getting to know each other. It really was innocent."

"Not the best judgment for a Hollywood star."

Lana lifts one eyebrow. "Like movie stars are known for great decision-making?"

"True."

"Oh, he also got busted for marijuana," she says. "His publicist is handling that one."

I straighten and ease the kinks from my back. "Isn't pot legal in Oregon?"

"Not when you're smoking a giant blunt behind the wheel." She rolls her eyes. "That's why Amy brought him home. Well, that and the Mercedes was meant to be a gift for his daughter."

"She's not old enough to drive." Not that I'm surprised Cash is the kind of guy to give gifts without learning what his kid needs. "Whatever."

Lana looks like she's reading my mind. Like she knows the Hollywood drama isn't really what's bugging me. She's opening her mouth to say something when the side door opens, and Nick strides through.

"Leaving now." Lana drifts away, giving me a meaningful glance before ducking out the door.

I tear my eyes off my sister to watch Nick marching toward me. He surveys the empty kennels and whistles. "Must have gone okay."

Clenching fists at my sides, I will myself not to react. "Yep."

"Come on, Lo." His gaze is wary as he approaches, the sawdust scent of his skin filling me with melancholy. "You're not still pissed about things, are you?"

Is he kidding right now?

I cross my arms over my chest because clenching my hands makes my fingers hurt. "You called the police on our guest star without contacting us." I throw up a hand when he starts to argue. "Please. I understand why you got cops involved. What I don't get is why you didn't tip us off. Didn't text Coop to say, 'oh, by the way, your buddy's been arrested.' Text Mari to let her know we had an HR problem or Lana on the PR side—"

"Because I didn't want to worry you if it wasn't necessary." He drags an exasperated hand over his head. "You're a champ at rolling with it when things go wrong. If it happened—and I wasn't sure it'd go down like that—I knew you'd handle it then."

"That was not your call to make."

"Okay," he says, huffing out a breath. "I didn't deal with things like you would. I handled it, okay?"

"That's not the point." I grit my teeth, struggling to keep a grip on my composure. "Honesty, Nick. *Communication*. That's what's missing here. You brought me dinner, for God's sake. It didn't cross your mind to say something then?"

His jaw clenches as his expression goes flat. "I knew how important this thing was to you. I wanted to avoid upsetting you."

Anger blurs my vision. "How's that working out?"

"Not great." He sighs. "I didn't mean for it to happen like this."

"How did you expect it to go?"

Nick pinches the bridge of his nose. "I figured you'd lose Cash. Maybe not the worst thing with all the Judson star power you've got out here. You don't need a guy like that."

My blood's full-on boiling now. "I see. You're a producer now?"

"That's not what I meant." His jaw tightens again. "Look, I wanted to make sure the asshole was held accountable."

I frown at him. "And you thought giving me a heads-up would prevent that somehow?" When he doesn't respond, my mind fills in the blanks. "Wait, let me guess—you figured if you told me what happened, I'd send Lana in with her mad PR skills, Dean goes in with lawyers, and the whole thing gets covered up. Is that what you thought?"

He doesn't answer right away. When he does, there's an edge to his voice. "You and I both know how this shit goes down in Hollywood."

"We're not in fucking Hollywood." I'm shouting now, but I don't care. "This is my show. My livelihood. My community."

He sighs and drags a hand over his head. "I know how invested you are, which is why I wanted to handle things."

"Goddammit." He's still not getting it, and I'm not sure what else to say.

"Lauren, come on." He touches my arm, and I ignore the ripple of nerves shooting to my shoulder.

With a shuddery breath, I draw back. "No."

"No what?"

I take a deep breath. "I need a partner who communicates with me. Who trusts me with all the information regardless of what he thinks I'll do with it." I pause, pretty sure this part hurts the most. "Who respects me enough not to assume I'd trade ethics for ratings."

"Lauren." He drags a hand over his head. "I didn't think you'd cover it up if he really did it. But we've both seen how things happen."

I turn away, hardly hearing him anymore. "We're done here."

"Good. Okay." The hope in his voice confuses me for a moment. "Let's get out of here," he continues. "We can go someplace and talk about—"

"No, I mean we're done." My voice sounds more forceful this time, and I turn to face the confusion in his eyes. "Look, I'm tired and hungry and pissed, so yeah—I'm filtering through all that. But I can't be with someone who goes behind my back. Who doesn't *have* my back."

He stares at me. "You've gotta be kidding."

"What?"

"You're running away again."

I cross my arms and stare him down. "I'm staying right here. And I'm telling you I can't do this again. Anymore. Whatever."

Nick shakes his head, looking more pissed than apologetic. Not that he's apologized. Just *"I thought I was doing the right thing,"* or *"I didn't want to upset you."*

That's not even close to *"sorry."*

He's staring at me like he's waiting for smoke to come out of my head. "You're serious."

I nod, not trusting my voice. Not trusting that I won't break down bawling like a big, emotional baby. Blame the hefty dose of humiliation, followed by a whirlwind day. "Yes," I manage, squishing the syllable from a throat pinched tight with hurt.

Here's where he could apologize.

Or where I could step up and ask to talk things through.

But I'm too tired, and Nick's too stubborn. We're at an impasse.

Gold-brown eyes search mine. Then he blinks and steps back. "Fine." He takes another step and grabs a hammer off the table. "I just stopped by to grab this anyway."

"Great." I give him my shark smile, the first time in ages I've needed it. "You got what you came for then."

He stares at me a long time, gold-brown eyes searching mine. "Not even close."

Then he turns and walks away.

CHAPTER 15

CONFESSIONAL 846
ARMBRUST, NICK (OWNER, ARMBRUST RESORTS)
MY FAMILY, WE'RE BIG ON PROVING OURSELVES. PROVE YOU CAN GET THE PROMOTION. PROVE YOU CAN BUILD A MULTI-MILLION-DOLLAR BUSINESS. PROVE YOU'RE THE SMARTEST, THE FASTEST, THE MOST SUCCESSFUL.
I DON'T KNOW, MAN. MAYBE THERE'S BETTER THINGS TO PROVE.

* * *

I'm sitting in the brewery knocking back the last of my drink when Cooper slides in across from me.

"Drinking away your troubles?" He clucks his tongue like Mama would. "Not a great plan."

I shove my empty glass in front of him. "It's ginger beer. Smell it."

He shoves the glass back. "I'm not smelling it. I trust you."

Sighing, I signal the waiter for two more sodas. "Want anything besides the drink?" I ask Coop. "Tots or fries or for me to take the big-ass hint you just dropped and admit I fucked up not trusting your sister?"

Coop looks at the server. "We might need a minute."

"I'll get those sodas." The waiter backs away fast, leaving me alone with the guy whose movie star smile just sent three women in the corner booth swooning.

Cooper leans back against the seat, oblivious to it all. "Look, I don't know what all went down. I'm not asking, either."

"So why are you here?"

He shrugs and pulls a bunch of bent metal from his pocket. It takes me a sec to see it's one of those wire puzzles. He starts working it without breaking eye contact. "I love my sister. I don't like seeing her unhappy."

"And I made her unhappy." It's the truth, but I still wish he'd argue.

He looks at me a long time, fingers working bent bits of steel. "You made her happier than anyone's ever made her," he says finally. "But sadder, too. If there's one thing Lauren hates, it's being undermined. Feeling blindsided or embarrassed or—"

"You know what I hate?" I shouldn't say this, but it doesn't stop me from running my dumb mouth. "I hate guys who game the system. Who take advantage of young girls."

Coop quirks an eyebrow. "You know a lot of folks who *don't* hate that?"

"You know what I mean."

He shrugs and thanks the server for our sodas, pausing to ask how the guy's son is doing in school. When the waiter's gone, Coop turns back to me.

"Want to know my first big memory of Lauren?"

That takes me by surprise. "Uh…sure?"

He takes a sip of his drink, then sets it carefully on a coaster. "I was five, maybe six. Which I guess would make her fourteen or fifteen? Mari was maybe twelve."

"Okay, got it." I don't know where this is going, but he's got my attention. "What happened?"

"Our mom was hounding Mari. Getting on her case about an audition she wanted Mari to go to, while Mari's got her face buried in a book just ignoring her." He laughs and spins his drink on its coaster. "Modern-day Mari would call that passive-aggressive, I guess."

"All right." I want him to get to the part about Lauren. "What happened?"

He leans back against the booth again, arms flexing. A passing server nearly drops her tray. "Mom won't let up, and Mari's face keeps getting redder and redder, right? So Lauren walks in. She sees what's going on, looks at our mom. Looks at Mari. Puts her hands on her hips and yells, 'I'm going on the audition! You can't make us compete for the same role.'"

I stare at him, not understanding. "But Lauren doesn't act." She never did, as far as I know.

"Of course not," he says. "But she knew that'd get our mom off Mari's back."

Frowning, I try to grasp what he's driving at. "Isn't that the same shit she's giving me grief about? Jumping in and trying to help someone who's not asking for it?"

"That's the thing." Coop leans forward, reaching for his drink. "The second Mom left, Lauren went to Mari. I was hiding behind some speakers, being a shit little brother, so I couldn't hear everything. But I heard most of what she said."

"Which was?"

"Lauren puts her hand on Mari's back. She says, 'I know you said you didn't want to do the audition. You still sure?' Like they'd talked about it before, right? And Mari looks up, her eyes all big behind the glasses. She sniffs and says, 'Yeah, but you don't have to go in my place.' And Lauren just pats Mari's back and gets that smile she has, you know?"

I do know that smile. "At fifteen?"

Cooper grins. "She was a badass kid. She looks Mari right in the eye and says, 'Don't worry. I'll bomb the hell out of it.'"

Admiration twists in my chest. "That sounds like Lo."

"Doesn't it?" Cooper chucks the rest of his drink, then sets down the empty glass. "I'm the last guy to give advice. God knows I've screwed up more than all the other Judsons combined."

"You look pretty good from where I'm sitting."

"My point," Coop continues like I haven't interrupted, "is that it's cool to help people. Noble, even. But not without seeing if they really want help. Otherwise, you might be making things worse. You get what I mean?"

I do, and it's making me downright depressed. "What do I do?"

He laughs and stands up. "Hell if I know." He slams a handful of change on the table in front of me, the clatter echoing in the brewery. "That's for you to figure out."

Still chuckling, he strides toward the exit. At the last instant, he turns, looping past the table of women who've been watching him since he sat down. For a second, I think he's asking for phone numbers, but no—they're handing *him* slips of paper, their eyes lit with eagerness.

Autographs. He's signing autographs, smiling and making eye contact with each person at the table. Someone pulls out an empty chair, but Coop waves them off and steps back, still smiling, but there's a sadness in his eyes I'm not sure anyone else sees. Seconds later, he's striding out the door.

I look down at the table and see it's not pocket change in front of me. It's Coop's metal puzzle, solved. The two rings sit side by side, glinting beneath the overhead light, barely touching each other.

* * *

It's nearly ten by the time I'm back in my cabin with the door shut tight and a throbbing wad of guilt in my head. Cooper's words linger in my brain, but they're not the only ones.

"Prove yourself, son."

What the hell did I prove in the last twenty-four hours? I'm not sure it's what my granddaddy had in mind. It's sure as hell not what Mama meant when she said it.

I'm dialing her number before I ask myself if it's a good idea.

"Baby." She answers without preamble, her voice light with cheer. "Is everything okay?"

"Of course. Can't I call my mama to say hi?"

"Hmph." She's not buying it one bit. "The cabins are coming along?"

"Yeah." I drag a hand over my head, not sure where to start. "You talked to Lexi lately?"

My sister planned to call Monday about her move to Juniper Ridge, but I won't spoil it if she hasn't.

"She called a few nights ago." Mama's voice sounds bemused. "Isn't that something about her and Abe moving?"

"It is." I tread carefully, not sure how to read her tone. "Lexi seems happy enough about it. Abe, too. The department's lucky to get him."

"Mmhmm." Mama laughs, sending me shockwaves of surprise. "Who'd have thought? My baby girl makes some interesting choices."

Wait. "You're not mad?"

"Mad? Why would I be mad?"

She sounds truly baffled, so maybe I picked the wrong word. "Disappointed, then. It's not what you wanted for Lexi."

"What I want," she says slowly, "is for my kids to be happy."

It sounds simple when she puts it that way, but I know it can't be. "That's not what you told me when I wanted to quit law school."

"What did I tell you?"

I'm not sure if she's testing me or if she really can't remember. I also can't believe I still recite the words from memory. "You said, 'Prove yourself, son. Your granddaddy didn't work twelve-hour days in the hot sun sending his kids to college just to have his grandson turn around and throw it in the trash.'"

"I said that?" She laughs as I choke back disbelief. "Yeah, that sounds like something I'd have said. What about it?"

I blink at a blank wall as my brain slowly recalibrates. "But—you hated when I gave up law school to work construction."

"Damn right, I did."

There's the Mama I know.

But her fire cools quickly, her voice shifting to toasty-marshmallow embers. "Honey, I wanted you to think hard about your choices," she says. "Doesn't mean I'm the one who should be making them for you. It's my job to help you if you need it. To push you to think hard about what you want and what you need. But in the end, that choice wasn't mine. It should always be on you, and I'd never want to take away one of your choices."

Like I did to Lo.

I swallow hard, closing my eyes against the surge of emotion. "Autonomy."

"What's that, now?"

"Autonomy," I say again, pushing the words past the pinch in my throat. "It was never about any one job or decision. What you said—it was about pushing me to make informed choices."

Mama's quiet a long time. "What's this about, baby? If you're not happy with your job, you can always change it."

I take a deep breath. "The job's fine. Great, I mean. I've got a great career."

"That's all I ever wanted for you."

I can't believe I never realized that before. "I think I screwed up." With another deep breath, I let out the rest of the story. Reconnecting with Lo. How good it's been this time, how happy we've been. How I might have just screwed up the best thing that ever happened to me. *Again.*

Mama listens quietly, asking a few questions in her soft lawyer voice. "You sound serious about her."

"Yeah," I say slowly. "The thing is, I'm in love with her again."

"Again?" Her thunder-warmed laugh vibrates my ear. "Child, you never *stopped* loving that girl."

I swear to God, my mother's a mind reader. Maybe all moms are. "I thought I had it all figured out this time," I say. "That I learned my lesson the first time around and figured out how to be the perfect guy for her."

"Baby, there's no perfect person for anyone. Just two imperfect people working their hardest to screw up as little as possible. And you *will* screw up. So will she."

The way she's talking—like there's a future instead of big, bleak abyss—lets the air out of the dark balloon hovering over me. "You think I could win her back?"

"I think you can do anything you put your mind to. I didn't raise quitters. Just two headstrong kids who pick paths that sometimes leave me marveling at how different you are."

My eyes feel like someone's scrubbed them with sandpaper, and I blink a few times to get the feeling to go away. "Tell me what to do."

Mama laughs hard at that. "I could never tell either of you kids what to do. Just point out the landmines and hope you don't step on too many of them."

"Where are they?"

"The landmines?" She chuckles. "Don't embarrass her. Don't undermine her. Give her space to cool down when she needs it. Communicate like hell, then let her make her own choices. Same as you'd want from her."

I swallow hard, finally getting it. "Give her the kind of autonomy you wanted me to have."

"Now you're getting it."

The sandpaper sting is back, but this time I learn to sit with it. "Anything else?"

She's quiet a long time. "You know she's a romantic, right?"

"How do you mean?"

"She and Lexi swap romance books the way you and your buddies traded baseball cards."

That's…okay; that actually kinda makes sense. "You think I should do something romantic?"

"I think it's worth a try." Her warm vanilla voice ripples over me. "You can't mess things up worse than you already have."

"Thanks a lot."

"Oh, go on now. It's not just on you. If I know that girl, she's kicking herself right now for her part in things."

I'm not so sure about that, but I'm sure of one thing. "I want to be the one to fix it. To apologize first."

"That's my boy."

Rubbing my eyes, I'm flooded with gratitude for family. For the fact that I can mess up a dozen, a hundred million times, and they'll always have my back. "I love you, Mama."

"Love you, too, baby. Now go on and get your girl back."

"I will." As I hang up the phone, I begin to make a plan.

CHAPTER 16

CONFESSIONAL 848.5
JUDSON, LAUREN (PRODUCER: JUNIPER RIDGE)
I NEVER PRODUCED A BIG ROMANTIC COMEDY BLOCKBUSTER. NEVER WANTED TO, I GUESS. HAPPY ENDINGS ARE MY JAM, YOU KNOW? I LOVE READING THEM. LOVE WATCHING THEM.
I JUST CAN'T FIGURE OUT HOW TO MAKE ONE MYSELF.

* * *

One day later, my heart's aching like I slammed it in the silverware drawer.

As I paw through forks and spoons, I struggle to recall why I came into this damn kitchen in the first place. My sisters and friends sit waiting for me around the breakfast table on my back deck, but I'm in here staring at cutlery and trying not to cry.

Why am I here again?

I glance at Sharkira's tank, hoping she has answers. "Don't look at me like that," I mutter, watching her hunker happily in her crooked house. "Just because you found your bliss doesn't mean everything's rosy."

Maybe not, but it might mean Nick's instincts are better than I thought. Two dozen decorations met with cichlid disdain, but Sharkira's happy as a clam in her house. She watches from the doorway, gills flapping as I trail my fingers over soup spoons and try to remember what I needed.

Unconditional love.

Laughter.

Companionship.

The best man I've ever known.

I had all of that and tossed it out. Was the Cash Beckett catastrophe worth wrecking the best thing that ever happened to me? *Twice.*

What kind of idiot throws away a damn good second chance?

Pride didn't snuggle me in bed last night. It's sure as hell not helping me find what I need in this drawer.

"Tea ball!" I shout. Pawing through the drawer, I find the fancy infuser and fill it with Mari's favorite Earl Grey. I set it on a tray next to Lana's mug that says "WAP" with a drawing of a cat in a soaking wet rain slicker.

There's juice and muffins outside already, so I grab a couple more mugs and the coffee pot and trudge back through the living room. I hate how hollowed-out I feel. With a belly full of blueberry muffin, I shouldn't be this empty inside.

Nick hasn't called. Not that I blame him since I made it pretty clear last night I wanted out. I'm trying hard to muster that same anger I felt twelve hours ago, to hold some shred of certainty I did the right thing.

The only thing certain is that I miss Nick. I miss him more than I did the last time we split.

Pasting on a smile, I step out onto the back deck. "Let's see, decaf for Gretchen?" I set the mug in front of her, watching her hand skim her still-flat belly. I'm guessing we won't wait long for a baby announcement.

Jessie shoots a knowing look at her sister. "Be right back." She stands and scoops baby Joy from her carrier. "This one needs brunch, too."

"You're welcome to stay out here," I call after her. "We've all seen boobs before."

Jessie smiles and slips past me. "But you haven't seen a nuclear level three diaper change."

"True." I pass out the rest of the mugs, handing the biggest to Vanessa. "Is my brother still torturing you with bad coffee?"

Vanessa takes a sip before setting her mug on a coaster. "He made the world's most disgusting coffee the first time we met," she says for anyone who hasn't heard how she and Dean got together. "Lucky for me, he's mastered some kitchen skills since then."

"So, there's hope for clueless men everywhere." Lana gives me a look over the rim of her mug, feigning sweetness and light. "Even if they screw up sometimes."

I sigh and drop into an empty chair between her and Mari. "Thanks for the hint, Captain Obvious."

"No problem." Lana grabs a slice of strawberry Danish from the plate in the middle of the table and bumps Mari with her elbow. "Here's where you say something wise and psychologisty."

Mari straightens and gives me an appraising look. "You haven't spoken with Nick?"

"No," I admit, gut pinching with guilt. "I'm still angry."

"Ah, the cornerstone of any good marriage." Colleen appears at the edge of my deck with Patti beside her, holding a basket wrapped in red linen. "Hope we're not too late. Had to wait for the cinnamon knots to come out."

"Oh, yum!" Lana drops the Danish and eyes the basket hopefully. "The ones you made last week?"

"Same recipe." Patti sets the basket close to Lana and claims an empty seat near the head of the table. "Sweet and spicy."

"No wonder Lana likes them." That earns me an eye roll from my kid sister.

My middle sister looks more pensive. Mari plucks a cinnamon knot from the basket and gives Colleen her famous shrink stare. "I'd love to hear your theory on anger as a relationship cornerstone."

"Ah, I'm mostly kidding." Colleen settles in beside her wife and pours a glass of juice for each of them. "But it's true some relationships run hotter than others."

"And not just in a sexy way." Patti takes the glass. "You've got your couples like Gabe and Gretchen—sweet as pie, not a lot of headbutting to be had."

"Can't argue there," Gretchen agrees, then makes a face. "Well, as long as he's not forgetting to tell me big stuff like—oh, I don't know—that he's a freakin' famous Hollywood director hiding in a remote mountain cabin?"

"That'll do it." Patti smiles at the memory. She was there the day Gretchen turned up brokenhearted and mad as hell. "You two even squabble sweetly."

"Sometimes," Gretchen agrees, taking a bite out of her cinnamon knot. "We've had our moments."

"What did I miss?" Jessie returns to the table, and I notice Patti's eyes lingering on the sleeping infant in her arms. Jessie sees it, too. "Did you want to hold her?"

"I'd love to." As Jessie tucks the baby into Patti's arms, Patti looks at Colleen and smiles. "Isn't she the spitting image of Joey as a baby?"

"I can see that." Colleen bends to grab a fallen baby bootie. "'Course, he was five when we met. I never saw Joey this tiny."

"Sure, but his baby photos are all over the house."

Jessie's shifting in her seat, probably itching for a subject change that isn't about babies. I'd give her one if I could think of anything besides Nick. What if I'm too late to apologize? What if I drove the last nail in our coffin?

I glance at Mari, biting my lip. "I want to film another confessional."

My sister eyes me carefully. "That's between you and Gabe, isn't it? Keepers of the production schedule."

"I need your help with this one. I need—" I take a deep breath. "I want to apologize. To Nick. On camera."

For giving up too easily. For walking away instead of talking things through. For so many things, really.

Mari doesn't answer right away. "Won't that be embarrassing?"

I nod and look down at my hands. "That's why I need to do it."

My sister's hand closes over mine. "I'll do what I can to help."

"Same," Lana says, scooching closer with a mouthful of cinnamon knot. "We're here for you, hon."

"Is something burning?"

Gretchen's voice yanks me from my funk. I sniff the air, not sure where the smell's coming from. "I'm not baking anything."

Lana wrinkles her nose. "Is that smoke over there?"

I look where she's pointing and *holy crap*. "That's Nick's cabin." I bolt from my chair, sending it slamming back against the rail. The baby starts crying, and I shout apologies as I sprint toward the smoke.

What if he's hurt?

"Lauren, wait." Mari's voice makes me spin in time to catch the fire extinguisher she's thrusting at me. "We should all go."

Vanessa drops to a crouch and starts unscrewing my garden hose. "In case he doesn't have one," she says. "Go! We'll catch up."

Tucking the fire extinguisher under one arm, I take off running. My heart pounds in my head as I race down the gravel pathway between long banks of cabins. I pass the construction zone, grateful it's not one of the new buildings on fire. But my bigger fear, the one choking my throat as I get closer to his cabin—

"Nick!" I force my voice past the lump in my throat. "Nick, where are you?"

"Here." His voice sounds strained and far away. "Son of a—"

He stops as I round the corner and skid to a halt on the grass. The first thing I see is the burning teddy bear. "What the hell?"

Nick frowns. "This isn't going how I planned."

Whipping out the fire extinguisher, I aim the nozzle at the flames. Praying I'm doing this right, I pull the trigger. "Gah!"

White foam hisses out, coating the flaming stuffed animal as well as Nick's arms. "Sorry, I didn't mean to get you."

"S'okay." He coughs as a wave of smoke blows back on him. "You can stop now."

I lower the fire extinguisher and survey the damage. The charred bear flops to one side, a bedraggled burn victim with a pink bow around its neck. Beside the charred plushy is an old-school boombox. Beside *that*, a basket of apples.

I look at Nick in confusion. "What's going on?"

"A grand gesture," he mutters. "Like in movies and romance books?"

"I'm familiar," I say, biting back a smile. "What do burnt bears and boomboxes have to do with it?"

He sighs and kicks the boombox. "I tried to go all out," he mutters. "The boombox to broadcast our song. I've never seen 'Say Anything,' but I know that's how it's supposed to go. The thrift store owner swore it worked."

The threat of a smile tugs harder at my mouth. "Did you buy batteries?"

He shoots me a look. "Yes, I bought batteries. You think I'm an idiot?"

I politely say nothing, and also don't look at the bear. Nick's eyes shift to the smoldering form, and a smile spreads over his handsome jaw. "All right. I'm not exactly knocking it out of the park."

"What happened to the bear?"

He nudges the charred form with his toe, and an arm falls off. Nick sighs. "I wanted a bonfire like we had at that B&B. The night with the s'mores when—"

"I remember." I can't hold back the smile any longer. "And the bear for the county fair?"

"I always felt bad you gave up the one I won you," he says. "Wanted you to have your own."

"He's bigger than the one you won for me."

"A lot crispier, too."

Footsteps pound behind us, and I turn to see my ladies gathering at the edge of the lawn. Mari, Lana, Jessie, Gretchen, Vanessa, Patti, Colleen. They freeze when they see Nick.

"Whoa," Lana says, summing up everyone's thoughts.

"It's a grand gesture." I feel oddly protective of Nick's attempt. When I meet his eyes, I give him the smile I've been stifling. The real one, not the shark variety. "I think it's sweet."

"Yeah?" Hope glimmers in his brown eyes. "How sweet is this?"

He yanks up his shirt sleeve and my mouth waters at the sight of one dark, rounded bicep. "Uh…pretty sweet?"

"Not my arm." He touches a band of silvery lettering inked on his dark skin. "It's supposed to say 'Lauren.'"

I stare at the letters, gaze snagging on the extra e. "Do we know anyone named *Laureen?*"

Patti peers at Nick's arm. "Laureen Harper, the wife of Canada's twenty-second prime minister," she calls helpfully.

Mari nudges her glasses up her nose. "Laureen Oliver, an American politician who co-founded the New York State Independence Party."

"Thank you." I press my lips together to tamp down a smile as I turn back to Nick. "Tell me that's not a real tattoo?"

Nick scowls, though there's humor flashing in his eyes. "Apparently, I mistyped my instructions for the temporary tattoo place. Also, the apples have worms."

I blink at the basket. "Um—"

"Saw a bunch of 'em on the ground by the property line near

Tia's place." He kicks the basket and a dozen pockmarked apples tumble toward the fire. "Remember apple picking?"

"I remember everything." Tears prick my eyes, and I'm pretty sure it's not the smoke. "This is all so sweet."

"Yeah?" Hesitating, he steps forward and puts his hands on my hips. "Lo, I screwed up. I undermined you and embarrassed you, and I'm sorry. All the things I promise not to do again if you give me a chance."

"Jerk."

Nick blinks. "What?"

"You had to beat me again, didn't you?" I choke on something halfway between a sob and a laugh. "I wanted to apologize, but just like with 'I love you,' you had to say it first."

Relief flashes in his eyes. "You wanted to apologize? To me?"

I swallow hard, chest pinching with emotion. "I'm sorry, too," I say. "I let my temper take over, and I walked away instead of sticking around to work things out."

"Yeah?" His eyes search mine, like he knows it can't be this easy. "You're right about me. I'm probably always going to be a take-charge kinda guy. It makes me a good businessman, but a shitty boyfriend. I'll try to do better by you, but I'm gonna screw up."

"So will I." I'm pretty sure about that. "I'll lash out when my pride's hurt, but I'll work harder to hold my temper. And I'll stick around instead of walking away. I owe you that. I owe *us* that."

He grins. "So you forgive me?"

"Only if you forgive me."

A hushed *"aww"* goes up from the ladies behind me, but I keep my eyes on Nick. It's the two of us who need to work through this. Who have to figure out how to build a house we can both live in.

"The crooked house!" I squeeze his biceps. "Proof you sometimes know what someone needs before they do."

Confusion creases his forehead. "Sharkira likes it?"

"Loves it," I say. "So do I." I rush ahead, wanting to be first to say it this time. "And I love you. So much, Nick."

"Good." He steps back. "Because there's one more part to my grand gesture." He bends and reaches into a bucket like the kind I've seen on jobsites holding tools.

Instead of a hammer, he pulls out a rectangular jewelry box. I stifle a gasp, though it's too large to be a ring. I don't wear much jewelry these days, but I'll wear a screw on a chain around my neck if Nick's giving it to me.

"Lauren." He drops to one knee, and I gasp for real this time. "We don't have to do this now. I'll wait forever if you need more time. But sooner or later, whenever you're ready, I want to marry you."

He flips open the box, and I stare. I'm not sure what I'm looking at. On the left is a massive platinum sparkler. It has a pear-shaped pink diamond at the center, with dozens of smaller stones at the edges. It must be more than eight carats, and before I left Hollywood, it's exactly the ring I wanted.

"I talked to your mom," he says softly. "A long time ago, she told me to come to her if I ever planned to propose. Said she knew the exact ring you wanted."

I nod, recalling that long-ago conversation in a moment of mimosa-fueled weakness. "That seems like a lifetime ago."

"I know." Slipping the ring out of the box, he holds it up. "Lauren from two years ago would have rocked this ring. You still can, if you want."

He holds it out and I open my hand. Thick fingers press it softly into my sweat-slick palm, and I'm surprised by how light it is.

"It's a fake." He grins. "Glass and stainless steel. Seemed like a dick move to assume what you'd want on your finger for the rest of your life, so I bought a placeholder for now. You get the real deal if you want it."

"A placeholder." I turn the ring over in my hand, relieved he didn't spend zillions of dollars on it. "It's beautiful." I swallow back the lump in my throat and meet his eyes. "But I'm not sure it's me anymore."

"I know." His grin holds a hint of cockiness as he takes the pink stunner and crams it back in the box. "That's why I had this second one made. The one in the middle, that's Oregon Lauren."

"Oregon Lauren?"

He slips out the center ring, a smaller size and style. "It's called a miner's cut," he explains as he holds the modest diamond up to the light. "Vintage. Old mine cut diamonds have a smaller table with a high crown and larger facets than modern diamonds." He makes a face as he holds it out. "I just learned what all that stuff means. Those are Oregon sunstones on the sides."

I gasp again, tears prickling my eyes. "Oh my God."

Seeing my reaction, he slips the ring on my finger. I tilt my hand, mesmerized by the ring's uniqueness. "I love how it's a little asymmetrical."

"That's the idea." He tips my hand to catch the sunlight. "That one's real, by the way. But the jeweler promised to take it back if it's not what you love. That's what the third one's for."

"The third one?" I drop my gaze to the tiniest band of silver. I almost didn't see it tucked in the lush velvet with the two bigger rings. Squinting at the polished surface, I notice the curlicue script. "It has writing on it?"

"Yeah." He slips the band out slowly and holds it up. "It says, 'I choose you.'"

More gasps from the ladies behind me, and an "aww" I'm pretty sure is Lana. I blink back tears, keeping my focus on Nick.

"You had it made?"

He nods and slips out the smaller ring. "It's meant to be a message. Like—hey, if you don't dig either of these rings, we can pick something together. In case you don't want me choosing for you." He meets my eyes with a sheepish smile.

"That's the idea, but it seems kinda cheesy now that I'm saying it out loud."

A tear slips down my cheek as I reach out to touch the ring. My fingertips trace the words as I lift my gaze to his. "I choose you, too." I look down at the ring on my finger, staggered by his thoughtfulness. "For the record, I'd say yes if you proposed to me with a screw."

He lifts an eyebrow. "Say what?"

My cheeks heat up as I realize I may have messed up our tender moment. "What's the thing a screw goes into?"

The ladies shout suggestions behind me.

"A bolt!"

"A nut!"

"A self-drilling drywall anchor!"

Pretty sure that last one was Gretchen, but I'm not turning around to look. I've got my eyes on Nick, the love of my life. My *fiancé*.

"You like the ring?"

"I love it." I curl my fingers like I'm trying to hold it on, pausing to admire the sparkle of the sunstones. "And I love you."

"I love you so much, Lo." He starts to put the thin band back in the box, but I touch his hand.

"Wait." I let my fingers glide to the engraving. "The words. Can we have those engraved on something?"

"Sure." He pulls it back out and slides it on the ring finger of my right hand. It doesn't quite go over the knuckle, but I can read the words from here. "You can have both if you want. Whatever you want, girl. It's all good, as long as we're together."

"'I choose you.'" I'm reading off the ring, but I mean each word from the bottom of my heart. When I lift my gaze to his, he's watching me. "I choose you, too, Nick. Forever and ever, even when we mess up."

"That's my girl." He plants a kiss on my knuckles, then clambers to his feet and grins. "We're getting married?"

"We are." I throw my arms around him, conscious of applause behind me. "You have no idea how long I've wanted to marry you."

"I might have a clue," he says, laughing a little. "Better late than never."

I laugh, too, breathing against the warm skin of his neck. "Maybe we'll have that etched on our rings."

"Love it." He kisses me then, slowly at first. Things heat up in a hurry, with Nick's fingers splaying in the small of my back. I graze his tongue with mine, going up on tiptoe to take him in. He feels so good pressed against me, all hard muscle and lean lines. We're perfect together.

No, not perfect.

We *fit*, and that's what matters.

"Hey, guys?" Lana coughs behind us. "Not to ruin the moment, but the bear reignited."

Nick jumps back and grabs the fire extinguisher. I edge away as he squeezes the lever to shoot a fresh swath of white on smoldering fur. I cough and laugh and tilt my hand in the firelight, admiring the soft sparkle.

This.

This is what I want. Not perfection. Not a marriage where no one ever screws up. We'll both make missteps. Dozens of them, hundreds in our lifetime together.

But our love for each other—that'll take more than a flagging fire extinguisher to snuff out.

"My hero." I pull him close again as he drops the red canister and reaches for me. "It was all worth the wait."

"Sure was," he says, and pulls me up for another kiss.

EPILOGUE

CONFESSIONAL 859
<u>Armbrust, Nick (Owner, Armbrust Resorts)</u>
Coming full circle.
I've always liked that phrase, even before Luxury Resort Magazine *used it in a headline about my project in Jackson Hole. The place that used to be a trailer park, then overpriced condos that burned in the early aughts? We went in and built this beautiful little circle of cedar cabins to be a rehab center for folks needing free services. Always felt proud of that one.*
What was I saying? Rebirth, right.
Isn't it great to know you don't have to get it right the first time or even the second or third? What counts is that you keep moving in the right direction. That your heart's in a good place.

* * *

My last sip of pumpkin stout leaves me feeling loose and blissful, or maybe that's the woman tucked under my arm. Shifting my gaze to Lo, I can't help grinning.

"Have I told you how hot you look in red?"

She laughs and grabs the ends of her pigtail braids, which have little red ribbons on the ends. "I'm dressed like a lumberjack in your old flannel shirt," she huffs. "And I'm going to kill Lana for doing this to my hair."

"Maybe wait a few minutes on the murder." I jerk a thumb at the game booth behind us and nearly knock the caramel apple out of someone's hand. "I've gotta win the Hammerschlagen first."

Lo rolls her eyes, but I know she found it sexy when I showed her my practice swing. Apparently, the ability to drive a nail into a stump with one blow of a hammer is a turn-on for my girl.

"Leave it to Lana to find the weirdest, most obscure games to round out Juniper Ridge's first Oktoberfest," she says.

I grin and set my empty beer stein on a stack of hay bales. "Weirder than the yodeling competition or the chicken dance contest?"

"Don't knock it." She sets down her empty cider mug and wraps her arms around my waist. "Who knew your sister had mad yodeling skills?"

I wave to Lexi as she rumbles by in the back of a horse-drawn wagon. She's perched on a hay bale like a queen with Abe and the girls tucked around her.

I've never seen my sister this happy.

When I glance down, Lauren's flashing her ring in the firelight from the bonfire beside us. Her cheeks pinken when she catches me watching her. "I still can't believe you picked the perfect ring," she says.

I slide a hand under her parka to cup one perfect ass cheek. "Or that you found the perfect guy?"

"So modest." She thumps me on the chest, then lets her palm trail over my pec. "I wish you didn't have to leave next week. You sure you can't let someone else get things started with Armbrust Vermont?"

"You know I'll be back before the week's over." I can't stand being away from Lo for any longer than that. "Want me to send you a postcard to stick in your keepsake box?"

"Yes, please." She wraps her arms around my waist and snuggles closer. "Did I tell you about the betta fish?"

I brace myself for a bloodbath story. "Sharkira didn't kill it, did she?"

"No way I'm trusting them in the same tank. But I set the betta tank next to Sharkira's aquarium, and they seem to like looking at each other through the glass."

"That's as good as it gets for some, I guess." I'm damn glad Lo and I don't need parameters like that around our relationship. "Speaking of weird relationships, did I see Cash Beckett got together with his baby mama?"

"We'll see if it lasts." Lauren's expression holds a healthy dose of skepticism. "Lana thinks it might be a PR stunt to play off our season finale. Time will tell."

"That it will." Right now, it's telling me Lo and I are rock solid. That we're wired to stand the test of time, to grow together no matter where life takes us.

Lauren's gaze skips sideways, and I watch her brows crease. "At what point do you think Cooper and Amy will realize they're meant to be together?"

"No way." I turn us so we've both got a view of my buddy watching the pretty police chief. He's pretending not to see her, but the longing in his eyes tells a different story.

Just as she passes, Amy's boot snags on a hay bale. Cooper leaps, catching her by the arms. He looks into her eyes, then moves back like he's been burned.

Lauren gives a knowing little hum. "Seems like a good sign when one person's catching the other." She cocks her head at me. "You don't think they belong together?"

"I think we're not meant to meddle in someone else's life." I've damn sure learned that lesson. "If they need a nudge getting together, they'll ask. But we've gotta let them figure it out for themselves."

Lauren laughs and tips her head back, leaving me to admire the smooth slope of her throat. "Who is this wise and worldly man and what has he done to my husband?"

Husband.

I love the sound of that, even though we're not there yet. The wedding's a few months away, but we may as well be married already. We've spent every night together, planning, dreaming, building our future.

I had no clue it could be this good.

"I've always been wise." I can hardly say it with a straight face. "Just took you long enough to recognize my infinite wisdom."

She laughs and stretches up to kiss me. "That's your takeaway for our relationship?"

Hardly. I've learned so much since Lo and I got together again. How to help without undermining. How to be a good partner. How to communicate like a damn champion.

We've both been learning. Mari even hooked us up with a couples' counselor who's giving us premarital pointers. I guess relationships require more care and feeding than we knew the first time around.

"Oh!" she says, pulling me back to the present. "Did I tell you Jessie's coming back for the holidays? We'll get to see baby Joy's first Christmas."

"That's great." I grin and blow a kiss to my nieces making another pass on the hayride. "Rosa and Nala already gave me their Christmas lists. Nala asked for a box of tacos and a pet tyrannosaurus."

"What did Rosa ask for?"

"A rock tumbler." A trip to the Oregon Coast landed them with more agates than they know what to do with. "Oh, and 'mature stuff.'"

"Mature stuff?"

I shrug. "That's what the list says. I figured it's better not to ask."

"Probably smart." Lo waves to Tia, whose petting zoo has turned out to be the highlight of Oktoberfest. Next to that, Patti and Colleen are leading a talk on native wildlife of the region. Patti holds up a photo of a fox and a bunch of small hands shoot into the air.

"Their son's still coming out for Christmas?"

Lauren doesn't even ask who I'm talking about. That's how connected we are these days. "Patti says the Navy gave him an extra-long leave. It's the first holiday they've had with him since he became a SEAL."

"It's shaping up to be a damn Christmas special."

She squeezes me tight and looks up into my eyes. "Know what I love?"

"Me?"

Her grin gets bigger as her arms go tighter around me. "That goes without saying."

"What else?"

"I love how we're learning together. How we've figured out ways to take charge without taking over." It's embarrassing how much I've embraced the shrink-speak, but I keep going. "Complementing instead of undermining, you know?"

"I do know." She smiles, and my heart bangs against my ribs. "Know what else I love?"

"What's that?"

"That Griffin's making cider for the brewery," she says. "And that they've got four different kinds on tap."

I laugh and tug the end of a braid. "Is that a hint?"

"I mean, if you're heading there anyway for a refill…"

"Say no more." I scoop up her cider stein and my beer mug from the hay bale. "Which flavor do you want?"

She smiles. "Surprise me."

"Deal." I always will, but only if it's what she wants. "You've got the sausage handled?"

She shoots a salacious look at my crotch and nods. "Yep. But first, I'll make a bratwurst run. Meet you back here in five?"

"All right." I grab the mugs in both hands, so damn happy I could explode. Maybe I won't pick the exact drink Lo would have chosen for herself. Maybe she'll pile too much sauerkraut on that vegan bratwurst they're slinging.

It's all good. In the end, we'll make it work. It won't be pretty or perfect or wrapped up in a big bow.

But it'll be ours.

I've made it two steps when she calls my name. "Hey, hottie."

Not my exact name.

"Yes, ma'am?"

I turn and she flings herself into my arms. "Couldn't let you walk away without a kiss."

As she lays one on me, I think this is the happiest I've ever been in my life. As we draw apart, I look deep in her eyes. "I love you, Lo."

"I love you, too."

With one more kiss, she turns and strides away, the woman who came back to me. Who'll always come back—and me to her—for as long as we're both breathing.

***

Thanks so much for reading Nick and Lauren's story. As you've probably guessed, we're gearing up for a messy match-up between Cooper Judson and Police Chief Amy Lovelin.

First, though, we've got a mystery to solve. Who the heck fathered Jessie Laslo's baby, and why is she so cagey about it? What are the odds Patti and Colleen's Navy SEAL son knows something? (Answer: Kinda small, but it's Romancelandia, after all…)

You'll get your answers in a special holiday novella headed your way. Want a sneak peek at *Show of Honor*? Keep reading for a glimpse!

YOUR EXCLUSIVE PEEK AT SHOW OF HONOR

CONFESSIONAL 869

Carver, Joseph (Lieutenant, US Navy SEALS)

I've always loved the holidays. Not the stuff you see in Hallmark movies where it's all snowflakes and mistletoe and kids yelling carols. We moved around a lot when I was a kid. One year we spent Hanukkah on Antigua where my moms were studying the velvety free-tailed bat. Another year, Christmas in Egypt for the fennec fox. We were never what you'd call "traditional." Not by a long shot, but we had fun, and there was tons of love.

Love, and some really weird animals.

* * *

"Here you go, kiddo." Mom sets a plate of sufganiyot on the café table in front of me, golden pastries still steaming from the fry oil. "This one's boysenberry, this is red currant, and this here is Oregon huckleberry."

"Wow." My mouth waters as I decide which to grab first. "I missed this."

Just like when I was a kid on the first day of Hanukkah, I snatch a hot jelly donut off the plate and bite into it, powdered sugar dusting my dress whites like I'm caught in a snow flurry. I should have changed at the airport, but I was too eager to surprise my moms before the coffee shop closed.

"Hhhhhawt!" I gulp cool café air, coughing as I inhale powdered sugar. Glancing up from my massive mouthful, I see my parents grinning.

"Pay up, Patti." Mama Clean—the name I gave her at five when I couldn't say *Colleen*—holds out her palm to Mom. "Told you some things don't change."

Mom rolls her eyes and forks over the cash as I devour the rest of the treat. "It's good to have you home."

"It's good to be here." *Home* is relative, since their work as wildlife biologists took us all over the world. With both of them settled at this old cult compound, splitting their time between biology, baking, and mothering this tiny town's residents, it's the homiest I've felt in years.

I grab the red current sufganiyah and blow on it this time. "How long has it been since we did the holidays together?"

My moms look at each other and have one of their conversations no one outside our family could ever translate.

"Was it the year we went—"

"No, it was after that." Mama Clean shakes her head. "Big snowstorm in—"

"That's right, he was in boot camp when we were in Jackson Hole." Mom makes her thinking face. "Maybe the year we—"

"Maine? No, you broke your arm that year. What about the time—"

"I don't think so." Mom frowns. "He had BUD/S training during our research project for—"

"The bobcats, right. Do you think it was—"

"A long time," I finish, since they could do this all day. "I'm still kinda stunned the Navy gave me three whole weeks."

It would have been two, but my grandfather passed in October when I was sweating my balls off in Al Anbar explaining to terrorists why they shouldn't blow up embassies.

I may not have said it so nicely.

But the end result is an extra week with family. My parents weren't expecting me 'til next Tuesday, and Mom burst into tears when I walked into their coffee shop. She squeezed me hard, murmuring about her baby, her *hero*, her brave Navy SEAL boy. I know she's hurting from losing her dad, and I glance at her now to see how she's holding up.

Mama Clean squeezes her shoulder and gives me a small smile. "We're glad you're here." She gives Mom another squeeze, then scoots around the café counter to straighten a fox in her nativity set. Apparently, it's too close to the cougar guarding the manger. "They've got lots of creative holiday stuff planned for Juniper Ridge."

Like her comment cued it up, the door swings open, and three women stride in talking a mile a minute. One blonde, two brunettes. Sisters, from the look of them.

"We've used the same costume shop for decades." The blonde pauses to gulp from a mug marked with a trio of cartoon reindeer having an enthusiastic threesome. "How could they screw it up this badly?"

The brunette with the long straight hair folds her arms like she's in charge. "I'm getting on the phone right now to read the fucking riot act to whoever—"

"Lauren, stop." The wavy-haired brunette shoves her glasses up her nose and sighs. "There's a new study on the psychology of customer service that found—"

"Ladies." Mama Clean steps out from behind the counter as Mom watches with a bemused look. "I'd like you to meet our son, Joseph."

"He's a Lieutenant in the Navy. A *SEAL*," Mom calls proudly as my gut balls up like a day-old fritter. "Joey, meet the Judson sisters—Lana, Lauren, and Marilyn."

"Mari." The one with glasses sticks out her hand. "I apologize for the ungraceful entrance. We've got a small holiday crisis."

"What's the problem?" Solving crises is kinda my jam, though it often involves explosives.

The blonde—Lana, I guess?—blows a shock of hair off her forehead. "Today's the kickoff for our big holiday bash, and half the costumes are borked."

"Borked." Lauren snorts. "The Santa costume came with a clown nose and a rainbow-striped beard."

Mari straightens. "Which is *fine* because Juniper Ridge is inclusive, and we fully support the LGBTQ community." She frowns. "The clown nose notwithstanding. Soph's at home making a new beard with cotton balls and crochet yarn."

I'm guessing from the pride in her voice that Soph must be Mari's kid. There's that gut twist again, reminding me I'm miles from adding any branches to my family tree. My moms gave me a kickass childhood filled with aunts and uncles and cousins and a grandpa who hung the damn moon and then gave it to me. I always figured I'd have kids of my own.

But family life doesn't mesh great with active duty, so hell if I know why I'm getting all sappy about it.

Meanwhile, Lana's hellbent on sounding hopeful. "Dr. Williams has her own traditional kaftan for Kwanzaa, so we're fine there. And there's no issue with our shipment of dreidels. This event could still happen without a hitch."

"It's the fucking Nutmeg Bear." Lauren huffs a frustrated breath and looks at me. "I don't suppose you feel like dressing up like a wild animal so a hundred runny-nosed kids can climb on you?"

"Nice, Lauren." Mari gives me an apologetic look. "Ignore her. We're all frustrated, but that doesn't give us license to—"

"I'll do it."

The three women blink. Hell, even I'm surprised.

"It's the holidays, right?" I shrug like it's no big deal, even though I'm seriously wondering what I've agreed to. "Sounds like you're trying to do some sort of inclusive holiday thing, which is great."

Lana eyes me up and down, taking measurements with her eyes. I'm used to it, but not like this. "Not a lot of squish, but your lap looks big enough. The costume should fit."

Mari regards me with a serious stare. "Our brother's wife offered to be the Nutmeg Bear, but the costume that showed up is a triple-XLT."

Mama Clean laughs, making her long gray braid sway. "Gretchen's tall, but not *that* tall."

The sisters size me up as I wipe my hands on a napkin. "When do you need me?"

"Now." Lana winces. "Sorry. I'm guessing you just got here?"

"It's fine." I shove the last sufganiyah in my mouth and stand up, dusting my hands. "You have the costume here?"

"It's at Gretchen and Gabe's," Lauren says. "I'm running over there now, so you can come with me."

"Roger that." May as well seize the chance to stretch my legs, and besides, I want to see the compound with a fresh dusting of snow. I've been here only once, and it was way before the Judsons moved in. Back when my parents had the place to themselves, researching the elusive Sierra Red Fox. "Do I need to bring anything?"

"Just your body." Lauren pivots for the door as her sisters shout thank yous from behind.

I hustle after her, surprised how fast she moves for someone a foot shorter than me. There's an engagement ring on her left hand and an air of authority in how she strides through the snowdrifts.

"So how are things going with the whole self-contained community?" I drag my brain for what my moms shared about how the Judsons bought this old cult compound and hired all the cops and grocers and nurses to turn it into a tiny town. "Is it more about the social experiment or the TV show?"

"Depends who you ask." She slings me a wry glance. "Those of us on the production side like Gabe and me get focused on the ratings. Mari's the shrink, so obviously the psychology stuff is her pet project. Everyone else falls somewhere in the middle."

"Sounds like a team effort." Kinda what being a SEAL is all about.

Lauren grins like I've said it out loud. "I'm betting your brand of teamwork involves way more ass kicking and firearms." She sounds almost envious as she tugs off her glove with her teeth. "The show's ratings are strong, and Mari's published articles in all the big psychology journals. Guess we're doing well, to answer your question. Here we are."

She stomps up the steps of a two-story cedar cabin, kicking snow off her boots as she rings the bell. While we wait for someone to answer, she studies me with curiosity. "You and Patti have the same eyes. Such a cool color. I've only seen one other person with eyes like that."

"Maybe I have a secret sibling." I laugh because it's possible. "I'm a donor sperm baby, so—"

"Hey!" A woman with long caramel hair throws the door open, making "sperm" the first word I've said to a stranger. A stranger whose pregnant belly makes it clear she's seen the stuff. "You must be Joe. Mari texted that you were headed this way. I'm Gretchen; come on in."

She swings the door open and leads us through a cedar-paneled living room that looks like it's from a catalogue for mountain home furnishings. Tall ceilings and lots of natural light, with a red plaid blanket tossed on a tan leather couch. "Costume's in the guest room," Gretchen continues as she leads us down the hall. "I tried it on, but I swam in it. I wasn't sure they'd find anyone it could fit. My husband's a big guy, but not humongous, you know?" She stops and winces. "Sorry. Was that rude?"

I laugh and shuck my jacket, ducking so my six-five frame clears the bedroom doorframe. "It's okay. I gave up my dreams of being a horse jockey years ago."

Lauren backs away. "I've gotta run. Was that the portable snow maker by the door?"

"Oh! Yes, just grab it." Gretchen gives me an apologetic look. "I'm so sorry, but I have to run, too. The costume's in the closet. Just ignore my sister's stuff. She doesn't fly in until tomorrow, so the guest room's all yours if you want to change in here."

Lauren shouts from the other room. "I'll come back to grab you in a few minutes. Thanks again, Joey."

"Joe," I murmur, even though they're both gone. Through the frosted windowpane, I see the two of them hustling toward a big wooden lodge. Must be where the party's happening.

Tugging the curtains closed, I strip off my dress whites and fold them on the end of the guest bed. A decade of military service hammered it home how to care for a uniform, and I'm wishing I'd brought a hanger. I didn't even stop by my moms' cabin to drop my seabag. That's how eager I was to see them, though I'm sure by now Mama Clean has schlepped my stuff back to their place. I can hear her in my head, tutting at Mom as they set me up in the main bedroom.

Patti, you know that boy needs a bigger bed. He'll be more comfortable in our room, and we'll take the guest room.

I've learned not to argue. Not to offer cash to buy a king for the second bedroom because deep down, they love snuggling in the double for a few nights.

I finish pulling on the bear costume, surprised how well it fits. It's meant to be roomy with plush brown fur padded thick around the middle. I turn to the mirror and lift my arms, chuckling at the paw pads dotted in pink hearts. There's a matching pink bow around my neck, which I straighten before tugging on the big hollow head.

God. If my SEAL team could see me now.

Jesus, Butch. You look like a rabid rat.

That's my nickname, Butch. A reference to my last name, Carver, which somehow morphed into Butcher, then Butch for short. Don't ask. I'm so used to answering to it that I forget sometimes it's not my real name.

I sit on the padded bench at the foot of the bed to straighten the paws on my feet. Probably should have considered the snowy path before I dressed in head-to-toe plush, but there's a sturdy rubber sole. I'll be okay with barely an inch on the ground, but there's more white stuff on the way tonight.

A door bangs at the other end of the house, and someone stomps through the living room. There's a soft squall, almost like a baby. Gretchen must have another kid? The crying quiets as a sweet female voice soothes and shushes and sings a few lines of "Santa Baby."

That gets me grinning inside the bear skull. Mama Clean's favorite Christmas song. I remember how she'd dance me around the house, singing her own version of the lyrics. She'd swap out gifts like diamond rings and yachts for her own favorite luxuries —Swarovski binoculars, a subjack for her laptop—as Grandpa grinned behind his paper and Mom made latkes in the kitchen. I always felt lucky having two holiday traditions. To have the perfect family to share them with.

Footsteps pull me to the present as someone hurries down the hall. I start to stand but freeze when I see her.

Holy shit, it's her.

Her.

My legs won't work, and neither will my voice, which doesn't matter since Jessie starts talking the instant she spots me.

"Oh, good, Gretch—you're here." She whips her sweater off

over her head, revealing the full, round breasts I met that magic night last year.

But this is no sexy striptease, and I still can't speak. Doesn't matter, since Jessie's not pausing for breath.

"I wasn't sure if my text went through, since I had to shut down for the flight. I took my chances getting an earlier one with everything closing down for the storm. You wouldn't believe the traffic out of Seattle. Everyone scrambling to get out before the snow comes, and Joy—" Her voice softens, which has the opposite effect on me because she whips off her bra and tosses it on the bed. "Joy got a little airsick, poor baby, and spewed like a geyser. It was worse than Stacey Sills on that girls' trip to Vegas when she drank all those cosmos after you got the lap dance from that stripper—what was his name?" She snaps her fingers, and I know this is my moment to say something, *anything*, to stop this train from flying off its tracks.

But she's talking again, bare breasts moving lush and lovely as she bends to dig through the dresser.

"Anyway, you look amazing," she continues.

With her perfect posterior inches from my face, I can't get enough air. Can't figure out what twilight zone I've stumbled into that this Ghost of Christmas Past is hovering half-dressed in front of me.

I didn't think I'd ever see her again.

"I wasn't sure what to expect," she's saying as she whips a bright pink bra from the bureau and hooks it around her ribcage, breasts swaying as she wriggles the cups around in front. "Nutmeg Bear? What the hell is that? But no, you look awesome. Fabulous. Ugh, unlike my tits. I swear they look like deflated soccer balls, minus the weird black and white hexagons. Hey, what time does this thing start, anyway?"

That's my cue. My moment to pry off the bear head and clear up this misunderstanding. As I raise my arms to do that, I realize my hands are sweaty, and my gut's clenched like someone kicked me.

I fumble with the loops holding the head on and tug it off. I set it slowly on the bench and sit blinking and baffled as hell.

But there's one thing I'm sure of as Jessie gasps.

"Jessie." I lock eyes with bright blue ones I've seen in my mind for three-hundred-and-forty-two days. "It's nice to see you. Your breasts look perfect to me."

***

Want to keep reading? Click to pre-order *Show of Honor*! https://books2read.com/u/3JRaYE

DON'T MISS OUT!

Want access to exclusive excerpts, behind-the-scenes stories about my books, cover reveals, and prize giveaways? You'll not only get all that by subscribing to my newsletter, I'll even throw you a **FREE** short story featuring a swoon-worthy marriage proposal for Sean and Amber from *Chef Sugarlips* in the Ponderosa Resort series.

Get it right here.
http://tawnafenske.com/subscribe/

ACKNOWLEDGMENTS

There's no way I can possibly thank Savannah J. Frierson adequately for the help with brainstorming, fine-tuning, idea bouncing, eye opening, authenticity reading, and editing on this book. Your input on Nick's life experiences as a Black man in rural Oregon were invaluable, and I'm eternally grateful for your work with me on this project. You're one of the kindest, savviest, most patient professionals I've met in my career, and I'm damn glad I found you in my quest for a sensitivity editor.

Thank you to my street team for your cheerleading and ARC reading, and for weighing in on everything from book covers to character names. Thanks especially to Rogina Dowling, Cherie Lord, and Erin Hawkins for catching typos in the ARC. Without you, I'd have no idea where to put the damn hyphens in the preceding paragraph. Thanks especially to street teamers who helped choose Lauren's ring, especially Nicole Weathers, Tina Hobbs Payne, Annie Hill, DeAnna Caudillo, Jackie Hunter Harmon, Lora Brothers Matthews, Sarah Kessler, Daphne Chase, Rosie Burke, Linda Ketter, Dana Waugh Strotheide, Victoria Martin, Julie Keating Schumacher, Dawn Bekenyi, Lucretia Ruiz, Stephanie Galan, and Amanda Dotson.

Thank you to the amazing Lauren Blakely for all the hand-holding on the audio side of this series. I'm proud to have you as an agency-sistah and colleague, and I'm in awe of all you do to elevate your fellow authors.

Huge thanks to Benjamin Charles and Stella Hunter for your work on this audiobook. I wasn't planning to do audio right away, but the instant I heard your voices, I knew I'd found Nick and Lauren.

Thank you to Terri Lynn Coop for your stories of Mr. Big Fish. Combined with memories of my own Mean Yellow Fish and the late Jack Black the Ghostknife, they gave me the inspiration for Sharkira.

Huge heaping gobs of gratitude to editor Susan Bischoff for the brainstorming and edits, and to Lauralynn Elliott for fine-tuning all my typos and comma vomit. Thanks also to Wonder Assistant Meah Cukrov and Special Agent Michelle Wolfson for being vital parts of my team (not to mention all-around awesome humans).

Hugs and kisses and awkward snuggles to my whole family, including Cedar Zagurski and Violet Zagurski, Aaron "Russ" Fenske, Carlie Fenske, and Mr. *not-a-GD-baby* Paxton, and the world's best parents, David and Dixie Fenske.

Special thanks to Craig Zagurski for being the best husband I could hope for, and for never flinching when I ask you to spend the weekend searching for photos of sexy, shirtless men. Love you, hottie!

ABOUT THE AUTHOR

When Tawna Fenske finished her English lit degree at 22, she celebrated by filling a giant trash bag full of romance novels and dragging it everywhere until she'd read them all. Now she's a RITA Award finalist, *USA Today* bestselling author who writes humorous fiction, risqué romance, and heartwarming love stories with a quirky twist. *Publishers Weekly* has praised Tawna's offbeat romances with multiple starred reviews and noted, "There's something wonderfully relaxing about being immersed in a story filled with over-the-top characters in undeniably relatable situations. Heartache and humor go hand in hand."

Tawna lives in Bend, Oregon, with her husband, step-kids, and a menagerie of ill-behaved pets. She loves hiking, snowshoeing, standup paddleboarding, and inventing excuses to sip wine on her back porch. She can peel a banana with her toes and loses an average of twenty pairs of eyeglasses per year. To find out more about Tawna and her books, visit www.tawnafenske.com.

ALSO BY TAWNA FENSKE

The Ponderosa Resort Romantic Comedy Series

Studmuffin Santa

Chef Sugarlips

Sergeant Sexypants

Hottie Lumberjack

Stiff Suit

Mancandy Crush (novella)

Captain Dreamboat

Snowbound Squeeze (novella)

Dr. Hot Stuff

The Juniper Ridge Romantic Comedy Series

Show Time

Let It Show

Show Down

Show of Honor (coming in 2021!)

Just for Show (coming soon!)

Show and Tell (coming soon!)

Show of Hands (coming soon!)

The Where There's Smoke Series

The Two-Date Rule

Just a Little Bet

The Best Kept Secret

Standalone Romantic Comedies

At the Heart of It
This Time Around
Now That It's You
Let it Breathe
About That Fling
Frisky Business
Believe It or Not
Making Waves

The Front and Center Series

Marine for Hire
Fiancée for Hire
Best Man for Hire
Protector for Hire

The First Impressions Series

The Fix Up
The Hang Up
The Hook Up

The List Series

The List
The Test
The Last

Standalone novellas and other wacky stuff

Going Up (novella)
Eat, Play, Lust (novella)

Made in the USA
Las Vegas, NV
19 September 2021